ST. MARTIN'S
PAPERBACKS

LOOK FOR THESE OTHER HOT NOVELS
BY BRENDA JACKSON

THE PLAYA'S HANDBOOK

TASTE OF PASSION

SLOW BURN

UNFINISHED BUSINESS

THE MIDNIGHT HOUR

AVAILABLE FROM ST. MARTIN'S PAPERBACKS

ISBN 978-1-250-00326-3

9 781250 003263

50799

EAN

NO MORE
PLAYAS

A NOVEL BY *NEW YORK TIMES*
BESTSELLING AUTHOR

BRENDA JACKSON

"Sexy, sexy, sexy . . . You'll cheer on this strong woman and honorable man." —*Fresh Fiction*

SLOW BURN

"An entertaining story . . . Jackson brings back beloved characters from her popular series, and the reunion is exceptionally satisfying." —*Romantic Times BOOKreviews*

"A good solid story with fiercely tender and intensely romantic protagonists." —SingleTitles.com

UNFINISHED BUSINESS

"Jackson is a master at juggling two plots at a time, and *Unfinished Business* proves no exception. A perfect balance of tension and chemistry is created as Christy and the somewhat domineering Alex battle unknown criminals—as well as their unresolved attraction to each other." —*Romantic Times BOOKreviews*

"Hot and sexy." —*Romance Reader at Heart*™

THE MIDNIGHT HOUR

"A super-hot hero, a kick-butt heroine, and non-stop action! Brenda Jackson writes romance that sizzles and characters you fall in love with." —Lori Foster, *New York Times* bestselling author

Also by Brenda Jackson

NO MORE
PLAYAS

BRENDA JACKSON

St. Martin's Paperbacks

This is a work of fiction. All of the characters, organizations, and events portrayed in this novel are either products of the author's imagination or are used fictitiously.

NO MORE PLAYAS

Copyright © 2005 by Brenda Streater Jackson.

For information address St. Martin's Press, 175 Fifth Avenue, New York, NY 10010.

Library of Congress Catalog Card Number: 2005048003

ISBN: 978-1-250-00326-3

Printed in the United States of America

St. Martin's Griffin edition / October 2005
St. Martin's Paperbacks edition / April 2012

St. Martin's Paperbacks are published by St. Martin's Press, 175 Fifth Avenue, New York, NY 10010.

10 9 8 7 6 5 4 3 2 1

To all my wonderful readers, who thought
Dr. Lance Montgomery deserved another chance.
And most important, thanks to my Heavenly Father,
who gave me this gift of writing.

Pride ends in destruction; humility ends in honor.
Proverbs 18:12, Living Bible

1

Lance

A man of genius makes no mistakes.
His errors are volitional and are the portals of discovery.
—*James Joyce*

He stood in the shadows, an uninvited guest among hundreds, watching with deep pain as the woman he loved was united in marriage to another man.

The minister's words tore into Lance Montgomery even though he knew that losing Asia had been entirely his fault and there was no one else to blame.

"Do you, Asia Monteen Fowler, take this man to be your lawfully wedded husband—to live together after God's ordinance—in the holy estate of matrimony? Will you love him, comfort him, honor and keep him, in sickness and in health, for richer, for poorer, for better, for worse, in sadness and in joy, to cherish and continually bestow upon him your heart's deepest devotion, forsaking all others, keeping yourself only unto him as long as you both shall live?"

Lance held his breath and prayed that the bride would realize she didn't love Sean Crews and that—

"I will."

With Asia's affirmation, soft but spoken loudly enough for all present to hear, another sharp pain tore into Lance. He wanted to scream out that there was no way she could love Sean Crews when she loved *him*. He tried screaming but couldn't find his voice.

Instead, the minister's words flowed through the church. "Inasmuch as Sean and Asia have consented to unite together in marriage before this company of friends and family, and have pledged their faith and declared their unity by giving and receiving a ring, they are now joined. By the power vested in me by the State of South Carolina and Almighty God, I now pronounce you man and wife. Sean, you may kiss your bride."

The moment Sean took Asia into his arms and kissed her, the scream Lance hadn't been able to release before suddenly burst from his lips. Everyone in the church turned to stare at him, but Asia and Sean continued kissing. Lance continued to scream until his throat felt raw, but it was all for nothing. He had lost her. . . .

Lance bolted upright in bed and sweat poured down his face. He'd had another dream. No, it had been another damn nightmare.

He dragged a hand down his wet face. This had been the third time in two weeks that he'd been consumed by visions of Asia and Sean's wedding—a ceremony that hadn't taken place yet—and each dream took something out of him, chiseled away more of his heart.

He sucked in his breath when the phone rang. Glancing over at the nightstand, he checked the caller ID. It was his good friend Sam. At first Lance wondered why Sam would be calling him so late, but a quick glance at the illuminated clock showed that it wasn't even ten o'clock yet. Right—he'd gone to bed early after consuming more brandy than he had intended. Even more pitiful?—until recently, he'd never liked brandy. Scotch had always been his drink of choice.

He reached over the bedside table and picked up the phone. "Yes, Sam?"

"What's going on with you, Lance?" Samuel Gunn said, not wasting any time lighting into him. "Lyle and Logan called today, claiming you're not taking their calls. Even your dad called today asking about you. It's not like you to not keep a check on your old man. What the hell is going on? I've called you several times, and you didn't call back."

Lance threw back the covers and pivoted to sit on the edge of the bed. He had avoided his brothers' and father's phone calls. Too much pain surrounded his heart, and he hadn't wanted to talk to anyone. "Look, Sam, I can't talk to you right now, and—"

"The hell you can't. I'm downstairs in the lobby. I'm coming up, and your ass better let me in."

There was a click in Lance's ear when Sam hung up the phone. Lance closed his eyes and inhaled deeply. Although he knew it was utterly impossible, he was convinced he could still pick up Asia's scent from the one time she had been in his home. She'd lain in this very bed while he tasted her, pleasured her, did everything short of sexual intercourse. The moment he had eased his face between her legs, he had inhaled her delicious feminine fragrance, and then he practically devoured her. It was as though an ache had moved from his groin to settle in the muscles of his tongue, making it throb relentlessly, and he knew of only one way he could satisfy the pulsating sensation. For the first time he could remember, he had held tight to a woman, had clung to her while exploring her intimately. Later, feeling her climax while his tongue had been inside her—kissing her in the most intimate way a man could kiss a woman—had been the single most erotic thing he had ever done in his life. And by the time he finished, he had fallen madly and completely in love with her.

Lance decided to put on a pot of coffee, since there was no telling how long Sam would be staying. Although a part of him wasn't up for company, there was no way he could keep his best friend out. The two of them had always been there for each other, from the time they were tots attending Mrs. Mary's Little Lambs Day Care, forging a bond that had lasted all of their thirty-three years.

After slipping into a robe, he walked to the living room. He had left the blinds open, and the view of Lake Michigan from his twentieth-floor window was magnificent tonight. He loved living in Chicago.

On his way to the kitchen, Lance caught a glimpse of *The Playa's Handbook,* a book he had written—and his ultimate downfall. Oh, the sales were great, since it was still in its twentieth week on the *Times* best-seller list. He had signed a very lucrative two-book deal, and his agent, Carl Kilgore, was already breathing down his neck about when he'd start penning the next million-dollar seller. Even now he should be doing research, deciding on the topic for his next title, but his mind had gone blank. For the first time in his life, he knew how it felt to have writer's block.

He had been tempted to tell Carl just where he could take the book and shove it, since Lance blamed the fact that he had lost the one woman he had ever loved on its existence.

He shook his head. *Love?* Yes. Love. Of all people, he, Dr. Lance Montgomery, had fallen in love—and had fallen hard. If anyone would ever have suggested such a thing to him months ago, he would have cursed them out and cut off their damn head. The word *love* had not been a part of his vocabulary. His motto was that he didn't love women, he played them . . . and he played them well. Over the years, he had perfected a strategy that guaranteed him any woman he wanted. Even the haughty of the haughtiest couldn't resist the Lance Montgomery charm when he laid it on thick. He had been dubbed the "king of the playas," the man whose playa's card would never expire. He had proudly written those books that glamorized the art of being single, and he'd found it downright amusing when *The Playa's Handbook* got a rise out of the female population. At the time the uproar hadn't particularly fazed him. If anything, it had annoyed him that the women were quick to place blame on him and not where he felt it belonged—on females themselves and the games they were known to play with men. No matter, controversy was good for sales, and so was adverse publicity—the book had quickly shot to the best-sellers' list, and it was still there.

But then something had happened to him.

He met Dr. Asia Fowler, a fellow relationship psychologist whose books directly contradicted his. Their opposing styles made them unwitting adversaries. From the moment he had met the simply beautiful and stunning Asia, he had wanted her. In his bed. He had been totally convinced that lust was driving his obsession, and nothing more.

He had been ruthless in his pursuit—daring, bold, relentless. And when he'd gotten her just where he wanted her, right on her back and in his bed, his good fortune became his downfall. He experienced emotions he had truly believed could not and did not exist.

Instead of accepting his fate, he rebelled like hell and pulled a stunt that had hurt the woman he loved. He could never get back in her good graces. Now she was engaged to marry another man, and there wasn't a damn thing he could do about it.

He turned his head from the coffeemaker when he heard the doorbell. He went to open the front door for the man whom he considered his best friend.

"You look like hell, man," Sam Gunn said, walking into Lance's condo. He turned around to face the entry and looked Lance up and down. "When was the last time you shaved, and what's going on with your hair?"

Lance leaned against the doorway. He had let himself go over the past two weeks, and it was just like Sam to mention it.

"At least I've been taking a bath every day," Lance muttered.

"Glad to hear it, smart ass. So what has you in a funk? Last I heard, that damn book of yours was selling like hot cakes, which means you're getting richer, but as far as I'm concerned, you can burn the damn thing."

Lance lifted a brow as he moved away from the door

and strolled toward the kitchen. "And what do you have against *The Playa's Handbook*?" he tossed over his shoulder, curious to hear what Sam had to say. One thing an author didn't do was trash his own book, but if others did it, then . . .

"Plenty. Besides nearly screwing my brains out with this zodiac-obsessed woman, it almost messed things up for not only me but for Phillip and Marcus, too. We read your book and decided to put our stuff into action. We were so busy being playa wannabes that when we finally met good women, we didn't know how to act and almost screwed things up."

"You met someone?"

Sam smiled. "Yeah, man. You know I was in a bad way after all that went on with Kim. Her affair really hurt. And marrying the guy before our signatures were even dry on the divorce papers only compounded the pain."

Lance nodded. He had talked to Sam a lot during that difficult time. "But you did meet someone?"

"Yes. Her name is Falon Taylor, and we met when she moved into my apartment complex a few months ago. At first I tried keeping her at a distance, not wanting to fall in love again—not thinking that I ever could, anyway. We started out as friends, and now it's escalated to more than that." Sam grinned. "I even broke the number one rule in your handbook and gave her the key to my apartment."

Lance studied his friend for a long moment. Then a sincere smile touched his lips. "I'm happy for you, man, and glad things worked out."

Now it was Sam's time to study Lance. Lance was not

a person who gave his blessings to serious relationships. Sam crossed his arms over his chest. "Okay, Lance, what's going on? Promoting happy endings these days? You're definitely not yourself."

Lance rubbed his face. Sam was right. He needed a shave. He said, "I screwed up, man. I met someone, too. I actually connected with a woman—and not just physically. I fell in love and fell hard but . . . I lost her. I lost her, and now she is going to marry someone else."

Sam heard the anguish, the torment, and the pain in Lance's words. "Damn," he said softly, shaking his head. "You actually fell for a woman. You?"

"Yes. Crazy, isn't it?"

"No," Sam said, "I don't think it's crazy. Nor do I think you should throw in the towel. If this woman hasn't gotten married yet, then there's still a chance."

Lance shook his head. "You don't know what all I did."

"Then let's talk about it."

Lance didn't say anything for a long moment, and then he nodded. "Okay. Let me finish making a fresh pot of coffee."

"So there you have it, man." Lance pulled a long draw from his beer and then set the bottle aside as he leaned back in his chair. He and Sam had decided to skip the coffee.

While talking, he'd felt like he was in a shrink's office, stretched out on the sofa and spilling his guts. Sam had listened without saying anything. Of course, Lance had omitted the intimate details of his relationship with

Asia, but he'd told Sam enough to convey exactly how much he had hurt the woman.

"So you screwed up big time. What are you going to do to get your ass out of this mess?" Sam asked.

Lance couldn't help but smile. That was Sam for you, definitely a straight shooter. His friend didn't believe in bullshitting around the bush. "I'm not sure there is anything that I can do."

Sam leaned back, took a swig of his own beer, and then exhaled a derisive snort. "Sure there is. From the way things look, you've already kicked yourself for messing things up. Now it's time to take action and do whatever you have to do to get her back. But first you need to come to terms with the reason you did what you did: why you panicked when you saw yourself falling in love with her. I think it goes back to how you've come to think of women over the years, Lance, starting with your mother."

Lance forced out a careless laugh. "My mother?"

"Yes, your mother. She wasn't the best in the world."

Lance thought about the woman who had deserted his father, brothers, and him; running off with another man and taking six-week-old baby Carrie with her, and leaving everyone speculating that the child belonged to her lover and not his father.

"What does my mother have to do with anything?"

"Come on, Lance, you're the one with the Ph.D. in psychology, so you know more about it than I do. There has to be a deep-rooted reason why you've always thought so little of women. Even when we were in high school, you acted like an asshole toward them. I think you should finally analyze the ramifications of that and just how your mother's desertion may have played a part in it. You have issues, and you need to *resolve* those issues before trying to get Asia back."

Lance studied his beer bottle for a long moment, and then he looked up at Sam. "She doesn't want to have anything to do with me, man."

"When did you ever give a damn about what a woman wanted? And it will be in your best interest not to start now, especially if it means giving up without a fight." Sam took another sip of his beer and then said, "If you really love this woman, then you need to get your shit together before it's too late. You're good at whatever it is that you do, Lance. Instead of using your skills as a negative, you should use them as a positive, pulling in all your creative abilities to win her heart. And whatever you do, you have to be sincere about it."

Lance considered Sam for a moment and then inclined his head. "I really love her, Sam. I thought I'd never say those words, but I can say them about Asia."

"Then let her know how you feel. Winning her back won't be easy, but if you love her as much as you say you do, then you should try."

Lance thought about how Asia had warmed his frozen heart, unthawing it. She was a truly remarkable woman who deserved more than a loveless marriage to Sean Crews. "There's no way I'm going to give her up," he said, knowing he would do whatever he had to do.

He remembered the obsession and the urgency with which he had wanted her in his bed, and the tactics he'd used when he'd been pushed beyond rational thinking. He had met her after she'd given a speaking engagement in New York, and from the first, he had been knocked off balance, struck right between the eyes. And although he had a feeling that she'd been attracted to him, she'd maintained that cool reserve even when he had pulled out his best lines and all his smooth moves. And the more she resisted him, refused to give him the time of day, the more fascinated he became. He saw her as a rare exotic breed of woman. And now the thought of her marrying someone else was totally unacceptable.

"I'm going to get my woman back, Sam. And I won't stop until I do."

"Hey, now you're talking," Sam said, smiling. "Before you get all fired up and start working on some devious plan to accomplish that goal, how about coming to dinner next Saturday night? I want you to meet Falon."

The next morning, shaved, showered, and after making an appointment to visit his barber, Lance walked over to the window and looked out, the phone still in his hand. The next person he needed to call was his agent, but before he did that, he needed a moment to reflect.

Last night he had gotten the best sleep ever: no dreams, no nightmares, nothing to make him toss and turn. And upon waking, he felt more in control, with a keen sense of resolve.

He gazed out the window. It was early, and crowds of Chicagoans were out and about, hurriedly strolling down Michigan Avenue. Thanksgiving was two weeks away, but still, the storefronts were decorated for Christmas, and for the first time in years he was looking forward to the holidays. No Christmas alone this year. Nor did he plan to share it with his brothers and sister. He was determined that, no matter what it took, he would be spending Christmas and New Year's with Asia.

With his spirits high, he walked over to the sofa, sat down, and placed a phone call to his agent. "Good morning, Carl. This is Lance."

"Lance, where the hell have you been? I've been trying to reach you for two weeks. I got a call from your editor, and they are tired of me stalling. They want a proposal from you by next week."

Lance massaged the bridge of his nose. "I'll see what I can do."

"And what the hell does that mean?"

Lance raised his eyes to the ceiling. "It means you'll have the proposal by next week, but I need more time to write the actual book."

"More time? The completed manuscript is due next month."

"There's no way I can have the book done in a month."

"You're going to have to try, since they're pushing for a May release date."

May! That meant Carl would be breathing down his neck until the book was finished. Carl didn't know it yet, but the way Lance felt about Asia changed everything in regard to the book, especially his way of thinking when it came to men–women relationships.

For years he had written about the pitfall of falling in love and the risks of being true to one woman. He knew his different mind-set would be a hard sale to his agent and publisher, but there was no way he could write another book like the ones he'd done in the past. Upon waking that morning, he had decided that the title of his next book would be *No More Playas*.

"I'll do my best, but I need you to do me a favor."

Carl hesitated before asking, "What kind of favor?"

"Do whatever you have to do, but I want Dr. Asia Fowler's schedule. Not just her touring schedule like you got me before, but I want a glimpse at her entire appointment book."

"Are you mad? What is this obsession you have with that woman?"

Carl didn't know the half of it, Lance thought, laughing. It was the first time he had laughed in a long time, and he liked it. "Yes, I'm mad, all right." *Madly in love,* he decided not to add.

"But if you want me to finish the book, you'll do that favor. Otherwise, I'm going to put writing the book on hold and research the information myself."

"Dammit, Lance, how am I supposed to find out what you want?"

"I'll leave that completely up to you and your creative abilities. Good-bye, Carl."

Lance could hear Carl mutter a few curse words as he hung up the phone. For the first time since hearing about Asia's engagement to Sean Crews, he felt hope. All he had to do was remember the way Asia had looked at him the last time he'd seen her, and it was obvious he had hurt her deeply. She wouldn't forgive easy. Hell, she probably ranked him right up there with her ex-boyfriend David Crews, but all that would change—and soon.

He had to believe what was wrong between them could be fixed. He had his work cut out for him, but no way could he lose her. If it took everything he owned, he was determined to repair all the damage he'd done and earn his way back into Asia's affections. And Sam was right about one thing: He did need to consult a psychologist and work on those larger issues he had with women.

Asia might as well get prepared for his comeback, because there was no stopping him now. He was a man on a mission.

2

Asia

Nothing in life is to be feared.
It is only to be understood.
—*Marie Curie*

"I can't believe you're really here," Asia Fowler said, smiling as she glanced across the kitchen table at her sister. She had been surprised to open the front door earlier that morning and find Claire standing on her stoop. During their last conversation, Claire had indicated she would try to come back to the States for a visit the week between Christmas and New Year's, but Christmas was still a month and a half away.

Claire grinned over the rim of her coffee cup. "Hey, it's only for a short while, so don't get attached. And if I remember correctly, you're the one who owes me a visit."

Asia chuckled. "Yes, I do owe you one, but I can never keep up with what country you're in from year to year, Dr. Fowler." Claire had a doctorate degree in education and worked for the State Department.

Claire shook her head, smiling. "Hey, I don't move

around that much, but I always said I wanted to travel, and my job affords me the luxury. So what's been going on with you?" she asked, although she already knew most of the story . . . at least their mother's version. According to Annie Fowler, the worse possible thing was happening: Asia was marrying Sean Crews, David's brother.

David Crews had been bad news for Asia from day one, but nothing anybody ever said or did could make Asia see that. Asia had even stopped speaking to the family for a whole year once because of David's lies. He had kept her obsessed and dangling on a string for five years while he used her, played around on her, and eventually married another woman the day after spending a night in Asia's bed.

In Claire's book, David Crews had been a dog of the lowest kind. Sean was the complete opposite, but he was still David's brother, and that was too close to home— too much of a family affair. No matter how good a friend Sean had been to Asia, you just didn't marry the brother of your former lover. It could definitely put you in an uncomfortable position at family gatherings. And knowing what an ass David was, Claire figured it would be just like him to say to Sean while passing the potatoes, *"Did I ever tell you about the time your wife gave me one hell of a blow job?"*

"I'm sure you got the message I left on your answering machine a couple weeks ago that I'm marrying Sean."

Claire met Asia's gaze after taking a sip of coffee and placing the cup down in the saucer. "Yes, but I was hoping I heard wrong. I thought you were through with that family."

Asia frowned. "You've met Sean, Claire. He's nothing like David."

"That might be true, but he's still David's brother. Don't you think that's too close for comfort? What happens when you run into David at family gatherings?"

Asia shook her head as she stood. "I'm over David—you know that."

"Yes, but does he know that? You know what an arrogant son of a bitch he is."

"Yes, but David is not my concern."

Claire nodded. "And can you look at me and tell me with all honesty that you love Sean?"

Asia met her sister's stare. "Why all the questions?"

Claire fired her sister a glare hot enough to melt blocks of ice. "Well, can you?"

"There are different degrees of love, Claire," Asia said, before walking toward the sink.

"And what degree do you have for Sean? And what about Lance Montgomery? How does he fit into this?"

Asia turned around abruptly, almost dropping the cup she held. She gave her sister a penetrating glare of her own. "What do you know about Lance Montgomery?"

Claire lifted an arched brow. *Bingo. Melissa is right!* Melissa James was Asia's close friend as well as her literary agent, and she had joined them for lunch earlier that day. Claire and Melissa had gotten a chance to talk privately when Asia excused herself to go to the ladies' room. Melissa was also concerned with what was going on in Asia's life.

According to Melissa, there was a whole lot of chemistry flowing whenever Asia and Dr. Lance Montgomery were within a few feet of each other. She had seen it on the set of a television talk show Asia and Dr. Montgomery had done together.

"I heard that the two of you seemed to have a thing for each other a couple of weeks ago," Claire said.

A frown touched Asia's features, and Claire knew her sister was going to deny it. "I can't stand the man. Whoever told you that—and I'm sure it was Melissa—was wrong."

Claire smiled. "Oh, I see," she said, and she really *did* see and wondered if Asia did. The good doctor Montgomery had definitely rubbed Asia the wrong way . . . or was it the right way?

Although she lived outside of the country most of the time, Claire had heard about the well-known and controversial Dr. Lance Montgomery. Somewhere she still had an issue of *Essence* magazine that had run a feature story on him. When she read his first book, *How a Brotha Can Avoid Getting to the Altar,* like a number of other women she had gotten riled up that any man could publish such a thing. Men had a problem with commitment already, and the book only reinforced, even encouraged, the problem. She had considered the book the most moronic piece of trash she had ever read.

But it seemed a lot of men didn't think so, and the book hit the *Times* list within a week of being released. Bookstores couldn't keep it on the shelves, and whether his book was a direct cause of the numbers or not, a survey taken a year after the book was released showed a drop in marriages over the previous twelve months. She, personally, didn't credit the book as being a factor, but a number of women did, which didn't make Dr. Montgomery very popular with single females.

Then to add insult to the injury, he had come up with a book titled *The Playa's Handbook*. Claire had purchased the book a few months ago for entertainment purposes only, and after reading it, she thought it was worse than the previous one. Not surprisingly, it, too, had become a runaway best-seller.

Sipping her coffee, Claire studied Asia while she loaded the dishwasher. Her sister had suddenly gotten quiet, and she wondered if perhaps Melissa really was right and something *had* been going on between Asia and Lance Montgomery.

She remembered becoming engrossed in the *Essence* article about the highly educated man who had roots in Gary, Indiana. The cover photograph had depicted a very handsome figure who oozed success, confidence, and virility. He had a reputation for being impeccably groomed at all times and smart when it came to investing, which had made him a millionaire since his first book appeared five years ago. In other words, he had certainly come a long way from his lowly beginnings.

But what Claire had really found intriguing was that he actually believed the garbage he wrote. After reading the article, she had come away with the conclusion that the man had issues. She knew there was something about him in that photo that his dashing smile and tailor-made clothes hadn't been able to hide. There was a rawness, ruthlessness, and brashness that made a man like David look like a Boy Scout.

At first, when Melissa had dropped Montgomery's name in connection to Asia's, Claire had panicked. It was like her sister was jumping out of the frying pan into the fire. The last thing Asia needed was a man who was a bigger dog than David. But something Melissa said had intrigued her. Melissa was convinced Asia had knocked the good doctor off balance.

Claire, of all people, knew how much Asia had grown emotionally over the years, and another man like David wouldn't stand a chance with her. But still, if there was a possibility that Asia and Montgomery had really connected as Melissa claimed, then why was she marrying Sean? Claire knew for a fact that Asia loved Sean as a friend, not a husband.

"So, have you picked a date yet?" Claire asked.

When Asia met her gaze, Claire saw a brief flash of sadness, and then it was gone. "Yes, I want a June wedding, but Sean wants to get married sooner. If he had his way, we would marry Christmas Day."

Claire took another sip of her coffee. Christmas was next month. "Why the rush?"

Asia shrugged. "I guess he's anxious for us to get married."

Claire nodded. *He probably wants to do it before you come to your senses,* she thought. A few years ago, she had made a vow to keep her nose out of Asia's life, but this marrying Sean business was pushing her to break that vow. In fact, she was determined to do so.

"Have you decided how long you plan to visit? You know you're welcome to stay here as long as you want," Asia said.

Claire smiled. "Thanks. Since Thanksgiving is in a couple of weeks and Christmas is next month, I might take an extended leave and not return to Africa until the first of the year." *Not until I'm sure you're not making the second biggest mistake of your life.*

* * *

Later that night, Asia couldn't sleep. Across the room, a log broke apart in the fireplace grate with a pop and, without bothering to look up, she knew that the piece of wood was burning and sparking, mimicking how she felt.

Damn. This was the second time she had allowed *him* to invade her dreams, to make her suddenly feel a heated rush. She wondered if Lance had placed some sort of curse on her. Here she was, engaged to marry the most decent man she'd ever known, and she couldn't stop dreaming about *him*. She sighed and slowly shook her head. She doubted that she would forgive Lance for showing her just how weak she still was.

She had endured months—no, years—of regaining her dignity and her self-esteem after David. And falling for a calculated strategy that had gotten him just what he wanted, she had become another notch to add to Lance's bedpost.

She turned her head from the thick pillow. No, they hadn't gone all the way. She was still celibate. Yet she feared that he wasn't wrong when he had told her that even that had been his choice. She knew he could have easily eased between her legs and pounded into her, and she would have loved every minute of it. She had almost begged for him to do it. Instead, he had taken her another way, a way more intimate than any man had before and with a finesse that even now took her breath away.

Outside rain tapped against her window. She remembered how before she could even leave Lance's apartment, Rachel Cason had shown up. He had used those same lips that hours earlier had teased her on another woman's mouth while Asia stood and watched. She didn't doubt that after she left, he had taken Rachel into his bedroom and made love to her. And Melissa and Claire wondered how she could hate him so? But then, they didn't know everything, and if it were left up to her, they never would. Being played by one man was bad enough, but having been screwed over by two was the worst.

Asia jumped when the phone rang. She reached over to her nightstand and quickly picked it up. "Hello."

"I miss you."

She couldn't help but smile. "I miss you, too, Sean. Where are you?"

"Zaire. I'm about to perform surgery on a man who's going to lose both legs without it."

Asia nodded. In a show of goodwill, the United States government had created a task force of some of the most noted medical doctors in the country, all in private practice, to occasionally travel together and perform acts of medical goodwill for individuals living in impoverished countries. "When will you be coming home?"

"A couple of days before Thanksgiving, but I was wondering if you wanted to fly over for a few days . . . so we can spend some time together."

Asia heard the edginess in his voice; she detected the restlessness, the desperate need. Of course, he wanted her. She was his fiancée, but still they hadn't slept together . . . at least not since that one night almost four years ago when he had come to tell her the shattering news about David.

It was Sean who had been there with her, to help her get through what had to be one of the worse nights of her life. In her drunken stupor, she had asked Sean to kiss away her pain, and they had made love, something she regretted upon waking the next morning with one hell of a hangover.

While she'd wanted nothing more than to drown in remorse, Sean had looked at her and confessed that he loved her, had always loved her from the moment David had first introduced them. That had been too much, and she had ended up asking Sean to leave, telling him that they could never be anything more than friends. And they had been friends. It was Sean who had seen her through some rough times and when she had wanted to give up, it was Sean who had convinced her not to.

What she'd told Claire earlier that evening was true. There were different degrees of love, and although she didn't love Sean with deep, undying passion, she believed that in time she would. How could she not grow to love a man who had played such a huge part in her emotional healing?

"Asia?"

Again she heard the edginess. It was there even when he said her name. She knew deep down that she wasn't being fair to him. It had been understandable for them not to sleep together before, but now that she had accepted his proposal and they were engaged to be married, there was no reason for abstinence. She knew it, and he knew it, as well. "Yes?"

"Will you fly over here so we can spend a few days together?"

Asia closed her eyes, wondering why it was so hard to make up her mind to sleep with the man she had agreed to marry. "Claire is here."

"What?"

She slowly opened her eyes. "I said Claire is here visiting. She arrived unexpectedly yesterday. It wouldn't be right to take off and leave her here alone, would it?"

"No, I guess not," he said, somewhat grudgingly. "How long will she be there?"

"I'm not sure. I don't think she's decided. I'm hoping she'll decide to stay through the holidays. It's been a while since we've spent any time together."

"And what about us?"

Asia raised a brow. "Us?"

"Yes, it's been a while since we've spent time together, too, Asia. Quality time."

She knew exactly what kind of quality time he was talking about. "Don't push me, Sean. You said you'd let it be my decision."

For a few moments he didn't say anything. "Yes, I know, but I hadn't figured it would take you this long. We've been engaged for almost three weeks."

She frowned. "And your point? Is it written somewhere that the moment we became engaged we were supposed to share a bed? And what if I said that I wanted to wait until our wedding night, Sean? What then?"

She and Sean shared a special friendship, but the one thing they couldn't agree on was sex. Why did the issue of them sleeping together have to muddle things?

"Asia, let's talk later. I can tell you're not in a good mood tonight, and I didn't mean to call and upset you."

She felt a thick lump form in her throat. He was right. She wasn't in a good mood, and she suspected she was half-crazy, as well. Here she had one of the nicest men she knew, who wanted to marry her, take care of her, and love her, yet she had been awakened from a dream of another man. A man who had been making love to her, making her moan. Just thinking about it made heat settle in all parts of her body. She knew it had to be guilt more than anything that was screwing up her mind.

"I'll call you later in the week. Tell your sister I said hello."

"All right."

"Good night, Asia."

"Good night, Sean."

Asia hung up the phone. She had heard the love in Sean's voice and knew that things couldn't go on this way between them. If she was going to marry him, then that meant she needed to share everything with him, especially herself. She hoped that by the time he returned to the States, she would be ready for their relationship to move to that level.

3

Lance

The greater part of our happiness or misery depends
on our dispositions and not our circumstances.
—*Martha Washington*

"Hey, man, I'm glad you could make it." Sam grinned
as he ushered Lance into his apartment.

"I wouldn't miss the chance to meet your lady," Lance
said, handing Sam his leather coat. When Sam had is-
sued the invitation, Lance assumed it would be a dinner
party with a few people, but from what he could tell, a
full-fledged throw-down was going on.

Sam chuckled. "Yeah man, I know. By the time Falon
and I finished with the invitation list, things had changed,"
he said over the loud music. "I hope you don't mind."

"No, I don't mind. I've been cooped up at my place
long enough anyway. It's time for me to get out into the
world."

"Hey, that's the right attitude. Come on and let me
introduce you to everyone."

Lance glanced around while he and Sam wandered
around the room and Sam made introductions. He had
visited Sam a couple of times since he'd moved into

this apartment complex, but certain telltale signs spoke of a woman's touch. There were framed pictures of flowers on the wall and silk flower arrangements sat on a couple of tables.

"Lance, I want you to meet my lady. This is Falon Taylor. And Falon, this is my best friend, Lance Montgomery."

Lance blinked twice at the woman who had walked across the room and into Sam's arms. Damn, she was a Beyoncé look-alike, a definite beauty. He held out his hand. "I'm happy to meet you, Falon."

Falon accepted Lance's hand in a warm handshake. "I'm happy to meet you, as well, Lance. I've heard a lot of nice things about you." She chuckled and added, "But I might as well come clean and say that before I knew you were Sam's good friend, I really didn't like you at all."

Lance wasn't surprised. "My books?"

"Yes. They aren't very women-friendly and that's not a good thing, *Dr. Montgomery.*"

Feeling oddly at ease with Falon's forthright honesty, Lance immediately decided that he liked her. She had as much sass in her talk as there was in her honey-brown eyes. Her eyes matched the fiery honey-blond hair that flowed down her shoulders and accentuated her cocoa-colored complexion. Yes, he liked her and thought that just as Asia was the perfect woman for him, Falon was the perfect woman for Sam.

He would even admit to feeling a tiny bit of envy the night Sam had told him about Falon. But then it had worn off, and been replaced by a determination to share the same thing with Asia that Sam had with his Falon.

He leaned in closer, for her ears only. "And what if I were to let you in on a little secret?"

Falon's eyebrows raised, her curiosity piqued. She glanced up at Sam, who merely grinned before she looked back to Lance. "What kind of a secret?"

"That I'm a reformed man."

Her brows lifted farther, and Falon knew the man standing in front of her was full of intelligence . . . as well as humor if he thought for one moment she believed what he'd just said. A reformed Dr. Lance Montgomery? There was no way.

"Well, I guess I have to take your word for it," she said. "I'm going to leave it up to Sam to introduce you to our other guests, but don't be surprised if the women corner you and read you the riot act."

"Oh, I'm prepared."

Falon shook her head. In addition to the intelligence and humor, she also saw a man who was highly self-confident. She decided that even with all that garbage he wrote, she liked him. "Enjoy the party, and make sure you eat as much as you want. I did all the cooking."

Lance nodded. "Sam told me you were a chef. The best."

She glanced up at Sam, and Lance could feel the love flowing between them. According to Sam, they were taking things slow, but Lance felt it wouldn't be long before they made future plans. In the back of his mind, he could actually hear wedding bells and for once the sound wasn't coming from Asia and Sean's wedding.

Asia and Sean.

Just the thought of them together caused a deep throbbing pressure to build around his temples. He couldn't think of them in the same sentence without wanting to go ballistic.

He watched as Falon stood on tiptoe and placed a kiss on Sam's lips. "No, *he's* the best, Lance."

Moments later, he and Sam were crossing the room to where two other couples were standing. He recognized the guys immediately: Phillip McKenna and Marcus Lowery. Phillip had been Sam's college roommate at Howard University, and Marcus was another of the guys from the hood where he and Sam had grown up.

Sam introduced Phillip's and Marcus's dates, Terri Davenport and Naomi Monroe. It didn't take much for Lance to figure out that Phillip and Marcus, like Sam, had found good women to love as well. He was happy for the both of them—especially for Marcus, who had lost his wife in a train accident a few years back.

An hour or so later, Lance had stopped counting the number of glares he had received from the women in the room. One woman had had the nerve to brush up against him and whisper the word *asshole* in his ear. Then another woman had almost followed him to the bathroom and told him he should take all his books with him and flush them down the toilet.

"Hey, man, you enjoying yourself?"

Lance took a sip of his beer. "Sure, I'm having a blast."

Sam barely suppressed a laugh and shot him a skeptical look. "So do you have a plan on how to get your lady back?"

"Yeah, but I need all the help I can get, so keep me in your prayers."

"You know I will."

Lance looked across the room to where Falon was, talking to Sam's sister Carolyn, who was in town visiting from Philly. "I think you've hit gold, Sam."

Sam followed Lance's gaze and smiled. "Yeah, I think so, too. She's a very special woman."

Until recently, Lance hadn't known that such a woman could exist. Now that he did know, he was determined more than anything to bring that special woman back into his life. He was prepared for the battle he knew would ensue. Not only would he have to deal with Asia, but there was also Sean Crews. The man wouldn't give her up without a fight, and he would definitely be a challenge. Competing for women was not in Lance's realm of expertise, but he was almost certain of one thing: Asia loved him and not Sean.

Now it would be up to him to make sure she realized that very important fact.

"Enjoying yourself?" Phillip McKenna asked the woman by his side. Not for the first time he thought of how much he loved Terri. They had been seeing each other exclusively for a couple of months, and every day he fell more and more in love with her. He had considered the M-word, although they had never talked about it. With one failed marriage behind him, he wanted to be sure. Now he was certain, and tonight he intended to ask her to marry him—and if she said yes, she and her daughter, Star, and he and his daughter, Chandra, would live together happily as one big family. Especially now that his ex-wife, Rhonda, had agreed to give him full custody of their daughter. Rhonda had gotten a big job promotion that was contingent on her moving to San Diego to start up another branch of operations there. Rhonda had surprisingly suggested that it would be best if he kept Chandra during the school year and that she could come out to California for extended visits during the summers. Phillip had quickly agreed, and they were supposed to visit with the attorney next week to draw up the custody papers.

"Yes, it's a nice party," Terri answered. "I'm rather surprised by Dr. Lance Montgomery. I thought if I ever met him that I wouldn't like him, considering the stuff he writes, but I do. He seems to be a nice guy."

Phillip smiled. "Yes, he is quite a charmer, isn't he?" Even he had to admit that Lance seemed to have developed a new attitude. Of course, he didn't know him as well as Sam did, but there had been a few times that he had been to Sam's place when Lance had been visiting.

He glanced down at his watch. He was eager to leave the party and take Terri home, especially since her little girl was spending the night over at her grandparents' house. That meant Terri had the house all to herself, and tonight he intended to fulfill more of her fantasies. He couldn't help but grin. His woman could become a diva in the bedroom, and he thoroughly enjoyed each and every moment the two of them spent there. But their relationship wasn't just based on great sex. . . . and it was definitely great. They also had the same interests and enjoyed doing a lot of other activities together, like playing tennis and golf and going camping.

"I'm thinking . . . ," he said softly, inching closer to Terri.

She glanced up at him and smiled seductively. "And what are you thinking?"

"That I would like to handcuff you to my bed and have my way with you," he said, desire shining in his eyes.

"Really?"

"Yes, really."

"Then what are you waiting for?"

The desire in his eyes deepened. "For you to say let's leave."

She leaned over, brushed his lips, and whispered, "Let's leave."

The sexy sound of her voice did things to Phillip. He intended to do more than handcuff her to the bed. Later that night, he would also ask her to be his wife.

"Thanks for taking me to the party, Marcus," Naomi Monroe said as she and Marcus Lowery entered her home. "And I'm enjoying the friendship I'm developing with Falon and Terri. They're a lot of fun to be around."

Marcus nodded and watched Naomi take off her coat and toss it across her sofa. He had admired her outfit when he first picked her up for the party, and was still admiring it now. Her dress wasn't overly flashy, but it had been an attention getter because she looked so good in it.

He and Naomi had begun dating seriously last month. Things had been rocky for them for a while, but spending time with her, he was seeing the truly special woman that she was. And deep down, he believed God had sent her into his life to help build him back up after years of being bereft and torn down and wallowing in grief and self-pity, all of which he had blamed God for.

Now he was going to church more—which definitely

made his mother happy—and thanks to Naomi, he was even a part of the singles group at church and found himself enjoying it.

"Would you like something to drink, Marcus? I still have tea left from dinner yesterday, or I can put on a pot of coffee."

"No, I'm fine, but I do want to talk to you for a second."

Her brow rose slightly as she went to the sofa and sat down. "All right. What is it?"

He crossed the room and sat down beside her. They had decided to take things slow. He knew her history: she had been abstinent for four years and was waiting for a good Christian man to come into her life. More than anything, he wanted to be that man, and although he wasn't a perfect Christian, he felt he was improving each day and building a deep commitment with his faith.

He had also come to realize that he had fallen in love with Naomi. He had really fallen in love. His wife, Dottie, would always hold a special place in his heart, and something Dottie had said to him in a dream a few months ago came so vividly to his mind now. *"You are a special man, Marcus, and there is a woman out there who needs you, and you will come to realize that you need her, as well. And one day you will also realize that you can love her as much as you loved me."*

Dottie had been right. Love had come back into his life, and he refused to make the mistake of denying it. Shifting his position on the sofa to face Naomi, he took her hand in his and met her gaze. There was so much he wanted to say, but he knew the most important thing was that he speak from his heart.

"You are a special person, Naomi, and I feel special just from being in your presence. You have that way about you. I've watched you—I've noticed you. No wonder my mother and so many other people at church think a lot of you. You have a heart of gold. And the way you volunteer your time to others, especially the senior citizens at church, is admirable."

She smiled. "Thank you, Marcus."

"And I guess all of that is just some of the reasons I feel for you like I do."

He watched her throat move slowly when she swallowed. "And how do you feel for me, Marcus?" she asked quietly.

He held her gaze. "I've fallen in love with you, Naomi."

He saw her eyes widen in surprise; then moments later he watched those same eyes fill with tears. He quickly wondered if they were tears of happiness or tears of despair. He reached out and wiped a tear from her chin with his finger. "Hey, me loving you can't be that bad," he said jokingly. "I know it might take time for you to reciprocate those feelings, and I don't want to give you the impression that I'm trying to rush you or anything, but I just wanted—"

"I love you, too, Marcus. I've always loved you."

Marcus blinked. Then he said, "Define *always*."

Naomi smiled. "*Always* means forever. Since high school, but you never noticed me. Then you left for college, and I gave up all hope of ever getting with you. It was during that time I made the mistake of getting married to a man I didn't love—to forget you. It didn't work out, and we were together less than a year."

She paused briefly before continuing. "I was hoping to get together when word got out that you were returning home from college. But then I'd heard you were seeing someone and later that you had gotten married. I tried getting on with my life, not ever thinking we had a chance to get together."

Marcus shook his head, smiling. "Let me get this straight. You loved me back in the day? While we were in high school? But I was older than you."

"Only by a few years, but it didn't matter. I loved you anyway."

For a moment Marcus remained silent. "And how do you feel about me now?" He needed to hear it again.

"I love you, Marcus."

Marcus leaned over and captured Naomi's mouth, kissing her deeply, completely. When the kiss ended, he pulled her into his arms. "I need you in my life. I'm so tired of being alone, sweetheart. Will you do me the honor of becoming my wife? If you say yes, I promise to love you always, too." He felt Naomi tremble and held her tighter. He pulled back slightly to meet her gaze.

"Yes, I'll marry you, Marcus."

He smiled. "And I don't want to wait forever. I want to start the New Year off right. How does a spring wedding sound?"

Joy touched Naomi's features, making the woman he loved even more radiant. "I think it sounds wonderful."

He grinned. "But the hard part will be keeping my hands off you until then. I intend to remain celibate for you until our wedding night. I want to be the man worthy of your gift, Naomi."

And then he leaned over and began kissing her again.

*   *   *

Before Lance Montgomery retired for bed, he received
a phone call from Carl. "Keep your fax machine on so
I can send you the information regarding Asia Fowler's
itinerary for the next couple of months."

Lance smiled. "I'm not going to ask how you got it,
but thanks."

"I just hope you know what the hell you're doing and
that you don't get yourself into any trouble."

Lance's smile widened. "Trouble? There won't be any
trouble."

4

Carrie

There is a way to look at the past. Don't hide from it.
It will not catch you if you don't repeat it.
—*Pearl Bailey*

This is the day.

It was another year, and for Carrie Montgomery it
was the anniversary of the day she had returned home
to her family. It was hard to believe it was just six years
ago that the three brothers she hadn't known existed
suddenly appeared to snatch her off the streets of Los
Angeles, where she had been living as a runaway. She
couldn't help wandering around her condo, wanting to
pinch herself.

Carrie had barely turned eight when her mother had
become an alcoholic and a junkie after moving in with
a man named Simon Anderson. When she wasn't hitting the bottle, she was shooting up, leaving Carrie in
Simon's "care." When Carrie couldn't take the sexual
abuse anymore, she decided that living on the streets
had to be better than what she'd been enduring. Simon's
threats of coming after her had meant nothing to her—
she had been willing to take her chances.

Living as a runaway those years hadn't been easy, but she'd made it the best way she could. She had become an accomplished thief and could defend herself when she needed to, and curse like a sailor, but she avoided getting caught up in anything like drugs. She had seen what had happened to her mother.

The day her brothers and their private investigator had found her, it had been hard to believe that the three men were telling the truth and that they weren't men Simon had sent to find her. And then to be told that she had a family living in Illinois, including a man who was more than willing to claim her as his long-lost daughter even if there was a possibility she'd been fathered by someone else—it was just too much. They told her their mother had run off with another man when Carrie was a few months old; she was their baby sister.

For reasons she never understood, Logan, Lyle, Lance, and the man she now considered her pop, Jeremiah Montgomery, had taken her off the streets, put a roof over her head and given her plenty of food to eat, and they claimed her as their own, showering her with more love than she could ever imagine, giving her a sense of self-respect, educational opportunities, and a future she never dreamed of having.

Now she was twenty-four, with a college degree, and working as a social worker in Tampa. She was the proud owner of a condo. She owed her family—her *real* family—everything.

Logan, who was a medical doctor with a specialty in plastic surgery, lived within a few miles. Pop was still in Gary; Lyle, a renowned heart surgeon, was living in

Texas; and Lance, a doctor of psychology, was living close to Pop in Chicago.

She checked her watch. She wasn't due at work until ten today and would make it a point to stop by and see Logan before she went in.

Especially today.

"Dr. Montgomery, your sister is out front."

At the sound of his secretary's voice, Logan glanced up from the patient's chart he'd been reading. A smile touched his lips. "Send her in. And Janice, please hold all my calls. We're not to be disturbed unless there is an extreme emergency."

He placed the chart aside as he stood. He had expected Carrie's visit today.

He imagined that there were things she had endured in the time before they found her that she wouldn't discuss with him, his brothers, or their father. They had promised not to push and had had to believe that one day she would find the strength to tell them about it and let them help her get through it. Maybe today was that day.

"Logan?"

He pulled himself out of his reverie and glanced toward the door when Carrie stuck her head in. "I'm here, Carrie."

Relief lit her face. He was letting her know that he was more than just here in his office—he was here for her, as a part of her life, and always would be. She walked into the room, closed the door behind her, and then walked right into his outstretched arms for his ready hug.

*   *   *

Although Carrie had arrived there late, good news had been awaiting her at the office. She had worked her butt off last year to finalize Jason Belmont's adoption with the Hendersons. Tom and Edith Henderson were good people and just what ten-year-old Jason needed in his young life.

Everybody wanted babies, but it was hard to find homes for preteens, especially children with both parents serving time. People tended to believe the saying "The apple doesn't fall far from the tree."

But the Hendersons thought differently, and after having Jason as a foster child for a year, they waited patiently for his parents to agree to give up their own custody rights so an adoption could take place. They had all met with the judge yesterday, and a final decision had been made today.

"Sorry to disturb you, Miss Montgomery, but this package just arrived for you."

Carrie glanced up from the case file she'd been reading. "Thanks, Helen."

The envelope Helen handed to her felt light, and the first thing Carrie noticed was that it didn't have a return address.

Once Helen left, Carrie pushed away from her desk and slit the seal on the envelope with her letter opener. The contents fell out on her desk.

She gasped at the five-by-seven photographs that stared up at her. The top photo was of a little girl, not much older than ten, clearly being sexually abused by a man.

She breathed deeply, recognizing the child in the

photo. The man in the photo with her was Simon. Those nights he had visited her bedroom, had the monster actually been taping her, too? These looked like snapshots from video—kiddie porn. Panic consumed her. Who had possession of these photos? Of the video? Who had sent them to her? Had Simon made good on his threat and finally found her after all these years?

She looked at the other three photos and felt sick to her stomach. Hands trembling, she picked up the type-written note that had accompanied them.

I thought you'd like to see this before the original footage goes up on the Internet. There are more where these came from. This could be embarrassing for your brothers if word got out. So, if you want to keep what's in the past in the past, then be willing to pay whatever amount I want.

I'll be in touch.
An Old Friend

5

Lance and Asia

Lance's limousine moved through the streets of Manhattan toward its destination: the *New York Times* Recognition Dinner. He had been invited to this annual event numerous times, but this was the first year he'd considered attending.

And only because he knew Asia would be there.

His guts clenched in anticipation. He also knew that Sean Crews would not attend. According to a very reliable source, Crews was out of the country, and Lance wished to God he remained just where he was. But regardless, he would not let the man interfere with his plans.

"We will be arriving in less than two minutes, Dr. Montgomery."

Lance nodded at the chauffeur and hoped like hell he arrived in one piece. The man who had introduced himself as Al when he'd been picked up at the Waldorf Astoria was quite a driver. With a physique more suited for a wrestler than a chauffeur, he seemed to think the streets of New York were his for the taking, and twice Lance had held his breath when they'd almost collided with yellow cabs.

"Here we are, sir," Al said, bringing the vehicle to a surprisingly smooth stop in front of Rockefeller Center.

Lance took a moment to glance out of the tinted glass. Numerous people were still arriving. Some he recognized, and some he did not. He couldn't help wondering if Asia was inside already. Just the thought of seeing her again, and within arms' reach, was causing his heart to thud in his chest. This time last year, he was a man who thought he was an expert when it came to noncommitted relationships. Now more than anything, he was a man who just wanted to be an authority on one particular woman. Tonight he intended to tell Asia that he still wanted her and, more important, that he loved her. He planned to say to her what he had not been able to say three weeks ago at the Pattersons' party, the same night her engagement to Crews had been announced.

Al opened the door for him. "Enjoy your evening, Dr. Montgomery."

Glad he had arrived in one piece, Lance said, "Thanks, and I fully intend to."

Claire touched Asia's arm and whispered, "Wow, this is some affair."

They neared a staircase in the middle of the huge ballroom. It had been lavishly decorated, and as Asia glanced around, she saw so had the patrons. "Yes, it is, isn't it?"

Everyone who was considered someone in the publishing industry, in addition to many well-known celebrities, were present.

"And your gown is exquisite, I might add," Claire added.

"And so is yours." Asia returned the compliment when they found themselves in front of a huge table laden with all sorts of mouthwatering foods. The decorations were a combination of the holiday theme as well as the theme of the party, Let Reading Take You Away. Various fountains spouted sparkling champagne, just in case you weren't quick enough to nab one of the waiters who were circulating among the guests.

"Mmm, this is delicious," Claire said, popping one of the many hors d'oeuvres into her mouth. "I don't want to think of how many calories I'm consuming."

Asia grinned at her sister. "Then don't think about it. Besides, it's against the law to watch your weight during the holidays." This, she immediately thought, is what she missed with Claire living so far away. They had always had a close relationship and always enjoyed spending time together. The only time their close ties had gotten severed had been during Asia's affair with David.

"I wonder what's going on over there?" Claire said, noting the small commotion going on at the entrance. It seemed the news media had moved into place, and cameras were flashing.

Asia shrugged. "It's probably some eccentric author who seldom attends, but decided to do so this year. Or it could be the Ernest Hemingway look-alike who showed up last year trying to convince everyone he was truly the man reincarnated."

Claire, whom Asia knew enjoyed reading Hemingway's work, lit up in amusement. "Really?"

"Yes, really."

"Then this I've got to see," Claire said, straining her neck to look over the crowd. Lucky for her, the mass of people parted within moments. Claire recognized the person who had caused such an uproar at the same exact moment that her sister did. Both women gasped.

Claire, who had never seen Lance Montgomery in the flesh, was awestruck at the man who strolled forward through the explosion of flashbulbs and the throng of reporters. Tall, dashingly handsome, and dressed in a black tux, he stood out, the epitome of everything male and then some. If there was a chance this man had piqued Asia's interest, then Claire could definitely see why. He was a man who caused a stir. She glanced over at Asia and saw that her sister hadn't taken her eyes off of Dr. Montgomery.

"He's gorgeous, isn't he, Asia?"

Asia snapped out of her trance, angry for having given Lance's entrance so much of her attentions. "The man is an ass."

Claire smiled. "Umm, that's the same thing I always thought about David."

Asia couldn't help but note that Lance's name was already being whispered around the room, no surprise since he'd never attended this affair before. But it was also being whispered for an entirely different reason. Women might find his work disgusting, offensive, and downright odious. But what they thought of the man himself was an entirely different matter. Evidently some of them were certain they could be the one to teach him a thing or two about women, if given the time alone with him.

"I'll put such a whammy on him that it will make

him see stars," she heard one woman whisper to another. "I'll have him begging for it in the end," the woman then added.

Asia was tempted to tell her that it would be the other way around, and even worse. Lance would put something on her that would not only have her seeing stars but would give her the equivalent of an earthquake and hurricane rolled into one. Not only that, in the end *he* wouldn't be the one begging. If he used his mouth on her, he would have her pleading in languages she'd never have guessed she knew.

"Well, what do you think?"

Asia lifted a brow at her sister's question. "I've told you what I think," she snapped.

Claire chuckled. "Not about Dr. Montgomery. We'd moved from that topic of conversation. Don't you remember I made a comment about what a beautiful gown that Senator Hillary Clinton is wearing?"

Asia sighed. She didn't remembering them changing the subject. "Well, it doesn't matter."

"What doesn't matter?" Claire asked, sipping from a glass of champagne.

"The fact that Lance Montgomery is here."

Claire didn't want to say so, but she had a feeling it did matter. Something *was* going on with Asia and Lance . . . or maybe something had been going on at one time. Asia usually hid her emotions well, but even from across the room, Lance Montgomery was obviously getting under her sister's skin.

She just *had* to keep her sister from making another mistake with another Crews. There was no way Asia could convince her that she loved Sean, and without love, the two of them didn't stand a chance with David around.

"Do you want to leave now?" Asia asked.

"No, the party is just beginning. Besides, rumor has it that Denzel will be here tonight, and I don't want to miss that for anything. I wish I'd brought his book with me. . . ."

When the media and photographers retreated to the background, Lance didn't waste any time scanning the crowd for the one woman he was here to see. Seconds later, he saw her.

She was standing across the room, talking to another woman, and the sight of her made him forget to breathe. She was wearing a stunning lavender slinky strapless gown with a fitted bodice that flattered her curves. He thought she looked gorgeous, and fully understood why he had always found her so mesmerizing, and why he had fallen so deeply in love with her.

He loved her with every part of his body, his mind, his soul, and he knew there was no way in hell he would allow Crews or any other man to have her. No matter what it took, he intended to sweep away all the vestiges of bitterness, anger, and misunderstanding between them. And one way to do that was to make her remember a very special time they had shared.

He quickly stopped a passing waiter. "Excuse me. I wonder if you could deliver this to the woman standing over there in the lavender gown?" Lance asked, reaching into his pocket and pulling out a lone diamond stud earring.

The man looked at the earring. "Is there a message that goes along with this, sir?"

Lance shook his head. "No." He was certain Asia would remember where she'd left it.

Once the commotion settled, there was no way Asia would allow herself to glance over at Lance. She hoped that with so many people in attendance, he wouldn't see her the entire night.

She had decided to tell Claire that Denzel or no Denzel, she was ready to leave. A waiter carrying a tray appeared before her. "Excuse me, ma'am, but that gentleman over there asked that I deliver this to you."

Asia met Lance's eyes. With a will of its own, her heart slipped into overdrive. She felt her palms get warm, and the area between her legs became unbearably hot. A part of her wondered why Sean didn't make her feel this way, and why Lance—and Lance, alone, even after all that he'd done—could make her body a mass of hot shameful desire. Even David hadn't made her feel this degree of wanting. It fascinated her how some men could turn women on, and others could not. Lance definitely had the knack—but *dammit*, she was happily engaged to marry Sean, she insisted.

Sean.

When she thought of Sean she tried to banish those illicit sensations flowing through her. He had called earlier today, when she and Claire had been out shopping. His message on her answering machine told her how much he loved her and how he missed her and that he was counting the days until they were together.

"Ma'am?"

Asia acknowledged the waiter and opened the palm

of her hand, ignoring her sister's curious expression. The man placed a diamond earring in it. "Thank you."

The man nodded and walked off.

Asia looked down at the earring, wishing she could forget everything about that one night with Lance. She had wanted a climax, needed one, and her traitorous body had practically begged for one. In Lance Montgomery style, he had delivered. He had given her pleasure in a way no man had ever done before and still let her leave without crossing the line—going all the way.

"How did Dr. Montgomery get your earring, Asia?"

Now was the perfect time to lie and say she didn't know, but her sister would see through it. "We had a date one night, and I guess I left it."

"A date? At the restaurant?"

"No, at his apartment—and that's all I'm saying, Claire."

Claire nodded. As far as she was concerned, that was enough. Asia had dinner with the good doctor at his apartment? Things were getting more interesting by the minute.

Claire turned when commotion erupted. Flashbulbs were going off everywhere. "Well, it seems that Denzel has finally arrived."

Lance crossed the room when he saw Asia and the woman she was with heading toward the door. He made it to them before they got there. "Good evening, ladies."

If looks could kill, he'd be a goner. Asia was giving him an angry glare. Standing in front of her was almost too overwhelming, and he was tempted to say the hell with propriety, pull her into his arms, and kiss her right then and there.

"Hello, I'm Claire Fowler, and I don't think we've met."

The woman standing beside Asia appeared to be only a couple of years older than she, and Lance quickly realized that they were sisters. She was an extremely beautiful woman. "No, I don't believe we have," he said, and accepted the hand she offered. "I'm Lance Montgomery."

She smiled and Lance thought yes, this was definitely Asia's sister. They had that same intriguing smile. "It's nice meeting you, Lance."

"It's nice to meet you, as well."

"I occasionally read your work when I'm looking for amusement," she said with a teasing glint in her eyes.

Her statement could have been taken as an insult, but for some reason he didn't see it that way, and he laughed softly. "Thanks. I'm glad I've been the source of your entertainment."

"I hate to interrupt this little chitchat, but Claire and I were about to leave."

He met Asia's eyes. "I was hoping that you would dance with me before leaving, Asia."

She took a step back. "Sorry to disappoint you, but you were hoping wrong because I—"

"I think the two of you *should* dance together."

Asia turned and narrowed her gaze at her sister, who merely dismissed the look with chuckle. "If the two of you haven't noticed, you're about to cause a scene. It's not often you can get two well-known adversaries in the same place. I'd say in a few minutes, the two of you will start getting hounded by reporters, who'll start asking questions—and they might be questions neither of you want to answer right now. So maybe it's not such a bad idea to get lost in the mist of the other couples on the dance floor for a while. Besides, I see someone I know over there, a guy who went to college with me at Georgetown, and I want to scoot over and say hello to him, so don't think you'll be deserting me, Asia." Claire walked off, leaving her sister alone with Lance Montgomery.

"Come dance with me, Asia." And before she could decline, Lance took her hands in his and led her toward the dance floor.

The moment Lance took Asia into his arms, she whispered, "You, Lance Montgomery, are an arrogant ass."

Lance was not stunned by her words, nor was he surprised. "And you, Asia Fowler, are the most beautiful woman I've ever had the privilege of meeting."

She glared up at him. "I'm sure you said the same thing to Rachel Cason that night." The moment they left her lips, Asia wished she could take back the words. The last thing she wanted was for him to know how much his actions that night had hurt her.

"No, I didn't tell her that. In fact I asked her to leave seconds after you did. The only woman who shared my bed that night was you."

"Am I supposed to believe that?"

"I'm hoping that you do, since it's the truth. I wronged you, and I want to apologize—"

"Spare me any explanations, and there is no need to apologize. Your true colors came out that night, Lance. I was operating with blinders on, but now I see clearly. All I was to you was a conquest, a challenge, someone you wanted to bring down a peg or two. Well, now the game is over, and I hope you got all the satisfaction that you wanted, and I pray after tonight we won't ever see each other again. In fact, I'm going to make it a point that our paths don't cross again."

She'd stopped dancing and had started to walk off. The only thing he could think about was that she was fighting him, putting distance between them, and he refused to let that happen. With a mixture of panic and desperation, he took her hand in his and quickly led her off the dance floor to a deserted area outside the hall. He pulled her beneath an empty stairway.

"What the hell do you think you're doing?" she asked when they came to a stop, snatching her hand from his. "How dare you—?"

His mouth swooped down on hers, seizing it in a sensuous assault, grinding her lips apart, forcing them to open to him. At first she resisted, as he had expected, but soon he felt the fight leave her, and her mouth slowly opened beneath his. Moments later, she wrapped her arms around his neck and pressed her body close to his.

He deepened the kiss as his mouth moved urgently and greedily on hers. He would melt her defenses and put a crack in that wall she had erected.

Lance heard a sound, almost a clicking, and lifted his head. When he looked down at Asia, her eyes darkened in absolute passion. Then when it hit her what they had done, she stared up at him in seemingly stunned anger. She raised her hand and slapped him. "You had no right to do that," she said in blazing fury. "I am an engaged woman," she said, backing up a step. "How dare you continue this game!"

Something snapped within Lance. He recovered the distance. "This is not a game, Asia. I love you."

"Love!" she choked out the word. "Give me a break. You wouldn't know the meaning of the word if it came up and bit you in the ass. I hate you," she all but screamed, not caring who was around to hear her words. Her chest rose and fell in sharp, fuming breaths. She took another step back. "And I'm warning you not to ever come near me again, Lance. If you do, you'll be sorry."

She turned and quickly walked away toward the ballroom, but not before Lance saw her tears.

Lance let himself into his hotel room. Tonight had not turned out completely the way he had wanted, but it was a start. Asia was angry with him; she was convinced she hated him. Those things he was pretty damn sure about. Another thing he was certain of was, besides those emotions, she also loved him.

Only a woman in love could have responded to him the way she had. He had known the exact moment she ceased to resist him and relinquished her entire being to him. Had they been alone near a bed, they would have made heated love on it. The one thing he knew about Asia was that she was not an impulsive person. Nor was she someone driven by passion to be reckless. She was a strong advocator that women should demand respect, love, and loyalty from the men in their lives; they should be in complete charge of every aspect of their life and under no circumstances should they let a man take advantage or get over.

Yet tonight, she had been driven by passion enough to give in to a need to kiss him, a man she considered her enemy. There was only one reason why she would do such a thing. Deep down, she loved him just as much as he loved her. But her hurt, pain, and anger were burying that love.

He reached up and rubbed the side of his face. It was still stinging from her slap. A bark of laughter erupted from his throat. Damn, but he'd deserved it. But to put it more bluntly, he and Asia deserved each other. And the way she had wrapped her arms around his neck and moaned his name into his mouth proved she wasn't as immune to him as she wanted to be.

And that key would eventually reopen her heart— their intense desire for each other, their passion. If for one minute she thought of having a future with anyone but him, then she had another thought coming. It was time to take things to the next level. Her warning for him to stay away from her meant nothing. The threat had fallen on deaf ears. Although the risk was large, the rewards in the end would be greater. And he had his eye on the ultimate prize.

Asia.

The woman he loved more than life itself. If he doubted that fact before tonight, after seeing her again, tasting her, inhaling her scent, and touching her, he knew it to be a definite.

He checked his watch. Pulling out his briefcase, he opened it up and retrieved the document that Carl had faxed to him last week. He slowly glanced over it, studying it in detail.

Then Lance smiled as he began planning his next strategy.

6

Carrie

"Talk to me, Carrie. What's going on? Why are you leaving?"

Carrie paused in her packing and met her brother's intense stare. "There's nothing going on, Logan. I just want to get away for a while, no biggie. You know me—it happens sometimes. A couple of months ago, I went to Chicago and spent some time with Lance. Now I want to go spend some time with Pops in Gary for the holidays. Quit worrying! I'm fine."

Logan had a feeling that she wasn't fine. She was running, but he had no idea what she was running from.

"Do you need anything, Carrie?"

Carrie met Logan's gaze. She loved all three of her brothers, but it was Logan who tolerated her shit the most. And it was Logan who was quick to put her in her place when she needed it. He was the big brother every girl should have. If things had been different while growing up, he would have been there to protect her from the likes of Simon Anderson.

But he hadn't.

"No, I don't need anything, Logan. I'm fine. I'm just burned out. I've worked on a lot of tough cases this year and I need a break. That's all. I'm taking a leave of absence from work and won't be returning until the first of the year. I plan to go to Texas at some point and visit Lyle, and drop in on Lance in Chicago, just in case everyone is too busy to get together at Pops' for Christmas."

Logan nodded. He didn't know his brothers' plans for the holidays, but he had intended on going home like he and Carrie had done every year since they'd been reunited. He knew his father looked forward to it.

Sighing, Logan checked his watch. He had to get to the hospital. He had surgery in a few hours. "Call me when you get to Pops', and let me know you made it there safe."

"I will."

He crossed the room and pulled her into his arms. "Take care of yourself, Pint," he said, calling her the nickname he had given her when she had first come home as a newborn from the hospital. She stood five-eight and had a willowy frame; he often got on her about not eating enough.

"I'll take care of myself, Logan. I promise."

Carrie snapped her seat belt in place and then leaned back as the crew prepared for takeoff. Her body shivered at the thought of leaving sunny Florida to head to icy cold Indiana. She had called Pops to let him know she was coming, and as she'd known, he'd been elated. He told her that something was going on with Lance, but he wasn't sure what. Lance hadn't been to see him in a couple of weeks, but when he'd finally come around last weekend, he was acting like a changed man, although Pops couldn't put his finger on what that change was.

Carrie settled in her seat, thinking that once she was settled in Gary, she would rent a car and drive into Chicago to see Lance. If something was going on with him, she needed to know about it. When she had visited him last month, she would swear he'd had woman problems. Lance would never let any female get under his skin. But still . . .

Thirty minutes later, the plane had leveled off in the air. The man sitting beside her was asleep, and she was grateful for that. She wasn't in the mood for conversation.

She closed her eyes, and immediately began thinking about the photos that were tucked away in her carry-on. Although she had every reason to suspect that Simon was the person who sent them, she had to be sure they hadn't fallen into someone else's hands. She'd have to hire a private investigator to find out what she wanted to know. Logan was a highly respected physician in the Tampa Bay area, so she didn't feel comfortable seeking out a private investigator there. She would take her chances with someone who operated a business somewhere in Indiana, not far from Gary. Although she was an innocent victim when the photos had been taken, she refused to let her brothers bear the shame and embarrassment of what had happened to her.

She also wanted a private investigator to find Edwina Montgomery. She wanted to look the woman in the face and tell her how her actions had almost destroyed her life.

She would return to Tampa the first of the year, secure in the knowledge that she had finally put the past behind her. Whoever was trying to blackmail her would be dealt with.

7

Connor

God has made all men to be happy.
—*Epictetus*

Connor Hargrove was a relatively happy man. And one thing he didn't believe in was missing an opportunity, especially when it came to women. Right now, he was happily watching as Debra Ervin removed the last of her clothes, slid provocatively on the bed to lie on her back, and shamelessly gave him a good view of the sweetness between her legs.

For the past two months, she had played hard to get, and tonight he would show her it had been a waste of time once he got the only thing he'd wanted from her anyway.

He tossed his jeans aside and quickly put on a condom then crawled naked onto the bed to join her and to give her the best ride of her life. She would think twice before holding out on him again, especially if she was waiting to hear the words he never intended to say to any woman.

"You still won't say it, will you, Connor?" she asked

in a voice so thick with passion that he felt himself get harder.

"No," he said before bending his head and kissing her lightly on the lips as he settled his body between her thighs. "I never say words I don't mean just to get a woman's stuff. Not even this is worth lying about."

He saw disappointment in her eyes. She wasn't the first who thought she could win his heart by way of his rod. Some women refused to accept that a happy man was a single man with no ties and who could slide between a glorious pair of legs without any hassles, commitments, or lies of love and affection.

"Love me, Connor."

He fought to hide his irritation. Damn, he had to hand it to her: she was persistent. "I can't do it, Debra. The only woman I love is my mama, so get over it and get ready for the best sex of your life."

He wasn't being arrogant. What he said was a fact.

He would make her giddy with pleasure, wet with joy, and screaming in ecstasy. He would also make her forget all this foolishness about only sleeping with men who loved her. He pulled her closer to him and began sinking into her wet warmth. When this was all over, she would realize he was a man who thrived on the physical and not the emotional. No linkage, just indulgence. There was nothing like a good hard workout in bed to keep your mind sharp. His sharp mind was what made him one of the best private investigators in the business.

He began pumping into her, lifting her hips to go even deeper, ignoring the pain of her fingernails digging into his back. He gripped her bottom when she began moaning his name, chanting disgracefully for him to do to her what he was doing anyway. And every so often, she would cry out that she wanted it hard.

He had no problem obliging. Hard was his middle name.

He increased the pace and began pumping into her like a madman, just the way she wanted it. She was tossing her head from side to side, delirious in passion, wrapping her legs around him tight, holding him captive . . . as if he planned on going somewhere. Their movements became urgent, desperate. He leaned over and nipped at her lower lip, which caused her to scream. She suddenly shattered, convulsing around him, trying to hold him with her inner muscles. The feel of her body gripping him, milking him, made his own pleasure explode. He threw his head back and thrust into her deeper, then held still as sensations took over his body, raced through him, and made him think that inside of her was one place he wanted to visit again.

With panting breaths and drained bodies, they slowly regained control of their senses. He leaned over and kissed her one more time before withdrawing his body from hers. He slumped down beside her, exhausted yet satiated.

A short while later, his fingers began drifting, seeking her out between her legs. Dammit, she was hot, wet, and puffy again. He needed to beat her stuff down some more. Whipping off the used condom and tossing it in a nearby trash can, he quickly grabbed another one to put on. He had no intentions of being anyone's baby daddy.

Without asking if she was ready for another round, he mounted her again. Not surprisingly, her legs parted for him like the Red Sea.

"Do you ever go down on a woman, Connor?"

He saw the hopeful gleam in her eyes. "No, I don't go down—just in."

And to prove his point, he swiftly entered her again, hearing her gasp. What he didn't say was that he had no problems going down on a woman, but only a special woman. So far no special woman existed for him, and until she did, the only place his tongue was going was in a woman's mouth.

"I will make you love me one of these days, Connor."

He smiled as he began pumping, lifting his head just enough to meet her eyes. Evidently he hadn't made things clear enough. "It won't happen, Debra."

He watched as she drew in a shaky, passionate breath. Sensations began overtaking her. "We'll see," she whispered.

Connor's breathing deepened, and so did his thrusts. "We sure will."

He spread his hand beneath her hips, deciding she talked too damn much. Her stuff was good but not enough to put up with the crap she was spouting. He decided that this would be his last time with her, and he might as well make it worth his while. He bent his head and began feasting on her breasts.

Within seconds, she screamed and creamed all over him as her orgasm hit her from all angles. He gripped her hips tightly as he thrust back and forth inside of her, catching up.

Finally, when he could breathe again, he withdrew and, without saying a word, got out of the bed. He began putting back on his clothes.

"I thought you were staying all night," she said, glaring at him.

"I thought so, too, but I changed my mind."

"Just like that?" she snapped.

He glanced up from buckling his belt, his expression serious. "Yeah, just like that. And let me give you some advice, Debra. Never tell a playa that your aim is to make him fall in love with you. Not that I think it's possible, but I personally didn't like hearing it. Besides, it makes me think that you could turn into a desperate woman, and desperate women are capable of doing just about anything."

He grabbed his jacket off the back of the chair as he headed for the door. "I'll be seeing you."

"I hate you, Connor."

He stopped, looked back over his shoulder and smiled. "Now you get the picture, baby."

He opened the door and walked out.

"Hey, Connor, we have a potential new client. Do you want to handle her case?" asked Brad Womack.

He, Brad, and another former Gary policeman by the name of Cameron Blue had quit the force to open up an investigative and security company in Portage. So far, business had been good—and he hoped it stayed that way.

"Why not? That last case was a piece of cake. The woman wanted proof that her old man was screwing around on her. The sad part about it was that he was screwing around on her with her brother."

"Ouch."

"Yeah, that's what I thought, too." Connor pushed himself away from the metal file cabinet and walked over to his desk. "What you got?"

"Possible blackmail. She wouldn't give me any specifics over the phone, just said she resides in Tampa, but wants things handled from here, since she'll be visiting in the area for about a month."

"That's fine," Connor said. "It's not like we don't need the business." The rent for this building wasn't cheap, and the cost for the remodeling they had done was still burning their pockets. But the three of them had agreed they wanted a classy place with state-of-the-art equipment. That was the only way they would draw in the type of clientele they wanted. So far, they took whatever they got, but he knew once they established a good reputation, the money for their services would start rolling in.

"So when is her appointment?" he asked, grabbing his Palm off the desk. So far they hadn't discussed hiring another full-time secretary after Debra had quit two days ago. The guys had joked about it, saying he needed to stop banging the hired help.

"Friday at ten in the morning, and her name is Carrie Montgomery."

Connor nodded. *Geez, blackmail.* He couldn't help but wonder what secrets Ms. Montgomery was harboring that she had to pay someone to keep.

8

Asia

"You might think Lance Montgomery is an ass, but he certainly has good taste when it comes to flowers. They are simply beautiful."

"Don't go there with me, Claire," Asia said harshly. Moments ago, a dozen of the most beautiful roses she had ever seen arrived at her apartment, and the card that had accompanied the arrangement hadn't been much better. It had simply said, *"It was meant for us to be together."*

She had crushed the card in her hand, thinking "the damn nerve of that man." She was engaged to Sean, but that hadn't stopped Lance from kissing her last night or sending her flowers today! The thought of his boldness—as well as his lack of respect for Sean's position in her life—pushed Asia to mindless fury.

"I gather you're upset."

"Of course I'm upset," Asia snapped, and then quickly apologized.

"And why are you angry? I think it's flattering that he's showing interest in you."

Asia's eyes blazed. "There is nothing flattering about it. What he's doing is merely playing a game, and I don't want any part of it," she shot out angrily.

Claire wasn't fully convinced that the doctor was only playing a game with her sister. She had watched Lance's reaction to Asia just like she had watched Asia's reaction to him. She knew of his reputation, but for some reason, as hard as it was to believe, she felt he truly cared for Asia. It had been there in his eyes when he looked at her. It was too bad that Asia refused to see it. "Are you sure he's playing a game, Asia?"

"Of course he is! He doesn't want me—he just doesn't want Sean to have me. He's obsessed with getting whatever he thinks he can't have. And do you know what I find the most infuriating about all of this?"

"No, what?"

"That in his warped mind he actually believes he has every right to me. He refuses to accept Sean's place in my future."

Claire took a sip of her coffee. She and Dr. Montgomery definitely had something in common there. She asked, "So, what are you planning to do?"

"Ignore him, his flowers, and his game. If he wants to waste his time by pursuing an unattainable goal, then that's his business. I, for one, refuse to be a party to it." Asia dropped the flowers, vase and all, into the garbage. "Now if you will excuse me, I have a book to finish." She walked angrily out of the room.

Claire shook her head as she went over to the garbage and retrieved the flowers. No matter what Asia said, they were too beautiful to be ignored, and if her sister didn't want to enjoy them, she certainly would.

She released a throaty chuckle as she placed the vase of flowers back on the table.

Dr. Montgomery had his work cut out for him, and Claire couldn't wait to see what was coming next.

9

Carrie and Connor

Connor stood in the middle of his office and stared through the plate glass window. His attention had been captured by a woman who was getting out of her car. He hoped like hell that she wasn't Carrie Montgomery.

Geez, that was all he needed: a client who was definitely catching his eye. He felt a stirring in his gut that he didn't want to feel. She was young, probably no older than twenty-one, and it was apparent the below-thirty-degree weather wasn't affecting her much. Although she had on a leather jacket, she was wearing a midriff shirt emblazoned with the words BORN TO BE WILD. His gaze then traced the planes of her flat stomach and spotted the small ring that was dangling from her navel. That short jean skirt she was wearing—pretty damn enticing, since it showed off thighs that were meant for riding and a gorgeous pair of legs. The short leather boots only added to the tempting package.

A rush of lust surged through his body when images

of him and this woman getting wild together in a number of wickedly sordid ways began playing in his mind.
He would love to see just how wild she could get.
"Down, Mr. P," he muttered to that part of him that was
pressing hard against the zipper of his jeans. "You
know when it comes to clients that I don't mix business
with pleasure."

When it became apparent the woman was headed
toward the doors of CCB Investigators and not the
Hallmark shop next door, he decided to get his body
parts under control before coming out of his office.

Carrie studied the painted sign on the door of CCB
Investigators. She had told Pops she was driving into
Chicago to do some shopping and to visit Lance—
which she fully intended to do after her meeting with
one of the investigators.

As soon as she opened the door and stepped into the
warmth of the building, a deep male voice stopped her
in her tracks. "Carrie Montgomery?"

She caught sight of a tall, dark, and handsome man
dressed in a pair of jeans and collared shirt. His facial
features were tough-looking yet compelling and his skin
was the color of semi-dark chocolate. He had intense
eyes beneath perfectly slanted eyebrows, day-old stub-
ble over a rugged sexy jaw. Those lips could probably
kiss a woman senseless. He was well over six feet tall,
and he had a muscular build.

She stepped back, tilted her head, and decided he
definitely deserved a second glance. Placing her hands
on her hips, she asked cockily. "Who wants to know?"

He came farther into the room, and she almost wished

he hadn't done that. The closer he got, the better he looked. "I do," he said, studying her intently. "My name is Connor Hargrove, and we have a ten-o'clock appointment."

Despite herself, Carrie couldn't help but feel a little flutter in her midsection. She couldn't remember the last time a male's presence had affected her this much. The man staring back at her had eyes that were dark as midnight, and a mouth that was tempting as chocolate. Then there was the lean line of his jaw and the hint of a cleft in his chin.

She thought she actually felt her breasts swell in the process. "Well, Connor Hargrove, yes, I am Carrie Montgomery."

"Then I suggest we go into my office and get down to business." He turned to walk off, dropping a smile on her first.

In just that short span of time, she had felt it—a jolt of static electricity that had flowed between them. There was no way he could not have felt it, as well. Long ago she had decided that she didn't trust men, and frankly didn't like them either—but there had to be a reason why a current of warm air was fanning around her navel and making goose bumps form all over her skin.

His footsteps slowed, and he glanced around. She swore she saw his eyes darken to an outrageously erotic black as he looked at her. "Are you coming?"

Carrie flushed. She actually wished that she *was* coming, literally, with this man buried deep inside of her. She gasped inwardly, not believing she had thought such a thing. But she had. She took a step back.

"No, I've changed my mind. Forget the appointment."

She turned to leave, but he quickly crossed the distance separating them and blocked the door. "What the hell are you afraid of?" he snapped. "If you're being blackmailed, then I'm the least of your worries."

Carrie doubted it. "Look, you're probably a good investigator and all, but I don't think this is going to work." His mouth twitched into another smile, and at that moment she knew he understood her dilemma. *Their* dilemma.

"Will it make you feel better to know that I don't do clients?" he asked huskily.

She wasn't all that sure his statement calmed her nerves or gave her the assurance she needed. "Only if it makes you feel better to know that I don't do men." When his brow lifted, she rolled her eyes before saying. "And no, I don't do women either."

A curious frown stole into his face. "And why don't you do men?"

Fair question, she thought, considering what she'd just told him. "What I mean is, other than my father and my three brothers, I don't trust men."

His face took on a serious expression. "If I take your case, you'll have to trust me."

Carrie lifted her chin. "I will, up to a point."

"Fine. Now we understand each other, so will you give me a chance and try me?"

Carrie felt a lump in her throat. That was her problem. The man standing before her was a total stranger, but for a reason she couldn't explain, she did want to try him. . . . Her mind filled with a lot of creative ways and positions: back, front, sideways, the wall, the table, floor . . . You name it, and she would certainly like to try it.

"Ms. Montgomery?"

She sighed. "I prefer that you call me Carrie, and yes, I will try you, Connor Hargrove."

Once they were seated in his office on either side of his desk, he said, "Now how about if you start from the beginning."

Carrie had no intentions of going that far back. Two things she heavily guarded were her privacy and her past. Besides, he didn't need to know the whole story. "I received this envelope in the mail two weeks ago. It had pictures in it."

He gave her a curious look. "What kind of pictures?"

She looked outside the huge window in his office. "Pictures of me and a man together," she said softly.

Connor leaned back in his chair, slowly understanding. "And now someone is threatening to give the pictures to your fiancé?"

"No, I don't have a fiancé. I told you—I don't do men, so I certainly wouldn't be engaged to one."

"Sorry. My mistake."

"The person threatened to put them on the Internet unless I pay up."

"How much are they asking for?"

"They haven't said yet. It was signed 'an old friend,' and that he would keep in touch."

Connor nodded. "And what makes you think it's a he? You don't think you have any girlfriends who may have turned on you and resorted to blackmail?"

NO MORE PLAYAS 73

Carrie slowly shook her head. Most of her life she had spent as a runaway, not befriending anyone. The only female she had befriended was an older girl named Serena, but she had died on the streets. "No, just like I don't trust men, I never trusted women either. I'm pretty much a loner."

"What about your family?" He remembered her mentioning something about three brothers earlier and saw the caution that lit her eyes with his question.

"What about them?" she asked, glaring at him.

"Evidently the person who is trying to get money out of you knows that you're willing to protect someone from seeing those pictures."

"Yes, my brothers. They are pretty well known nationally in their chosen fields. Two are medical specialists, and one is a psychologist." And that was as much as she would tell him about her brothers.

Connor said, "Look, if you want me to help you, you're going to have to tell me all I want to know. Otherwise, you might as well walk out of the door and invite these brothers of yours over to your place for the Internet viewing, or be prepared to pay this person who's trying to extort money out of you whatever amount he wants. I'm an ex-cop, and my goal will be to use whatever resources and connections I have to stop him or her before he causes damage."

Carrie inhaled deeply. He was right. The only way he could help her was if she told him everything he needed to know. More than anything, she wanted Simon stopped before her brothers found out about him and what he'd done to her years ago and what he was trying to do even now.

"I believe the person who is trying to get money out of me is the man in the picture with me, and I want you to do whatever you can to stop him."

Connor nodded. "I need to see the photographs he sent as well as the extortion letter."

Carrie hesitated for a moment before pulling the envelope from her canvas tote bag. She handed it to him and then slowly held her breath when he opened the envelope and dumped out the contents onto his desk.

"Holy shit . . ."

Those were the only words Connor could say as he looked at the photos that had come tumbling out. He recognized the little girl immediately, since she was merely a younger version of the young woman sitting across from him. She didn't look any more than seven or eight years old then. She had always been a beauty, and the thought that some bastard had . . .

He forced himself to look away from the pictures and look at Carrie. His stomach knotted when he saw tears glistening in her eyes. Somehow he could actually feel her pain, and, for the first time in his life, two emotions that he'd never shared with any woman, tenderness and a feeling of protectiveness, rammed through him. "How old were you?" he asked quietly. Damn, she'd been just a child, but someone had placed her in the hands of a pervert. How could anyone have done something so cruel?

She swiped at her wet cheek and said softly, "I was eight."

"And who is this bastard? You said his name is Simon?"

Carrie swallowed, searching for composure. "Yes, Simon Anderson. He was my mother's boyfriend at the time. While she was somewhere getting high, he was supposed to be taking care of me."

Connor's heart broke at the abuse she had endured. No child, no matter the age, should have gone through what Miss Montgomery had gone through. Damn, no wonder she didn't trust men.

"He is one stupid son of a bitch for sending these to you now. Evidently, he doesn't know that he can be prosecuted on these alone. In the state of Indiana, there is no statute of limitations on crimes done to a minor."

"He was never a smart man."

And he would be a damn unlucky one now that Connor was handling the case. He would make sure the bastard got what he deserved. "I will find him, Carrie," he said, meaning every word.

Carrie believed him. "And there's someone else I want you to find, as well."

Connor raised his eyebrow. "Who?"

"My mother. She's still out there somewhere, if she's still alive. She deserted my father and three brothers when I was barely six weeks old, running off with me and her lover to California. I can't remember a lot of the time before Simon, but not once did she tell me I had a family living in Indiana. In fact, she led me to believe I was the only child. One night I decided to run away. I managed to dodge the authorities, and sometimes I didn't and I was sent to live in foster homes."

She tossed her hair back from her face and said, "I hated the foster care system. Some people took you in because they got paid every month for putting up with you. I didn't make friends or any lasting relationships. When I was thirteen, I ran away again and lived on the streets until my brothers' private investigators found me."

"How old were you when you ran away the first time?"

"A little over ten."

Connor couldn't imagine a kid that young fending for herself on the streets of L.A. "How old were you when your brothers found you?"

"I thought I was eighteen, but my birth certificate said I was only sixteen. Somehow while I was on the run, I lost track of time. Birthdays didn't mean a lot to me then."

Connor could understand why. He came around the desk when Carrie stood. "If your mother is still alive, then I'll find her, as well. I understand your need to bury the past, get beyond it, and I'm personally going to make this Simon regret the day he ever laid a hand on you."

Carrie's throat tightened with emotion. She was stunned by his anger. "Thank you." She took a single step back, suddenly needing space between them. "I'd better be going."

"All right, but we'll need to meet again soon. I'll need to know the last known address for your mother and Simon, the city where you were staying, schools you had been attending . . . someplace where I can began my search." He reached out and picked up his Palm off his desk and checked it. "Is there a way for us to meet again next Tuesday?"

"All right. I'm in town visiting my father, so us getting together to meet won't be a problem."

"Good. How about at noon? And if you're hungry, we can always do a change of atmosphere and discuss things over lunch." He decided to add, "It will be strictly business."

"No thanks," Carrie said.

Connor studied her expression, knowing her guard was up. "Okay, we will meet here at my office again."

"All right." Without saying anything else, Carrie walked away. Connor didn't allow his feelings of compassion to relax until he heard her close the door.

Carrie went to bed early that night but was awakened by a nightmare as a wave of trembling shook her body. With the delivery of those pictures, her nightmares had started up again and the face constantly in them belonged to Simon. She and her mother had lived with him for almost four months when something happened that shattered her life and was the beginning of a hellish existence.

It had started one evening at dinner. As usual, her mother was sleeping off a drunken state, and she and Simon had been the only ones sitting at the table. She hadn't understood why he'd been watching her eat until later . . . the first night he'd come to her room. He had explained that he got aroused just from watching her eat. At the time she hadn't understood what he meant, but she soon did. She had tried to avoid eating around him but he wouldn't let her. And each time she did so, she'd known what would happen. Her stomach clenched tight at the memories.

After returning to her father and brothers she had demanded to eat alone for a long time. Of course they had found her request strange, and to this day they never understood why, because she had been too ashamed to tell them.

She knew Connor wondered why she had turned down his offer to take her to lunch for their next meeting, but there was no way she could sit across from him, or any man, his eyes watching her as she ate. It would trigger memories of those terrible days with Simon.

She heard the knock and then a comforting voice through her bedroom door. "Carrie, are you all right? I thought I heard you scream."

"I'm okay, Pop, just a bad dream," she called out, hoping he didn't hear the tremor in her voice.

"You sure?"

"Yes, sir."

All right, then."

As soon as she was sure he was gone, she settled back in bed and softly began crying for the childhood she never had.

10

Sean

"How about joining us in a celebration, Sean?"

Sean glanced over at Elizabeth Howard, a fellow physician. She was one of the doctors he usually teamed up with on these types of goodwill medical missions, and they had known each other for years. They'd even dated a few years back, but then they decided just to be friends. "Sure, why not? I have a lot to celebrate."

"How are those wedding plans coming along?"

He sighed, hating that question. He really didn't know how any plans were coming. He and Asia had decided that because of his schedule and her book-signing and writing commitments, a June wedding was best. Now he wished he'd talked her into marrying him before he had left the States. If he didn't know better, he would swear she was having misgivings about their engagement, and hearing that her sister was in town wasn't helping matters. Although he had never done anything to Claire personally, she detested all the Crews family, thanks to David. She thought her sister would be better off not having contact with any of them.

He still hadn't answered Elizabeth's question. "They're coming, Liz. We've decided on a June wedding, although if it was up to me, we would marry sooner."

She smiled, nodding. "Hey, it sounds like you're one of those grooms who don't intend to get cold feet."

"Not hardly." He had fallen in love with Asia Fowler the first moment David brought her home. He had felt guilty as sin for harboring such feelings, especially when he thought she'd be the one to finally capture his brother's heart. It didn't take long to realize that no woman could really touch David, and that he intended to add Asia to his long line of women. It had been hard to sit back and do nothing while David played her for a fool. David's marriage to another woman had been the last straw, and since his brother hadn't been man enough to tell Asia the truth, Sean had felt that he owed her that much.

"Meet us at the bar downstairs in a couple of hours. We've decided to have a partying good time our last night here."

Sean smiled and stepped off the elevator. "That sounds good to me."

Sean had showered, changed into a pair of khakis and a polo shirt, and was about to grab his hotel key off the bed when there was a knock at his door. He walked across the room to discover a bellman there. "Yes?"

"There's a delivery for you, Dr. Crews."

He lifted his brow as he took the envelope. He prayed

the work orders hadn't gotten changed to tell him he wouldn't be leaving the island after all. He went to the desk in the room, sat down at the chair, and opened the sealed package.

His mouth formed an angry line. Enclosed was an article taken from what appeared to be the *New York Times'* society page that included a photo taken of Asia and Lance Montgomery kissing. Beneath was the caption, "Enemies or Lovers?" The short write-up read:

> *It is a known fact in the publishing world that these two renowned relationship experts, Dr. Lance Montgomery and Dr. Asia Fowler, very seldom see eye-to-eye on anything. But it appears when this shot was taken, they were definitely seeing lip-to-lip. An added note of interest is that Dr. Fowler is engaged to marry the well-known orthopedic surgeon, Dr. Sean Crews.*

Tossing the article aside, he picked up the note that had accompanied it.

> *Sorry, Sean, but I tried to warn you that Asia was bad news. Now I hope after seeing this picture that you'll believe me when I say that she's only marrying you to get back at me. While you're over there saving lives, your supposed fiancée is here having an affair. Lucky for you the article was cut due to lack of space and never appeared in the paper. Someone I knew at the* Times *thought I'd like to have it.*

I hope that you'll finally admit that you deserve better.

David

Sean picked up the newspaper article again. He wanted to believe there was a reason for what he was seeing. He had known when he first met Dr. Montgomery that the man wanted Asia. He'd even known that something— Asia refused to say what—happened between them later that same night. All he knew was that Asia had called him the following day and had accepted his proposal. He had been too elated to ask questions at the time.

But then, he couldn't forget when Montgomery had shown up at the Patterson's party wanting to talk to Asia. He had never seen Asia be so hateful toward a man. He had known then that whatever Asia and Montgomery had shared, it had been brief, and it was completely over.

So he refused to take David's accusations at face value—although the article was pretty damn incriminating. There was only one person who could explain what the hell was going on, and that was Asia.

Tossing the newspaper aside, he picked up the phone. When a voice came on the line, he said, "Yes, this is Dr. Crews, and I need a flight back to the United States immediately."

11

Asia and Lance

Lance leaned back in his chair. The room had filled with women and men who had come to Atlanta to attend the AABCC, the African American Book Club Conference, and Asia, one of the keynote speakers, should be arriving any time now.

He had arrived at the hotel yesterday with his laptop in hand and had basically remained in his room, working on the book he still had to write. He was happy to see that he was making tremendous progress. But whether or not Carl and his editor would be pleased with the finished result was anyone's guess.

He figured there were over a thousand people attending the three-day conference, and although he had paid the conference fee and had received the registration tote bag, he had kept a low profile, not wanting to chance running into Asia. Timing, he'd decided, was everything.

"This crowd is awesome, don't you think?"

Lance glanced sideways at a woman who had leaned

closer to him to be heard. She appeared to be in her mid-thirties and on her face was a smile as well as a look of complete awe. He scanned his surroundings and had to admit there were more people here than he had expected. "Yes, there's quite a crowd."

"Twice the number from last year," the woman replied. "I know, since I come to this event every year. My book club, the Diamond Ladies, is from Boston. Book clubs are a wonderful way for readers to get together to bond and read a lot of good books."

Lance nodded and asked, "Have you read any of Dr. Fowler's books?"

The woman looked at him like he had asked a very ridiculous question. "Of course. I've read every book she has published. They are so inspiring and motivational. She went through a lot before getting her life back together, and for her to share her trials and tribulations with other women so they won't make the same mistakes is totally uplifting."

Lance had nothing else to add. However, the one thing he knew not to say was his name. He had registered for the conference under Carl's name, figuring what his agent didn't know wouldn't hurt him. He had a feeling that none of the women attending this conference would be fans of his.

"Have you read any of her books, Carl?" she asked after checking out his badge and seeing the fictitious name.

The first time Lance had read Asia's work it was for amusement. Only recently, after discovering how much he loved Asia, had he taken the time to go back and really read her books. And afterward, his admiration, as well as his love, only increased.

The woman next to him was right. Asia was inspiring and motivational, and he could see why so many women had come to hear her speak. He remembered the first time he'd done so in New York, back in August. He hadn't been the same since.

"Yes, I've read all of her books. She's a wonderful writer," he finally answered the woman.

"Yes, she is," the woman agreed, smiling.

The room suddenly got quiet, and Lance glanced toward the front of the room and saw Asia take a seat on stage. He couldn't ignore the rush of excitement that raced up his spine when he saw her. Then there was something else he was feeling, too. Profound love. He loved her in a way he never thought was possible.

"She's a beautiful woman, isn't she?" the talker next to him said. "If good-looking women like her get dogged out, I wonder if there's hope for the rest of us."

Things got quiet again while the moderator of the event introduced Asia, first listing her educational background then giving a brief summary of why she had decided to start writing her books. "That's a story only Dr. Fowler can tell," the woman was saying, "and I'm sure that she will, since it has helped to shape her into the phenomenal woman she is today. Each and every time I hear her story, my admiration for her goes up another notch. She is living proof that women can get their lives together and that we don't have to put up with any man's mistreatment of us. I introduce to some and present to others, our speaker of the hour, Dr. Asia Fowler."

Pride ran all through Lance as Asia approached the podium with such an awe-inspiring, confident, and feminine grace. With her shoulders back and her head held high, she smiled to the audience, who provided a deafening sound of applause as they got to their feet. A lump of emotion formed in Lance's throat as the group gave Asia the recognition and honor that she deserved.

Dressed in a two-piece business suit of lime green, she looked good in the outfit, which did a lot to capitalize on her curvy form. When the audience had taken their seats again, Asia looked out over the crowd, still smiling. A part of Lance hoped like hell she didn't see him . . . at least not yet.

"Hello, ladies and gentlemen. I am Dr. Asia Fowler, a woman who's been through hell but survived, and I'm here to tell my story."

Lance settled back in his chair. He had heard it before—that time in New York—but today he wanted to hear it again. And this time he intended to listen with a better pair of ears.

"Dr. Fowler, thanks for agreeing to take part in our Dine with an Author segment again this year," the conference coordinator was saying as she and Asia walked off the elevator and into the hotel's beautifully decorated lobby. "There were a number of book clubs who bid for the honor, but of course only the highest bidder could be selected. And they paid quite a lot to dine with you this evening. As you know, all proceeds are going to charity, and I'm happy to say the Sickle Cell Anemia Foundation will benefit greatly."

Asia smiled. The SCAF was special to her ever since

one of her closest friends from college had died from the disease more than seven years ago. "You're welcome, Rhonda, and I always look forward to meeting with my readers. I consider them special. What's the name of the book club, and where are these ladies from?"

"The name of the group is the Enchanted Book Club, and according to Linda Springfield, the person who coordinated Dine with an Author, the book club is from central Florida and this is their first time attending our conference."

Asia smiled. "I'm looking forward to dining with them tonight."

"And I'm sure they are looking forward to dining with you, as well. Emerils is the restaurant they'd chosen, and a limo is parked out front ready to take you there to join them."

"Thank you."

Asia walked out through the swinging doors and was met by a uniformed chauffeur. "Dr. Fowler, I'm Edward, your driver for tonight."

Asia smiled at the man. "Hello, Edward. I can't believe the difference in the weather here and what I left behind in New York," she said when he opened the door for her to slide onto the limo's backseat.

Edward closed the door and then quickly walked around the car to get into the driver's side. She leaned back, liking the feel of the leather seats and thinking that today had been busy but productive. She enjoyed attending conferences where she could mingle with her readers and—

The opening of the door cut into her thoughts, and she blinked when another passenger got inside swiftly, sliding into the seat beside her. "Okay, Edward, we can leave now. And I want complete privacy back here."

Asia inhaled sharply upon recognizing that voice, and then her gaze met a pair of disturbingly familiar dark eyes. Anger surged through her. "What do you think you're doing?" she snapped, scooting away from him, as close to the other side of the vehicle as she could get. The arrogant bastard, she thought, had the nerve to look amused.

"I'd think by now it would be obvious," he said, leaning back in the seat as the limo raced onto the interstate.

She was livid, fuming, enraged. "Nothing is obvious."

"Then let me explain things, Asia. I am a member of the Enchanted Book Club."

Asia pounded on the dark plate of glass that separated them from the driver. "Edward, I demand that you stop this car and put me out immediately!"

"You're wasting your time, Asia. He has orders not to stop this vehicle until we reach our destination."

She turned on Lance. "How dare you! You have no right to trick me and the conference organizers. And you have no right to keep me here with you against my will. I demand that he stop this car now."

"And do what? Put you out on the interstate?"

Asia glared at him. "Even that is better than being here with you and enduring your sick games."

"I'm not playing a game with you," Lance tried assuring her in a quiet yet husky voice.

"That's all you know how to do," she nearly yelled with eyes full of contempt. "You played a game with me from the first, and I refuse to let you do so again.

Since meeting you, I've been subjected to things I swore I'd never go through again, from intimidation to humiliation."

"What about love, Asia?"

"Love?" she repeated ferociously. "You don't know a damn thing about love. According to what you write, love is another word for bullshit."

His expression tightened. Yes, he *had* written that in his first book, dammit. "What if I told you I've come around and now think differently?"

"Then I would gladly tell you to go to hell because I personally don't believe you. Why can't you understand that I see what you're doing, what you're all about?"

"Which is?"

"You're pissed that I've agreed to marry Sean, because you were so sure you had me under your thumb, that I would be one of those women who see you as an addiction. And it's obvious that you're the type of person who dislikes losing, especially to another man."

All venom, she added, "Get over it, Lance Montgomery, because I am engaged to marry Sean, and I *will* marry him in June."

Lance was on the edge of his seat in a flash, his face mere inches from hers. "Why are you marrying him? You don't love him, dammit. You love me!"

Asia's mouth fell open. She gaped at him. "Where in the hell did you get an idea so ridiculous? I don't love you! I love Sean."

"No, you don't, and I'm sick and tired of you saying it! Admit it, you love me."

"I do not."

"Don't make me prove otherwise, Asia."

Asia drew in a fuming breath. "There's no way that you can. I've been in love with Sean for a long time."

"Now *that* is bullshit. The last time we were in a limo together, you said you loved Sean in a special way and it didn't take a rocket scientist to figure out what you felt for the man wasn't love but gratitude. There's a big difference. You are a woman who wouldn't intentionally hurt anyone. If you loved Sean—and I meant truly loved him in the full sense of the word—you would never have let me touch you that night. You wouldn't have let me do all those things that I did to you, Asia. And don't think I've forgotten our kiss. We couldn't get enough of each other. If you're in love with Sean, you damn sure wouldn't have responded to me the way you did. You're a woman who equates passion with love, which is why you had stayed celibate for so long . . . and the reason you're still celibate now."

Asia's eyes flashed fire. "You don't know that!"

"I wasn't sure until listening to your speech earlier today. Then I knew. You don't know how imagining you sleeping with Sean Crews was eating me up inside. But today I knew for sure."

"There's a reason we haven't," she said, despising him for dragging out her business. "Sean is out of the country, but when he gets back we will—"

"When he gets back, you will have thought about everything I'm saying, and there's no way you will in good conscience marry one man while being in love with another."

Asia was ready to explode. "Read my lips, Lance: I do not love you!"

"And read mine, Asia: Yes, you do—and I love you, too. With all my heart," he whispered huskily.

"No." Asia refused to give an inch.

"Then we need to prove a couple of things to each other, don't we?" Lance said, straightening and leaning away from her to settle back in his seat. If he stayed in her face one second longer, he would be tempted to kiss her, devour her, and make love to her right in the backseat. "First, I need to prove to you that I love you, and second, you need to prove to me that you don't love me."

"I don't need to prove a damn thing to you!"

"Yes, you do, Asia, and if not to me then to yourself."

"You're wrong."

"Then prove it. Give me a week with you, somewhere secluded, just the two of us, with you calling all the shots. If we sleep together, it will be because you want it and not because I forced it on you. If you don't want to make love with me, then you'll leave there still celibate. But if you do want to make love with me, I fully intend to fulfill your every desire and I will make sure you have no doubt about how much I love you. One week alone with you is all I'm asking for."

"No, I can't do that to Sean," she choked out.

Lance lifted his hand and took her chin gently, tilting it with his forefinger. "And you can't afford *not* to do that to him. I believe he's a good man who deserves a woman who truly loves him. A week with you is all I'm asking for. Think about it."

"There's nothing to think about, and your assumptions about me and my feelings are all wrong. The only thing I feel for you is loathing."

Lance held her gaze and then reached out and took a lock of her hair. It had tumbled over her shoulders, and now he twirled it around his finger. "You almost had me convinced of that, after the night of the Pattersons' party. But now I know differently, and do you know how I know?"

Knowing she wanted to know, was probably dying to ask but wouldn't, he said, "I could tell from our kiss that night. The way you responded when my mouth touched yours. And when you slid your arms up my back and wrapped your hands around my neck, I didn't want our kiss to end. I wished it could have lasted forever."

Asia fought against it, but her feminine muscles were clenching, filling the area between her legs with liquid heat. He leaned closer, and she thought he was going to kiss her. If he tried, she'd have to pull back and resist. But she knew if he did kiss her, there was no way she could deny him or the feelings he was causing to stir all through her. Lust, she convinced herself, was trying to take over her mind, and she refused to let it. This man had hurt her once, and she would not let him do so again.

She pulled back. The deep, heated look in his eyes was daring her to challenge him, and dammit, she would. She tilted up her chin and tossed her hair back over her shoulders, giving him her haughtiest look. "No matter what you say or think, I *would* prove you wrong."

"So you say," he countered with a smooth grin. "And I would prove I'm right."

They both felt the limo come to a sudden stop, and when they glanced out the window, they saw they had reached their destination. Lance said. "Enjoy your evening with the ladies. They have no idea who their anonymous book club member is, and I prefer keeping it that way. After all, the money I donated to assure that they dined with you tonight went to a very worthy cause, and I understand it's a charity that means a lot to you. Good-bye, Asia. I'm flying out tonight, returning to Chicago, and hope to hear from you soon." He smiled. "And if I don't, then rest assured you will definitely be hearing from me."

Asia's eyes narrowed and hardened. "That's called stalking."

"I disagree. It's going after the woman I want and love."

Asia watched in shock and disbelief as he opened the door and quickly slipped out and walked across the curb to another waiting limo, not looking back before the door closed behind him.

She blinked when her own door opened and Edward appeared. "We're here, Dr. Fowler."

Asia wanted to believe she had dreamt the past forty-five minutes but knew that she hadn't.

Lance leaned back in the leather seat. He had wanted to kiss Asia before departing but he'd pushed her as far as he dared for one night. But man, had he been tempted.

Lance shifted when he felt his cell phone vibrate in his pocket. He pulled it out. "Yes?"

"Where the hell are you?"

Lance raised his eyes to the ceiling. He had been in demand a lot lately. Sam had tracked him down earlier, wanting him to be the first to know that he had asked Falon to marry him and she had said yes. He and Sam planned on getting together later in the week with Marcus and Phillip to celebrate.

"Lance?" the voice asked impatiently.

Damn, his sister was one bossy woman. "I'm in Atlanta, Carrie."

"Oh. I drove up from Gary yesterday with plans to spend the night."

A corner of his mouth tugged up in amusement. "I'm sure you made yourself at home since my not being there has never stopped you before."

"Stop being a smart ass." A few moments later she said, "How are you doing? I heard you've been under the weather."

Drowning in self-pity is more like it. "I'm better now."

"Was there a reason for it?"

"Not one I care to discuss with you, brat. Hey, behave until I get back. My plane lands at O'Hare tomorrow at noon."

"You need me to come and get you?"

Lance started to tell her not to go to the trouble, but then he remembered the call he had gotten from Logan a few days ago. On that conference call, he had shared his suspicions with him and Lyle that something was going on with Carrie that needed looking into. If that was true, then he needed to check things out right away.

"Yes, that would save me the trouble of getting a cab. And for once, get out of bed at a decent hour so you won't be late."

Ignoring her string of obscenities, he clicked off the phone.

12

Asia and Sean

Asia arrived back in New York late Sunday afternoon. After placing her luggage in her bedroom, she walked over to the answering machine to check her messages.

Claire had left to spend a week with their mother, who lived in South Carolina, and wouldn't be back until after Thanksgiving. Once Sean returned next weekend, they would decide how and where they would spend Thanksgiving, whether they would have dinner in Detroit with his family or in South Carolina with hers.

Personally, she preferred not having to deal with the Crews this year. David had convinced his parents that she was the reason for his and Sean's strained relationship, and they believed him, placing the blame entirely on her. If Mr. and Mrs. Crews only knew the hell David had put her through during the four years they had been together, they would think differently. Sean had told her constantly not to worry about what his family thought. It didn't matter to him, and he loved her anyway.

Asia released a disappointed sigh when she saw that of all her numerous messages, none had been from Sean, and she so desperately needed to hear his voice, to wipe the images of Lance Montgomery from her mind. Lance Montgomery's arrogance and audacity never ceased to amaze her. And it certainly didn't help matters that he was so sinfully handsome; it was a shame.

Asia scowled. She didn't want to find him attractive. She didn't want a damn thing to do with him. And if he thought she was going to spend a week with him, then he had another thought coming.

She glanced down at her watch, trying to remember the difference in time zones between there and Zaire. God, she needed to talk to Sean, hear his voice. She needed to hear him whisper that he loved her so she could tell him that she loved him, as well.

She took a long, hot shower instead, and afterward, she slipped into a terry cloth jumper. Asia walked out of her bedroom the same exact moment there was a hard knock at her door. She started in surprise. Whoever it was evidently had a pass key to get beyond the security door downstairs. Since Sean was still in Zaire and her sister was in South Carolina, then it had to be Melissa, who was supposed to have dropped off her manuscript revisions while she was gone.

"I was wondering where the revisions were, Melissa," she began as she opened the door. Only to find her visitor wasn't Melissa.

"Sean!" She flung herself into his arms. Only seconds later did she note how he had hesitated putting his arms around her.

She must be imagining things. Asia placed a kiss on

his lips before taking his hand and pulling him into the apartment. Once he was out of the shadows, she could study his face, and she found rigid lines consuming his features. He wore a cool, distant look, something she had never seen on him before. "Sean, what's wrong?"

He stepped aside to remove his coat and then flung it angrily across the back of a chair. What the hell was going on? He wasn't acting like himself. "Would you like a drink?" she asked, giving him time to relax.

"No, I don't want a drink. I want an explanation."

Asia was surprised at his sharp tone. "An explanation about what?"

"An explanation about this," he said, pulling the newspaper article out of an envelope he'd been carrying and shoving it at her. She took it from him and gasped when she saw a picture of her and Lance kissing that night at the *New York Times* Recognition party.

"Luckily the article was pulled at the last minute due to space."

"How did you get this?" she demanded.

"Answer me, Asia," he bit out angrily, ignoring her question. He closed the distance separating them. "I want to know why you were kissing Lance Montgomery."

She would tell Sean only the truth. "I wasn't kissing him. He was kissing me."

"Doesn't look like you were putting up much of a fight."

He was right; she hadn't. "He caught me off guard."

"That's a damn poor excuse, Asia. Look at that photograph. The man is practically mauling you."

Asia threw the newspaper down, not wanting to look

at it any longer. "Don't you see what he's doing, Sean? Lance probably staged the entire thing and sent you that article, hoping they would—"

"Montgomery didn't send it to me," Sean all but snapped. "David did."

"David?" she asked shakily. The mention of his brother caused anger to overshadow the guilt she was feeling.

"Yes, David. Someone he knows works at the *Times*."

"And how convenient for him."

"Don't blame David, Asia, nobody asked you and Montgomery to put on a show for him, dammit," he said furiously.

She'd never known Sean to get upset like this. Okay, he deserved to be angry, but didn't he see what his brother was trying to do? Why were all the men in her life trying to sabotage her marriage?

"Do you know the first thought that went through my mind when I saw that newspaper, Asia? I thought, Damn, she's never kissed me that way or let me hold her like that. Just how intimate did you and Dr. Montgomery get?"

"That," she said, feeling a pulse of frustration deep in her throat, "is none of your business. What I did before I agreed to marry you is not open for discussion. Whether you want to believe me or not, I've been celibate for more than a year and—"

"Celibate by whose definition?"

Silence filled the room until Asia spoke. "I think it would be best if you left now, Sean. You've said enough."

"Maybe you're right," he said, snatching his coat from the back of the sofa.

"And maybe you should have this back," she said, tugging the engagement ring from off her finger, thrusting it at him.

Sean stared at the ring she was holding out to him. "No, I don't want to break our engagement, Asia, not if we can work through this. All I want is assurance that I'm the most important man in your life, that I'm the man you love above all else, because right now, I don't feel that I am."

"Sean, I—"

"No," he said softly. "We're both too angry to indulge in a decent conversation right now. I'm tired and you probably are, too. I'm staying at a hotel tonight and in the morning I'm flying out to D.C. to brief the brass on the time I spent in Zaire. I'll try calling you later this week to discuss how we'll spend Thanksgiving."

He left without taking the ring from her hand. Ignoring the newspaper article that was on the floor, Asia slowly sank down on the sofa. Why did her world start falling apart whenever she got within two feet of Lance Montgomery?

The one thing she'd never wanted to happen had happened: She had hurt Sean.

13

Carrie and Lance

Yep. Something was definitely going on with Carrie, Lance thought as he walked into his living room and paused to watch her standing at his window and taking in the sight of Lake Michigan. Although he knew the view was breathtaking, he had a feeling that someone else had her in deep thought.

She had been on time to pick him up earlier that day from the airport; then they had stopped and had lunch at a pizza parlor in downtown Chicago. After dropping him off, she had driven to some mall to shop, returning a couple hours later.

Carrie had been quiet through most of the dinner his chef, Stuart, had prepared. The one thing he and his brothers had discovered about Carrie over the years was that no matter what you wanted to know, you didn't push. She could clam up quicker than a politician keeping secrets. But whatever was bothering her, it was deep.

Standing at the window, she looked no more than a

teenager wearing a pair of tattered jeans and T-shirt. He longed to wrap her in his arms and never let go.

Instead, he strolled over to her. She glanced around when she heard Lance approach and smiled. "How's the book coming?"

He put his hands in the pockets of his slacks and leaned against his fireplace mantel. For the past couple of hours, he'd tried working on the book that was due within a few months—as Carl was quick to remind him, practically every day. It was slow going.

"It's not coming, but I'm sure it eventually will," he said.

Carrie gave him a long sideways glance when he came to stand in front of her. "You look tired, Lance. Worn out. Like crap."

He couldn't help throwing his head back and laughing. Carrie didn't mince words. "Thanks a lot."

She shook her head and smiled. Her expression soon turned serious. "It's a woman, isn't it?"

When he didn't answer quick enough, she said, "Never mind. Maybe it's best that I don't know."

He nodded, thinking that maybe it was best that she did. Logan had brought it to his attention last month that what Lance thought of women and how he treated them wasn't just his own business, since Carrie was at an impressionable age. The last thing his brothers wanted was for their baby sister to think that the way Lance operated was the norm for most guys—especially since she seemed to have a hang-up with getting interested in guys, anyway.

"Yes. It is about a woman," he finally said. "And Miss Nosy, that's as much as I'm going to say." As far as he was concerned, he had said enough. To admit that a woman was the cause of his distress was a big deal, and he was well aware that Carrie recognized that fact.

"She must be some lady."

Visions of Asia quickly formed in his mind. He smiled and simply said, "Trust me, she is."

14

Sean

"Are things all right, Sean? You left Zaire so suddenly."

Sean glanced over at Liz. The two of them, along with several other physicians who were members of the president's Goodwill team, were leaving the Pentagon, where they had spent the better part of the day. How he had gotten through the extensive meeting and provided the right answers was still beyond Sean. He had fought every single minute to keep his mind focused and not get distracted with thoughts of Asia.

"Yes, things are fine," he lied. His entire world could be falling completely apart. He desperately wished he could talk to someone about how he was feeling. Had he been wrong to react the way he had after seeing that article? Should he have considered the source and not put much stock into it? Damn, how can a man not put stock into a photograph that clearly showed his fiancée kissing another man?

"You know I'm a good listener if you ever want to talk."

He nodded as they walked together toward their rental car. They were staying at the same hotel and had decided to use one vehicle. When he had arrived in D.C. last night, she had already checked into the hotel. One thing he did know about Liz was that she was a good listener. She could always sense when something was bothering him, although he might try playing it off.

"Sean?"

He glanced up at Liz, realizing he hadn't answered her. "How about if we go out to dinner later this evening?" He knew she would be flying out to Memphis in the morning to visit family, and he would be leaving to return to Boston.

She smiled at him. "I'd like that."

Liz Howard felt intensely nervous while applying her lipstick. She shook her head, thinking those same hands of hers that expertly and skillfully opened, closed, and revived more hearts than she cared to think about were actually shaking at the thought of going out with Sean tonight. It had been a long time since they had gone out, just the two of them, without other doctors joining them.

It was important that she looked nice for Sean. Yes, he was an engaged man, and she wouldn't cross any boundaries. After all, she was a woman, and she wouldn't want another woman making a play for her man. But in her opinion she wasn't making a play exactly. She was merely making Sean aware of the fact that she was more than a doctor. She was also a woman.

And, she hoped . . . she prayed, that Sean would wake up and realize that marrying Dr. Asia Fowler wasn't the right thing to do. The old history with his brother David went too deep for Sean and Asia to ever be happy, and Liz was certain, knowing the ass that David was, that he would make trouble.

Oh, yeah, she knew all about David Crews. He had even tried hitting on her one night when he had flown to Boston to see Sean . . . as if she would be stupid enough to want *him* over Sean.

Her heart jumped suddenly when she heard a knock at the door. With trembling fingers, she adjusted the gold belt at her waist, grabbed her purse off the polished wood desk in the room, and taking a deep breath, she walked to the door.

"You look nice tonight, Liz."

Liz smiled, wondering. Over the course of the evening Sean had already told her that four times. "Thank you. You look good yourself. It's nice to come out of our doctors' attire once in a while and live like normal people, isn't it?"

"Yes, I suppose," he said.

He didn't say anything for a few seconds. He just sat there, looking into his wineglass and studying the dark liquid. "I hope you enjoyed dinner," he said, lifting his eyes to meet her gaze.

God, he was beautiful. "You know I did. Give me anything with shrimp in it, and it will make me happy."

He released a throaty chuckle. "Yes, I remember."

When he got quiet and began studying his wine again, she decided to ask, "Sean, is everything all right?"

He lifted his eyes and hesitated for a brief moment before saying, "I'm not sure if everything is all right, Liz. Asia and I had a big argument a few days ago."

She tried not to let the pain in his eyes tear into her heart. "All couples argue, Sean. Disagreeing every once in a while isn't a bad thing. Differences of opinions are expected. The important thing is for the two individuals to openly communicate, share their feelings."

For a moment, she was tempted while staring into the darkness of his eyes to say the words she had repressed for almost six years: *I'm in love with you. I've always been in love with you. I'll always be in love with you.*

"You're probably right."

"Probably? I know I'm right, Dr. Crews. Now, the best thing for you and Asia to do is to kiss and make up." She suspected that whatever Sean and Asia had argued about must be serious for him to be in such a gloomy mood. She needed to give him hope. "And I'm sure whatever the two of you argued about will work itself out," she said, trying to assure him.

He picked up his wineglass and took a sip before quietly saying, "I hope so."

15

Carrie and Connor

Just like he'd done a few days ago, Connor stood in his office and watched Carrie get out of her car. And just like before, his body responded just from watching her. He crossed his arms over his chest.

One thing was different though: he couldn't see her tantalizing belly. Thanks to the snow that had fallen that morning, and the below-ten-degrees weather, she had sought protection from the cold by wearing a heavy coat. It didn't reveal a damn thing.

She was sexy as hell, even covered up. He'd never had a thing for dimples before until he'd seen hers. One in each cheek was a total turn-on. Hell, he could have an orgasm just standing here looking at her.

Something else he had noted the other day was that even with her seemingly rough demeanor, there seemed to be something graceful about Carrie Montgomery . . . when she chose to be that way.

He had been attracted to her. That was a given. He

still was. That was a fact. But the attraction hadn't been
one-sided. He'd been around the block enough to know
what heat in a woman's berry-dark gaze meant. That
moment in the outer office when they'd first met, she had
stared at him so long that he'd been hard-pressed not to
cross the room and kiss the stare off her lips. Hell, hard-
pressed—he'd been hard, period. She had made for the
door when she caught on. He couldn't be blamed if there
were some things men just couldn't hide.

And speaking of hiding . . .

The moment she had left his office, he had done his
research. He knew everything he wanted to know about
Carrie Montgomery, including the fact that she was em-
ployed as a social worker in Tampa, Florida, owned a
real nice condo on the bay, drove a Mustang convertible,
and spent a lot of her free time at a gym working out.
She also did a lot of volunteer work with agencies that
benefited disadvantaged youths. He even knew the identity of the brothers she wanted to protect. Talk about a
small world, evidently she'd assumed that since his office was in Portage, that's where he lived. She might not
be too happy to discover he'd been born and raised right
there in Gary. In fact his cousin Marcus was good friends
with Sam Gunn, and anyone living in Gary who had
ever attended Roosevelt High knew that Sam was the
best friend of Dr. Lance Montgomery, well-known psychologist and relationship expert. And although Connor
didn't know her brothers personally, he had heard about
them and how successful the three of them were.

Connor's thoughts went back to Carrie. On the Internet, there were photographs of her taken with other
members of the agency where she worked. She had

been wearing a business suit, and her hair had been tied back on her head. He had to stare hard to make sure that it had really been her. Talk about a startling transformation. Evidently, at work she dressed the part of the staunch professional.

But then while at play . . .

He smiled when he remembered what she had been wearing Friday. There had been nothing professional about letting it all hang out, especially her stomach. But he had no complaints. In fact he had gotten turned on seeing that ring in her navel.

From what he'd been able to dig up on her, it appeared she was twenty-four, a dedicated employee, and didn't date much. She mostly stayed to herself, and when she did go out, it was to an occasional movie or baseball game with her brother, the well-known and renowned plastic surgeon, Dr. Logan Montgomery. However, in a couple of news articles, it was reported that one of the players on the Tampa Devil Rays, Ethan Carmichael, had been smitten with her. When she refused to reciprocate his interest, he had moved on.

She doesn't trust men.

Connor thought of the photographs she had shared with him and was consumed with anger. No one should have been subjected to the life she'd had, first as a child abuse victim, and then as a runaway. Once again tenderness and protectiveness welled up inside him. The woman was a survivor, but a part of him wished more than anything that there was a way he could soothe any past hurt she had ever endured. He was looking forward to finding this Simon what's-his-name and making sure he paid for his dirty deeds of the past. The man had to be brainless. He'd get jail time for exposing those photos. Either he was extremely stupid, or he was not the one trying to blackmail Carrie. For some reason, Connor was betting his money on the latter.

"Hey, Connor, your noon appointment is here," Brad said, sticking his head in the door and shoving his glasses back on his nose. "Should I send her in?"

"Yeah, send her in, and Brad, let me know when lunch arrives."

Carrie felt Connor's presence even before their eyes met.

Since meeting him on Friday, she had thought of him a lot, and the one thing she always remembered, in addition to how handsome he was, was the intensity of his eyes whenever he looked at her. And whenever she had thought of him, she had felt hot.

She hadn't wanted to feel that way, and even now she knew her only concern was to have him find who had sent her those photographs, to stop them before they got started in what they planned to do. But still, thanks to Connor Hargrove, he had reminded her she was a woman.

He was so angry when he'd seen the photographs. Watching his reaction to them had made their arrangement feel more personal than business.

She cleared her throat. "Connor."

He smiled sexily. "Carrie, please come in. I'll be glad to hang up your coat for you."

She nodded as she slipped out of her coat then handed it to him. "Thanks."

He placed it on the rack next to his leather one. "I was looking forward to our meeting today."

She raised an eyebrow. "Why is that?"

"So we can get down to business. I'm anxious to get started."

She wiped her damp hands on her jeans. What in the hell was wrong with her? She had met good-looking men before. Ethan hadn't been bad looking, and a lot of women had envied the interest he had shown in her. But she hadn't been attracted to him to this degree, and as crazy as it sounded, she would swear that there was some sort of warm, musky, and seductive scent that was emitted by Connor's skin, calling out to her in a totally primitive way. It was tempting her to do something thrilling as well as forbidden.

"Would you like to take a seat?"

What she really would have liked was to go somewhere and toss between the sheets with him.

"Carrie?"

She quickly moved toward the chair. "Yes, of course."

Connor suspected what was going on in Carrie's head was the same thing going on in his. The moment she had taken off her coat and he saw she was wearing another top showing all of her belly, he'd had to dig his heels into the floor to stop from crossing the room, dropping to his knees, and licking her navel. She had a stomach that was covered in smooth, soft-looking skin that just cried out to be kissed.

There was just something about her that made his male instinct go on full alert. He wanted her. He'd definitely liked the way she looked in a skirt the other day, but she looked good today in jeans, as well.

"Do you ever get cold?" he couldn't help but ask.

She settled back in the chair and shrugged. "Not particularly, and I'm proud of my body."

Connor swallowed. She had a lot to be proud of and then some.

"You needed information."

Her words cut into his thoughts, and he immediately felt guilty. He needed to get laid and soon. Her midriff T-shirt said SLIPPERY WHEN WET, which wasn't helping matters. He desperately wanted to see just how wet she could get.

The knock at the door nearly made him jump. He was grateful for the interruption when Brad stuck his head in. "Lunch is here."

"Thanks," Connor said.

When Brad closed the door, Connor glanced back at Carrie and said, "I ordered us lunch. I hope you like ham and cheese."

Sudden panic consumed her. "I told you I didn't want to do lunch."

It was on the tip of Connor's tongue to say they didn't have to do lunch. Instead they could do each other. But Connor figured that wouldn't be the thing to say. "You have to eat, and what's wrong with us sharing a meal while we get down to business?"

"Everything." She tossed the folder she'd brought with her on his desk. "Look, I need to leave. Look through those notes, and if you need anything else, just give me a call."

Before Connor could get around his desk to stop her, she had quickly walked out of his door.

* * *

When Carrie couldn't drive another mile, she pulled the car over into the parking lot of a Target store and sat for a while. She tightened her hand on the steering wheel. How could she have panicked like that? Connor Hargrove probably thought she was one giant moron for leaving his office that way. But she hadn't been able to help it. What was easy for some was hard for others. She knew that on occasion that was one hurdle she couldn't cross. While in college, she had sought counseling, and it had helped somewhat, but every once in a while, she would remember.

She sighed, trying to remember the last time sharing a meal with a man had bothered her. It had been a while ago. She chalked up the recent panic attack to the fact that someone, more likely Simon, was trying to breach the protective wall her brothers erected around her.

She was afraid.

She was afraid that her brothers would face embarrassment if word ever got out of what had happened to her, although it was not by her choosing. There was no doubt in her mind that Logan, Lyle, and Lance would hold her blameless, but still there would be talk, and she would do everything she could to protect them from that.

Carrie didn't want to get her hopes up, but Connor seemed pretty sure that he would be able to put a stop to Simon before he caused any mischief. And more than anything, she hoped that he would prove successful.

Later that night, Connor lay in bed and replayed in his mind the conversations he and Carrie Montgomery had shared in his office that day. He was pissed with himself for allowing his mind to spend even one second thinking about a woman who had such a deep mistrust of men that she seemed petrified at the thought of sharing a meal with one of them. He wondered what the hell that had been about? Why in the hell did he even give a damn? With a muttered curse, he flipped on his back and stared at the ceiling. The irony of it all was that he did give a damn.

What was there about Carrie Montgomery that captured his interest? Okay, he would admit she was fine, but then he'd had women who looked just as good, even more beautiful. But his vitals had never responded to any of them the way they were responding to Carrie. His body was responding to her in ways he damn sure wished it wouldn't. In a way, his intense attraction to her angered as well as disconcerted him. It just made no sense. And then there was her ability to touch him on a level beyond just physical desire. Although it was clearly obvious that she was capable of taking care of herself, there was something about Carrie Montgomery that brought out his protective instincts, as well as a degree of compassion he'd never known he had. He wasn't sure how that was possible, and why it was so with this particular woman.

Knowing he wouldn't get any answers tonight, he rolled back on his stomach, punched his pillow a couple of times, and forced his eyes closed.

He needed sleep.

He needed to get laid.

He needed to lick that part of Carrie's stomach that she liked exposing.

He opened his eyes when he realized that more than anything, whether he liked it or not, he needed Carrie Montgomery.

16

Lance and Sean

Lance looked out his window at Lake Michigan. It was morning, and he had just finished eating breakfast. Last night, the snow hadn't stopped falling. After Carrie left early yesterday to return to Gary, he had spent the rest of the day trying to formulate his thoughts for his book. He'd sat at his computer and managed to get in at least six good hours of writing time before calling it a day and going to bed.

Now he was wide awake and fighting like hell against the impulse of calling his travel agent to book a flight to New York and appear unannounced on Asia's doorstep—to beg if he had to for another chance. Now that he had seen her, talked to her, been in close confines with her, the distance separating them was killing him. He needed to be around her, to work hard to let her know he had meant every word when he'd told her that he loved her. He had ordered more flowers to be delivered to her. He had gotten a call from the New York florist who said Asia hadn't been happy getting the delivery. He told them it didn't matter, that he wanted fresh ones sent to her every few days with the same message: *I love you*. For a man who had never used the words, he was certainly using them a lot now.

He moved away from the window when he heard his phone ring. Crossing the room, he quickly picked it up. "Yes?"

"Dr. Montgomery, this is Tom from security downstairs. There's a Dr. Sean Crews here to see you."

Lance recovered from his surprise enough to say, "Send him up, Tom."

"Yes, sir."

Shoving his hands into the pockets of his slacks, Lance crossed the room to the door, vividly recalling the day the two had met. He'd arrived at the television studio where he and Asia were to tape a show and had walked up just in time to see the love-smitten man take Asia's hand in his, while whispering something low in her ear. Lance could truly say he had been confronted with his first bout of jealousy that day. While Asia made introductions, he noted that Crews's smile had been forced, brief, and cool. The man's antagonistic reaction hadn't surprised Lance. A smart man recognized his adversaries. He had found out enough information on Crews to know he was highly thought of in the medical profession as a skillful orthopedic surgeon. But most important, he had been a true friend to Asia when she needed one. And Lance even believed that he truly loved her. Under different circumstances, Lance would probably have liked the man.

But unfortunately, too much was at stake right now,

and he had no intention, regardless of how Crews felt about things, of losing Asia a second time.

Asia would be furious with him when she found out he had paid a visit to Montgomery. When he left D.C., instead of taking the flight to New York to meet with Asia to determine their plans for Thanksgiving, he had impulsively decided he needed to have a good heart-to-heart talk with Montgomery. Evidently, the man didn't understand the concept of gentlemen's honor when it involved an engaged woman. Maybe it was time someone educated him.

When the elevator stopped, Sean stepped off onto the twentieth floor. The moment he rounded the carpeted corridor and veered to his right, he noticed Lance Montgomery's condo's door was open. The man himself stood in the doorway, his hip casually leaning against the wooden frame . . . waiting for him.

Lance cut to the chase and asked, "What's the reason for this visit, Crews?"

Sean tried keeping the annoyance out of his voice. "I felt that we needed to talk."

Lance stared at Sean then admitted dryly, "Yes, we do."

He took a step back, and when Sean entered, he closed the door. He asked, "Would you care for anything to drink?"

Sean shook his head after removing his coat. "No. What I have to say won't take long."

Lance nodded. "Then say it."

Again, just like the first time they met, Sean's smile

was forced—brief and cool. "I want you to stay away from Asia. I don't understand what you think you're doing, but I want it to stop."

Lance crossed his arms over his chest and matched Sean's phony smile. Only a man who felt threatened would have the gall to show up and say such a thing to another man. "And just what do *you* think I'm doing?"

"You're blatantly disregarding the fact that she's engaged to be married. Although Asia has never denied or confirmed it, I have a feeling that you had your chance and blew it, Montgomery. Get over it. She is not a woman to be toyed with, and I resent you doing so. She has been through enough bullshit in her lifetime. She's someone who deserves total and complete happiness."

Lance couldn't agree more, and all the unnecessary pain she had endured had come from this man's brother. As far as Lance was concerned, that was too close for comfort. "Doesn't it bother you to know that although she might have agreed to marry you, there's a possibility that she's in love with another man—namely me?"

Sean chuckled. "You really think highly of yourself, Montgomery, to believe that. I saw Asia's reaction to you at the Pattersons' party. She can't stand you."

"At the risk of sounding conceited again," Lance said in a cool, implacable voice, "that is just a temporary state of mind. Asia is in love with me. She only agreed to marry you because I screwed up. If you don't believe it, then think about the timing of when she accepted your proposal. Asia loves you as a friend and nothing more, and I believe that deep down you already know that. Why are you willing to tie her to a loveless marriage? Like you said earlier, she is someone who deserves total and complete happiness."

When Sean didn't say anything immediately, Lance said, "If you love her as much as I think you do, then you would want to give her that, too, even if it means giving her up."

Sean gazed at him levelly and began putting back on his coat. "I *won't* give her up, Montgomery."

"Then I guess the battle is on, and I intend to win." He knew it was a huge physical effort for Sean to look cool, confident, and collected when he turned to walk out the door.

Before he reached it, Lance called out, "Crews. You owe it to Asia to make sure she knows what's in her heart. Don't take advantage of her vulnerability. If you do that, then you're no better than your brother was. Think about it."

Sean shot a cold glance over his shoulder at Lance before opening the door and walking out.

17

Carrie

"Baby girl, some mail came for you."

"Thanks, Pop," Carrie said, glancing up at him and smiling. Jeremiah Montgomery was a robust man who stood well over six feet tall. According to her brothers he had been a stern but loving father. To her he was the man who had accepted her, without question, as his daughter. Beneath his thick eyebrows were dark brown eyes that had probably seen a lot during his sixty-two years. As soon as he left the room, she leaned back in her chair and pushed away from the table where she'd been trying her hand at a crossword puzzle.

She had instructed her secretary to forward any mail that didn't appear to be business related. The moment Pop had handed her the legal-sized envelope, she had known what it was. It looked the same as the last one she had received.

A shiver of foreboding ran through her as she ripped

it open then cursed when the contents tumbled out. More photos. And the note read:

I want ten thousand dollars for every photo. I think they're worth it, don't you? And don't think about going to the cops. Remember if you care about your brothers and the embarrassment it will cause if these photos become public, then make plans to send the money. My next letter will provide all the details.

A Good Friend

Carrie wasn't stupid. Once she started paying this person money it would never end. There would be more photos and more demands for money. She knew she had done the right thing in hiring Connor.

The last thing she wanted was to talk to Connor right now, but the arrival of the photos gave her no choice. She had to tell him. Every time his name crossed her mind, her skin became somewhat heated; it actually tingled. It was her fault for finding the brotha so damn irresistible, so mouthwateringly handsome and fine. The memory of how he had looked when she'd walked into his office the other day made her pulse leap even now.

She was so absorbed in her thoughts that she actually jumped when her cell phone vibrated in the front pocket of her jeans. She stood to pull it out and swallowed deeply when she saw the name that appeared on the caller ID. It was Connor. Her thoughts of him might as well have conjured him up.

"Yes?" she answered.

"Carrie, this is Connor."

"Yes, I know, Connor. What can I do for you?" She quickly bit her bottom lip. That might not have been the best question to ask.

"Did I catch you at a bad time?"

It depends on your definition of bad, she thought. "No, I was just thinking about calling you anyway."

There was a pause. "Really? How come?"

"I received another envelope today with more pictures."

"Is the person demanding money now?" he asked after muttering curses. The tone of his voice was sharp, angry. She was glad that anger wasn't directed at her.

"Yes. Ten thousand for every photo. Unless there are more, that's ten of them, which means a hundred thousand dollars."

"Over my dead body. The bastard won't be getting a damn penny out of you. I'm going to see to it. I'm going to make sure his ass rots in jail."

She found his words comforting. "Thank you, Connor."

There was another pause. Then he said, "Hey, no sweat. That's what you're paying me for."

There, Carrie thought. He had made sure she knew that anything and everything he was doing was in no way personal. "Was there something you needed to talk to me about?" she decided to ask. She wanted things to be strictly business between them as much as he did.

"Yes. I got a lead on Simon Anderson."

Carrie stomach knotted. "You did?"

"Yes, and I'm flying out to L.A. in the morning."

"You are? Can I go with you?" The request was out

of Carrie's mouth before she could call it back. But then she didn't want to. She needed closure, and one way to get it would be to look Simon Anderson dead in his face.

"Why do you want to go?"

Carrie knew he had a right to ask. She also knew she had to make him understand. "I need to see him, Connor. I need to put this behind me."

For a few moments, he didn't say anything. "Okay, you can come along."

Carrie sighed. She suspected that he did understand. "Thanks."

They talked awhile longer. He provided her details of the flight arrangements he would be making for her, and then they said good-bye. Instead of placing the cell phone back in her pocket, Carrie placed it on the table then quickly put the photos and note back inside the envelope. The last thing she needed was for Pop to see them.

She was glad Connor had agreed to take her with him. Now she needed to let Pop know she would be going out of town for a few days. Her brothers would be coming for Thanksgiving, and she needed to put as much of this behind her as she could before then.

18

Asia and Sean

At around eleven o'clock in the morning, the day after his visit with Lance, Sean knocked on Asia's door. A seven-hour delay out of Chicago's O'Hare Airport had given him time to think. That Lance Montgomery was one arrogant son of a bitch.

But what if she is in love with Montgomery, like he claims?

Sean knocked on the door again, his jawline tightening. Both he and Asia needed to know the truth. The arrogant son of a bitch was right about one thing: Sean cared too much for Asia to take advantage of her vulnerability a second time. He would never forgive himself for doing so, and the thought that she would wake up one morning and decide she'd never loved him and wanted out of their marriage killed something inside of him.

The door flew open, and there she stood, in a pair of god-awful-looking sweats, her hair going every which way on her head and a pair of glasses propped on her nose. But at that moment, he thought she was beautiful.

"Hi," he said, leaning toward her and placing a quick kiss on her lips.

"Sean," she said in a rush. Clearly surprised. "I wasn't expecting you." She glanced down at herself. "I look—"

"Beautiful as usual," he said, meaning every word. Damn. Life wasn't fair. Would he forever be punished because his ass of a brother had met her first and had broken her heart? He forced that thought from his mind. "May I come in?"

"Of course you can," she said, moving aside for him to enter.

He waited a minute, feeling the tension in the air between them before stepping over the threshold. He knew his life was about to change forever.

"Would you like something to drink?" Asia nervously asked. God, she felt awful. This wasn't just any other man. This was Sean. The man she considered her best friend. The man she wanted to marry. The man she loved in a special way.

She wondered if she had lost all of that. Had he already judged her from that article David had sent him? If so, what else could she say in her defense? She had allowed Lance to kiss her and hadn't resisted . . . until later, when it hadn't mattered.

"No, I don't want anything to drink," he said, glancing around, seeing the area in the room where her desk and computer were located. It was cluttered with all her writing materials, which meant he had interrupted her at work. "Do you have a few minutes so we can talk?"

She shrugged. "Sure."

Sean reached out and captured Asia's hand, entwining their fingers. She felt his warmth but didn't feel the tingle she'd felt when Lance had touched her. She tightened her hand in Sean's. It didn't matter. She hated herself for even comparing.

He led her over to the sofa, and they sat down. "First, I want to say that I'm sorry for the way I acted the other day. I—"

"You had every right to act that way, Sean," she interrupted. "I should not have let Lance kiss me."

Sean didn't say anything for a few brief moments, and then he nodded. "Why do you think you let him do it, Asia?"

A tremendous sigh escaped her lips. "I don't know. It just happened. I have no excuse, but I am sorry that it did, and it won't again."

"Are you sure of that?"

Asia raised a single dark, irritated brow. "I said so, didn't I? Don't you believe me?"

"Do you believe yourself, Asia?" he asked almost tenderly.

She tensed before pulling her hand free of his. "Yes, but you obviously think not."

He leaned back against the seat. "I just want you to be sure of your feelings."

"And you don't think that I am?"

When a full minute passed and he didn't answer, she stood and walked over to the window and looked out while trying to suck in calming breaths, getting angrier by the second. She wondered why he was doubting things between them just because of that article.

"I went to see Lance Montgomery, Asia."

Abruptly Asia turned around and stared at him. "You did what?" she asked in a disbelieving voice.

Sean stood. "I went to see Montgomery, to let him know I think he crossed the line where you're concerned."

Asia stared at him, not believing what he was saying. Sean was a soft-spoken, kind, and noble person and nothing like the cold-blooded, manipulating shark Lance was. Lance was a man who didn't know how to take the word no for an answer, a man who was accustomed to getting whatever he wanted. She didn't want to imagine Sean and Lance, facing each other, both defending what they felt was their individual right to have her. The thought of that encounter angered her even more.

"You had no right to go visit him, Sean."

Sean covered the distance separating them. "As your fiancé, I had every right." Then he added, "He thinks you're in love with him."

"I'm sure he does. Me and every other woman on this earth. He's nothing but a conceited bastard. I hate him, and don't care if I ever saw him again."

Sean studied her. He saw the quivering of her lips, the tears she was holding back in her eyes. Lance had hurt her, but he knew her well enough to know that for the man to have had the ability to do so only meant she had felt something deep for him.

"You know what they say. There's a very thin line between love and hate," he replied unsteadily.

Asia placed her hands on her hips. "Just what are you trying to say?"

He had to know. He had to be sure. But most important, *she* had to know. She had to be sure. He loved her enough to risk losing her if it came to that. More than anything, he wanted her to be happy. Totally and completely.

"What I'm trying to say, Asia, is that as much as I love you and want you to be a part of my life, to marry you and make you my wife, I can't see us ever being truly happy as long as Lance Montgomery is going to be there, somewhere, always lurking in the shadows, looming between us."

"If he is looming between us, it's because you're letting him!" she snapped. "Don't you see what he's doing? He's deliberately coming between us, putting doubt of my feelings for you in your head and—"

"I know you love me, Asia."

"Then what is this all about?" she asked, feeling her world closing in.

"It's about knowing the degree of your love. Forever is a long time. I couldn't handle it if you decided ten years from now that you don't love me enough to stay with me anymore."

"That won't happen, Sean."

"We can't be absolutely sure of that."

She turned away, not wanting to see the uncertainty in Sean's eyes any longer. It took her a moment to compose herself before turning back around. "So, since you think I don't know my own mind and heart, what are you suggesting, Dr. Crews?" she asked bitterly.

"Time," he whispered huskily. "Time to be sure the decisions we make are the right ones. We should spend time apart, not as an engaged couple, to think things through. I'll come back and see you on New Year's Eve, and if you're still sure you want us to marry, that you want to be my wife, we can move forward and set a date. If you'll be in full agreement, I'd prefer not waiting until June but would like to marry in April. On my birthday."

"I'll still want to marry you, Sean. I'll still want to be your wife," she breathed softly. "And we will marry in April. Don't let Lance come between us."

He nodded and forced an assuring smile. "I won't. What's meant to be will be."

Asia fought the anger that was consuming her as she slipped off his ring. "Here," she said, offering it back to him.

He looked at it for a second. "No, you keep it until you give me your decision on New Year's Eve. When I slip it back on your finger, then we'll both know that's where it belongs and where it will stay, forever." Then he leaned down and kissed her tenderly on the lips.

19

Carrie and Connor

"You're all buckled up?"

Carrie raised eyes to the curved ceiling. "Of course I am. Do you think I'm a half-wit?"

Connor grinned as he reclined in his seat. "No, but you did mention how much you hated flying, so I was just checking to make sure you're okay."

Carrie snorted. "I can take care of myself."

Her comment drew a chuckle from Connor's throat. He was slowly but surely discovering that Carrie Montgomery was a lot different from most women.

Feeling her eyes on him, he tilted his head and met her gaze. "What?"

"You never said what happens when we get to L.A.," she said nervously as the plane began moving swiftly down the runway.

"I've made hotel reservations."

At her arched brow, his smile widened, and he added, "Separate rooms, of course, and once we get settled, we'll check out Anderson's last known address to see what we can find out. A friend of mine, an ex-cop who also owns a PI firm, drove by the place and said it looked vacant, like Anderson was out of town or something. Hopefully by the time we get there, he would have returned."

Connor watched as Carrie pushed a hand through her hair. Whether her agitation was from the plane tilting upward as it zoomed off toward the friendly skies or from the thought of possibly coming face-to-face with Simon Anderson again after all these years, he wasn't sure. At this point it didn't matter, especially when just watching her run her fingers through her hair was a turn-on for him. Even strapped in his seat, he could feel his body respond. Mr. P was reminding him of how long it'd been since he'd gotten laid. Damn. He reached into the compartment in front of him, pulled out a magazine, and placed it in his lap.

"What if he denies everything?" Carrie asked, leaning a little toward him to drown out the sound of the plane's engine.

Connor wished she hadn't done that. She smelled good—tantalizing and seductive. He cleared his throat. "Then he has a lot of explaining to do, since it won't take much for the authorities to figure out that he's the man in those photos, which would mean jail time. Like I told you the other day, the man has to be stupid."

He tilted his head back and closed his eyes, not wanting to think about another possibility that had begun forming in his mind, one he didn't like. What if Anderson *wasn't* the person trying to get money out of her?

He had another strong suspect, but until he checked into things further, he would keep the information to himself. Carrie had enough to deal with, and a part of him wanted to shield her from any additional hurt and pain she might encounter.

Carrie glared at Connor. "You said we had separate rooms."

He glared right back at her. Their connecting flight from Atlanta to L.A. had been the flight from hell. They had encountered enough turbulence in the air, and the last thing he wanted to deal with was turbulence here at the hotel with her. He simply refused to put up with Carrie getting a bad-ass attitude. "We do have separate rooms. This happens to be a two-bedroom suite, and it was all they had at the time I made reservations. Double occupancy, two bedrooms separated by a spacious sitting room, so what is your problem?"

Carrie stared at him in amazement that he would have to ask. "My problem is that I assumed I would be getting more privacy."

Connor frowned, wondering what could be more private than this. She had her own section, and he had his. What she did behind her closed doors was her business, like what he did behind his closed doors was his. A smirk formed at his lips when he said, "Why would you need more privacy? Do you have a tendency to walk around naked or something?"

Her glare deepened. "You wish."

Yes, he did wish—just the thought was a turn on.

"Look, Carrie, this is business, and like I told you in the beginning, I don't mix business and pleasure. Besides, it was your idea to come along and not mine, so stop the whining."

Her nostrils flared, giving him the distinct impression she hadn't liked what he'd just said. "Whining? You're accusing me of whining?"

"Yes."

She crossed her arms over her chest, which made her already short top raise up even more, giving him an even nicer view of her belly. "I don't whine."

"What do you call what you're doing now?" he goaded sweetly.

"I'm merely making a point."

"Oh, is that what you call it?" He turned and glanced around. He actually liked their room. It was set up like an apartment. In addition to the two bedrooms and living room, there was also a kitchen area with a table and chairs as well as a breakfast counter big enough for the both of them. She could stay on her side and he would stay on his. Piece of cake. "Look," he said, "I'm going to unpack and get some shut-eye. This difference in time is a bitch. You can knock on my door and wake me for dinner in a couple of hours."

She stared at him like he had asked her to actually strip naked or something. "I'm not eating dinner with you. I eat alone."

He started to say something then remembered the day she had refused to eat lunch with him at his office. Evidently that was one of her many hang-ups. "Fine, eat alone. Just don't bother me if you begin choking on your food or something."

"I'm old enough to know how to eat properly, thank you very much."

"Yeah, whatever," he said, grabbing his one piece of luggage and walking off toward the bedroom where he would be sleeping, and wondering just what else she knew how to do properly . . . or improperly.

Carrie glanced around her bedroom. The color scheme of peach and aqua was different from most hotels, and the splash of sun coming through the window gave it a lush translucent beauty.

She had to admit that her bedroom was nice, and since it had a separate bath she had made a mountain out of a molehill in arguing with Connor. But still . . . even with a spacious sitting room separating them, the thought that he shared part of her space was unnerving.

It didn't help matters that she had spent a lot of her time in flight covertly studying him—especially the sexy curve of his mouth, wondering how it would fit on hers. Then there were his hands. Large and strong look-ing, almost aristocratic. His nails were short, clean, and had a healthy appearance. She had speculated how his hands would feel stroking certain parts of her body be-fore his mouth took over. Thoughts of his mouth and hands had had her twitching in her seat for most of the flight. Unlike him, she had welcomed the turbulence, which had helped shake some sense into her.

But only up to a point. Back on land, it was an en-tirely different story.

There was no way she could ignore how he looked in a pair of jeans. Damn his soul, he was blessed with hav-ing the best looking butt she'd ever seen on a man. And the way his jeans hugged his backside as well as the way they clung to his firm thighs was enough to make your mouth go dry. Then there was the strength of his muscles and the ease with which he had managed all their luggage. Her exposed belly had clenched with total awareness when he moved those gorgeous muscles to do anything. Even when he had stood at the front desk signing them in, she watched how his shirt had molded to every masculine line of his chest. Magnificent.

Hoping that a good hot bath would erase thoughts of Connor from her mind, she quickly walked toward the bathroom.

Connor needed to sleep but couldn't. He was in a bad way. In frustration he grabbed his pillow and placed it over his face, thinking if he suffocated himself he would stop breathing, which meant he would also stop thinking about Carrie.

It also meant he would stop living.

He tossed the pillow aside, refusing to let Carrie Montgomery be the death of him. As far as he was concerned, there wasn't a woman out there to die for. They were a dime a dozen, and from the time he'd reached puberty and had figured out the differences between a man and a woman, and after eavesdropping on his older cousins' conversations about "getting some," he'd known he would grow up to enjoy women. And luckily, enjoying them had come easy for him. He'd had the art of seduction down pat by the age of sixteen, and when it came to sex, he could work his way inside any woman's panties. He definitely believed in equal opportunity. Although he had discriminating taste, he would do any female of legal age, no matter the race, creed, or color.

He smiled when he recalled the crazy white sicko he had taken off his cousin Marcus's hands a month ago. The woman had gotten a taste of black and had refused to go back, turning herself into a stalker, a damn nuisance. In distress Marcus had called on him to use his expertise as a cop to handle it. He chuckled every time he remembered just how he had handled it and to this day he hadn't told Marcus any of the details. What his cousin didn't know wouldn't hurt him. All Marcus knew was that whatever approach Conner had used had worked. Marcus didn't need to know all the fringe benefits that had come along with it.

The ringing of the phone almost startled Connor, and he reached over and picked it up. "Yeah?"

"I thought you were going to check in once you got to L.A."

Connor pulled himself up in bed to sit on the edge. "Jet lag screwed me up. I had planned to do it later," he said after recognizing Brad's voice. His friend didn't have to know the real reason he had gotten screwed up. "How are things going?"

"Fine. You got a call from a Stuart Miller out in L.A. He said he got some information on what you were asking him about."

"Good. Let me grab a pen to jot down his number." In addition to finding Simon Anderson, Miller was supposed to dig into information on Edwina Montgomery, as well. From what he'd been able to gather, her mother and Anderson split up not long after Carrie had run off. The man had literally kicked Edwina out on the streets, drug habit and all. It was clearly plain to see that Anderson—who'd later turned out to be a known pedophile—had not been interested in the mother but in the daughter. The bastard.

"Thanks for the info, Brad. I'll give Miller a call."

After his conversation with Brad, Connor decided since he couldn't sleep, he might was well make contact with Miller. They had met years ago at a police officer seminar in Atlanta. Miller, who'd had plans of one day establishing a private investigative firm, had been the one to plant that same idea into Connor's head, for which he was extremely grateful.

Connor's smile widened when he thought that another thing he liked about Miller was that the man was a true bona fide playa. During the weeklong seminar, he had had the female sex practically at his feet . . . and definitely on their backs. By the time the seminar was over, Miller had slept with most of the female attendees and had started hitting on a few of the hotel staff.

Since he needed to get laid, Connor decided that spending time with Miller this afternoon would definitely be more productive than time spent with Carrie Montgomery. Hopefully after their talk, his friend would be willing to take him around to a few of the "hot" spots.

Carrie had just slipped into her bathrobe and belted it around her waist when she heard the knock on her door. "Yes?"

"It's Connor."

She knew it was Connor. Who *else* would it be? She quickly made it to the door and opened it partway. "What do you want?"

Connor saw that her unpleasant attitude hadn't

wavered any. But no matter what mood she was in, he couldn't help notice her robe and think that this was the first time he had seen her with her stomach completely covered. He missed seeing her bare skin. Forcing his mind back on track, he said. "I'm going out for a while."

She raised a dark brow. "But I thought you were tired from the flight and wanted to take a nap."

He gave a negligent shrug. "That had been my plan, but I got a message from my contact. He wants to meet with me."

Carrie nodded. "Should I come, too?"

With Miller's reputation, the last thing he intended was for the two of them to meet. He shook his head, wondering why on earth he was suddenly feeling territorial. "No, you don't need to come. After we get a good night sleep tonight, we'll go check out Anderson's place tomorrow."

"All right."

Connor couldn't help noticing how quickly she had looked away from him when their gazes had held a tad longer than was necessary. That hadn't been the first time she had—whether she wanted to or not—acknowledged him as a man. And for a woman who claimed she didn't do men, that had to be pretty unnerving for her. But he was tempted to do more than just unnerve her. A part of him wanted to stir up all that passion he believed she had bottled inside of her. Damn, stirring up anything with Carrie Montgomery was the last thing he needed to be thinking about.

"I'll be back later," he said abruptly, turning to leave.

"Connor?"

He jerked his head around. "What?"

For a moment she didn't say anything, just stared at him and for a second he felt what he knew they were both trying to fight. Instant attraction. Animal lust. "Be careful."

Color swept her brown cheeks, and for a moment he was taken back, disconcerted, by the way she was looking at him, filled with concern. Did she have any idea how much her care for his safety touched him?

Bloody hell! He didn't want anything a woman did to touch him—unless it was giving him a mind-blowing orgasm.

His eyes narrowed. He threw back at her the same words she had thrown out at him on the plane: "I can take care of myself."

"What the hell you mean the bastard's in a nursing home?"

Stuart Miller held up both hands, laughing. "Hey, man, calm down," he said to Connor. "You said you wanted him dead, so this is close to it. After following up on a tip, I checked out the nursing home he's in, and Simon Anderson is in a pretty bad way."

Miller reached into the pocket of his jacket and pulled out a business card. "Here's the address to the place if you want to check it out for yourself."

Connor took the card and looked at it. If Anderson was as bad off as Miller claimed, that meant he was not the one who'd sent Carrie those pictures. "How long has he been there?"

"He's been there for about three months. Someone dropped him off in the ER at one of the hospitals after what looked like a possible drug overdose, which eventually triggered a stroke. I'm sure his history of drugs and booze didn't help matters any, and now he can't talk or move the majority of his body parts. In other words, Anderson is paralyzed. He just sits there every day and does nothing but stare into space. I saw him, and he looks pretty damn pathetic."

The bastard deserved it. He doubted that Carrie was the only child the man had violated in his lifetime. "I want to see him for myself. Just to make sure he's pathetic enough to suit me."

Miller nodded. "Okay. I told Lila to expect you."

"Lila?"

Miller smiled. "Yes, that's his nurse, and she's definitely a fine piece of work, if you know what I mean. She and I have gotten pretty friendly over the past couple of days."

Connor shook his head. Knowing Miller, he could believe that. "Did Lila say whether Anderson gets regular visitors?"

"No, in fact she mentioned that no one ever visits him, so they assume he has no family or friends."

Connor snorted. Someone had taken those pictures off the bastard's hands and had known just how to contact Carrie. "Thanks for the information, man."

"Hey, no problem. You know how I feel about pedophiles."

Yes, Connor did know. He'd heard that the reason Miller had left the police force early was due to losing his cool and almost beating the hell out of a man who'd kidnapped and abused a little girl. Miller had been the arresting officer and had given the man one good ass whipping before hauling him off to jail, something the Police Review Board had frowned upon. They had given him the choice of early retirement or facing strict disciplinary action.

For the next hour, they talked while lingering over beer and watching the women who passed their table as the sound of a saxophone filled the air. One woman in particular had been sitting at the bar staring over at Connor for the past thirty minutes. The look in her eyes said volumes. She needed to get laid as much as he did.

"Hey man, if you don't hit on her, I will."

Connor's gaze move from the woman to Miller. As much as he wanted to get his pleasure between a nice pair of legs tonight, a part of him held back, and he was too frustrated at the moment to question why. "Go ahead, man. I'm not in the mood."

"Hell, I'm *always* in the mood."

Miller quickly got up and crossed the room to the woman. He was about to run a game that would have her eating out of his hands . . . and no telling where else before the night was over. Connor shook his head and took another sip of beer, watching Miller and the woman head to the dance floor.

Already Miller had a possessive hand on the woman's ass, staking his claim for the night. It certainly seemed that his loss was his friend's gain. He watched them dance together, saw their measured movements, and noticed how good their bodies fit.

At that moment, he couldn't help wondering how he and Carrie would fit. Somehow he knew if they ever danced together, she would feel right in his arms. He could even imagine their bodies close, tight, and with the differences in their height, her head would come to rest just under his chin. And if he were to lean down and kiss her, he knew he would find that tempting chocolate mouth warm, tasty, and full of delicious pleasure.

"Would you like another beer?"

The waitress's question almost startled Connor. "No, thanks." When she walked off, he checked his watch. It was close to midnight. Chances were Carrie would be asleep about now.

He stood, threw some bills, on the table and tossed a thumbs-up to Miller before leaving the club. True to his word, Miller had taken him to a place filled with "hot" women, but no woman, Connor decided, was hotter than the one sharing a suite with him back at the hotel.

20

"Did your contact have any more information on Simon?"

Connor glanced up while lifting the covers off the breakfast that he'd ordered to be delivered to his room. After getting in last night, he had been surprised to find the light shining underneath Carrie's door, indicating she was still awake. Frustrated as hell, he had taken a cold shower, crawled between the clean cotton sheets, and had called himself all kinds of fool for not getting a piece off the woman at the bar when he'd had the chance.

"Yes, he had information," he said.

Carrie sat on the sofa and casually sipped her coffee. True to form, she was wearing a pair of jeans and a midriff top. And her belly was showing. He couldn't stop his gaze from flickering over the exposed area. He'd never had a fetish for a woman's stomach before but there was something about hers. . . .

"What kind of information? And would you look at my face and not my belly?"

Connor blinked. He crossed his arms over his chest. "I wouldn't look at your stomach if you kept it covered. Dressing like you do is only asking for trouble."

Carrie laughed. She had heard some of the same from her brothers countless times. "If you don't know, it's the latest style."

"Well, if you ask me, exposing yourself that way is one style you should stay away from."

"Nobody asked you."

Connor went back to uncovering the platters that were filled with his food. He glanced over his shoulder at her. "Sure you don't want any?"

"Didn't I tell you that I like eating alone?"

He turned and stared at her for a long moment then said, "Do you want to tell me why?"

"No. What I want is for you to tell me what the guy told you last night."

Connor sat down at the table, ready to dig in to his breakfast. A slow grin touched his lips. "What makes you think it was a man?"

Carrie placed her coffee cup on the table with a thump. "I don't know nor do I care. The only thing I want is to know what you were told."

Connor picked up the glass of orange juice, took a slow sip. They both knew he was deliberately stalling, trying to agitate her. Not many women refused to share a meal with him, and he was beginning not to like it one damn bit.

"Connor, what do you know?"

He decided to answer her, knowing she wouldn't

like what he was going to tell her. "Simon Anderson can't be the one trying to blackmail you."

Carrie sat up and inclined forward. "Why do you say that?"

"Because he's in a nursing home. He can't talk, and he's paralyzed. He's been there for three months."

He watched Carrie, knowing the impact of his words. She stood and walked over to the wet bar in the room where the coffeepot was located and poured another cup. She then walked back across the room and sank down in the love seat. "We'll never find the person who sent those pictures."

"I'll find them." He still wasn't ready to tell her of his next suspect. "You're going to have to trust me on that." He scooted closer to the table. "Now if you will excuse me, I'd like to eat my breakfast. The sooner I finish eating, the sooner we can go check out Simon Anderson at that nursing home."

Connor stopped walking just seconds before he and Carrie entered the nursing home. He touched her hand. "Are you sure you want to do this?"

Carrie glanced from Connor to the door, thinking that confronting Simon wasn't anything she *wanted* to do but was something she *had* to do . . . for closure.

"Yes," she said softly, swallowing the lump in her throat and returning her gaze to his. "It's something that I must do, Connor."

He studied her features, saw the determined glint in her eyes, and nodded. "Okay, then, let's go on in," he said, gently placing his hand on her back to guide her through the door.

Carrie was grateful for Connor's presence. It would be hard to come face-to-face with the man she had hated for so long. The man who had robbed her of the chance to grow up an innocent. The man she had considered a father figure until . . .

"You all right?"

Carrie nodded, knowing Connor had felt the shiver that had run down her body. "Yes, I'm fine."

After making a stop at the front desk and talking to the woman who'd identified herself as Simon's nurse, they walked down the long hall that led to Simon's room. Carrie wasn't sure what she would find. According to Connor, Simon was in pretty bad shape, but she had to see for herself.

When they reached Simon's room, the door was open and Carrie stopped and stood in the doorway, unable to tear her eyes from the man sitting in a wheelchair in front of a window. She eased a deep breath past the tightness in her throat, thinking that "pathetic" was too kind a word to use for how he looked. It appeared as if he'd had a stroke. He looked haggard and old and his face and hands were all twisted. He looked nothing like the huge, intimidating man he'd once been.

Connor's hand still on her back somehow gave her the strength she needed to take a step into the room. Simon gave no indication that he heard them enter; instead he sat there, staring out of the window. Carrie squared her shoulders and started toward him . . . then stopped. She glanced back at Connor.

For a split second he thought of going to her, pulling her into his arms and telling her that she didn't have to do this, but deep down he knew she did. Regardless of the condition Simon was in now, he had once hurt her in the worst possible way and she needed to let him know how she felt, even if his stroke-stricken mind didn't understand any of it.

"Tell him, Carrie. Tell him what you want him to know. Tell him how you feel," he whispered softly.

She nodded, turned, and walked over to Simon. He watched as she stood there and stared at him, her expression a mixture of anger and revulsion. There wasn't even an ounce of pity. "You bastard," she said, trying to keep her voice low, calm. "You took something from me that you had no right to take. I hated you each time you did it and swore one day I would grow up and kill you. But it seems that you might as well already be dead. You deserve each and every day you sit alone and in misery. I hope you continue to suffer."

Simon didn't say anything. He merely stared at Carrie as if he'd never seen her before. Moments later, when Carrie realized that he really didn't have a clue, she shook her head in disgust and walked off, her mouth trembling and tears streaming down her face.

Connor was there waiting. He held his arms out to her and she went into them, needing the comfort of strong arms. He pulled her into his chest, pressing her head against the soft material of his shirt. And then she cried uncontrollable tears. The heartwrenching sound of deep, remembered pain echoed in the room, bringing on even more tears that soaked through Connor's shirt and seemed to scorch through to his chest.

And while Carrie continued to cry, Connor continued to hold her, knowing she needed this kind of cleansing. He glanced over at Simon. The man was staring into space, unaware of his surroundings or anyone in them.

A short while later, Carrie slowly pulled back out of Connor's arms. She looked at him with tear-swollen eyes. "Can we leave now?"

Connor nodded as he looked down at her, feeling a degree of tenderness he'd never remembered having before. The intensity of it made his voice shake as he said, "Yes, let's get out of here."

Before leaving, they stopped at the front desk and he questioned Lila extensively, asking about anyone who paid Anderson visits, but she stuck to the same information she had provided Miller. The man didn't get visitors and there was no one listed in his records as being a family member.

"So what now?" Carrie asked quietly when they were seated in the car, still recovering from coming face to face with Simon. She knew Connor had asked her to trust him, to believe that he would figure out who was trying to get money out of her, but she was afraid to consider what might happen if he didn't succeed. The thoughts of those pictures being posted on some Internet site and her brothers and father finding out about it was too much to think about. Although they would see her as a victim, she couldn't face the humiliation.

"Now we go and check out Anderson's house," Connor said, interrupting her thoughts. "He might not get any visitors at the nursing home, but maybe if we looked around his place, it might give us some ideas of who his acquaintances might have been."

A half hour later they pulled up in front of the place that Miller had given Connor as Anderson's last known address. The refurbished-looking house was located in a recovering part of South Los Angeles.

"If anyone asks, I'm Anderson's long-lost cousin from Florida, and you're my wife."

Connor's comment interrupted her musings, and she merely nodded. Connor strode up to the front porch confidently, as if he had every right to be there, and she followed him.

The lawn looked unkempt, and weeds had taken over, killing out what appeared to have once been a flower bed. Connor tried the door, and not surprisingly, it was locked solid. "Stand next to me, close, to block my hand movement," he whispered to her.

Trying hard to ignore the feel of his warm breath on her ear, Carrie lifted a brow. "Why?"

"I'm going to pick the lock," he explained.

She watched as he took a paper clip from his wallet, bent it back, and inserted in within the lock. A few seconds later, she heard a click when the lock released.

"It's good to know there're certain things that I'm still good at."

Carrie thought about a number of other things he was probably good at doing but refused to let her mind go there. Besides, she really didn't have time to dwell on those things when Connor turned the knob and went inside the house. She quickly followed, closing the door behind them.

She glanced around. She distinctly remembered that no matter where they had lived, Simon had never been a good housekeeper, and it seemed nothing had changed. The place was cluttered at its best and untidy at its worse. Another thing she remembered was that her mother, when she wasn't on drugs or hitting the bottle, had been the one to keep the place fairly clean and livable.

Quietly, she followed Connor to the living room. The furniture consisted of odds and ends one would pick up at a flea market or thrift store. Nothing lush, vintage, or fancy but definitely cheap. "What are we looking for?" she asked, knowing he was the one used to playing Sherlock Holmes and not her.

He didn't look at her when he answered, but continued to glance around. "Anything that will give us a hint about Anderson's associates. He was dropped off at the ER at one of the hospitals and was later sent to that nursing home. He may not have family, but I find it hard to believe he doesn't have friends or associates. I'm curious as to who is keeping up the rent on this place. Someone must have come upon those pictures and decided to use them for extortion."

At that moment he did glance at her. "Come on. Let's see what's upstairs."

He fell in step behind her as she began climbing the stairs. He couldn't move his eyes off the lush backside in jeans in front of him. Whether he was viewing her from the back or the front, he liked what he saw—a little too much.

Suddenly, she almost lost her footing, and instinctively he reached out his hand to place around her, to help her keep her balance. "Be careful."

Carrie fought to regain her equilibrium. She hadn't realized Connor was following so close behind, and the feel of his arms around her waist was making goose bumps form all over her body.

Instead of saying anything, she resumed mounting

the stairs at a quicker pace. When she reached the landing, she glanced around. The upstairs looked as untidy as it did downstairs. Although what Connor had said made sense, she wasn't sure just what they were supposed to be looking for.

"Come on, let's go in here," Connor whispered in her ear, catching her arm before she went off in another direction. Again, his touch did crazy things to her insides, and she quickly dragged her arm free. She followed him into a bedroom.

Despite her best effort, she tried ignoring him while he began opening and closing drawers and looking under the bed. To regain her focus, she walked over to what appeared to be a bookcase, thinking the one thing she never remembered was Simon having a penchant for reading. Her eyes skimmed the spines of the books, and then she pulled out one to discover it wasn't a book at all, but a video case.

"Umm, this is interesting."

"What is?"

She motioned to what appeared to be a row of books. "Simon's hidden video collection." When she noticed they had been organized by year, panic began to crawl through her, and she began quivering at the thought of what the collection contained.

Knowing Anderson's background, Connor had an idea and quickly grabbed them before Carrie did. When he pulled them out a piece of paper slipped to the floor.

Carrie picked it up. The paper had a list of names, dates, and phone numbers. "Hey, look at this," she said holding up the paper. "It might be a list of his contacts."

"Just stop right there and put those things back where

you got them from. You have no right to be here, and I'm calling the police."

Carrie swung around the same exact time Connor did and came face-to-face with an elderly man brandishing a baseball bat and staring hard at them. "I've had a lot of break-ins in the houses I own," the man was saying, "and the police told me to call them if anyone trespasses on our property. And don't think I won't use this if I have to," he said, holding the bat up higher.

Connor said quickly. "You don't have to involve the police. My wife and I are related to Simon Anderson and—"

"That's not true. The only family he has is a sister, and she told us to watch out for people like you who'd come around, claiming to be relatives just to bother her brother's belongings. I promised her that I would make sure that no one did."

Connor looked surprised. "His sister?"

"Yeah, his sister."

Carrie eased a little away from the bookcase and lifted her hands in apology. "Look, we're distant relatives, so evidently Simon's sister forgot about us. If she told you to protect his belongings, then you do what you have to do and we'll just leave. There's no need to involve the police, and we're sorry if we've caused any problems."

The man's anger eased somewhat at Carrie's apology. He lowered the bat halfway. "You didn't cause any problems, but the two of you should leave. I gave her my word."

Connor, following Carrie's lead, reassured the man. "Okay, we're going. Do you know by chance when his sister will be coming back around? I really would like to talk to her."

The man shook his head, lowered the bat to his side. "No. She just shows up every so often to check on things. She says her brother isn't doing well and asked me to make sure no one comes in here and steals his stuff. She's good about keeping the rent paid every month, so that's the least I can do."

"And we do understand," Connor said, crossing the room and taking Carrie's hand in his. The last thing he needed was police involvement at this point. "It was nice meeting you."

Without looking back he led Carrie down the stairs by the hand, feeling Carrie's pulse leaping in her wrist. When they were sitting back in the car and pulling away, Connor gave a sigh of anger and relief.

"Damn, I wished we would have had time to grab those videos and the list of names and numbers. I'd come back later but the landlord is going to make sure he keeps his eyes and ears open. I'd like to know who this woman really is, since Anderson doesn't have a sister."

Carrie met his gaze when he stopped at a traffic light. "I'd like to know the same thing." Then with a smirk on her face, she said, "And as far as the videos and that list of names are concerned . . ."

She lifted her tote bag and emptied the contents on the space between them. "What the hell?" Somehow she had swiped a couple of the videos, as well as the list. "How did you manage to get these past that guy? I saw when you put everything back on the shelf."

Carrie's smirk deepened. "Let's just say it's a skill from the past."

* * *

"I'm going to get with Stuart Miller and have him check out a few things on this mysterious sister since we're due to leave tomorrow," Connor said as they walked back to their hotel suite an hour later. "But I plan on flying back next week."

"But next week is Thanksgiving. Don't you have plans with your family?" she asked as they entered the room.

"Just the usual, but they'll understand. It won't be the first time I've worked on a holiday. As a cop, I did it often enough." He stretched his hands. "Give me those videos and that list. I want to check something out."

She went into her tote and pulled out the items. "What?"

"I want to see what's on them and what I can find out about these names."

"I want to see what's on those videos, too. The one thing I noticed before the landlord walked in on us was that they were grouped by date and year. The one with the year my mom and Simon were together was missing," she said.

Somehow Connor wasn't surprised. "You don't need to see the videos, Carrie, and knowing what might be on them, I prefer that you didn't," he said, turning to leave.

When he reached the door, he turned around. He had expected her to disagree, to give him a lot of mouth, and was glad when she didn't. "I'll be back later. You should get some rest while I'm gone."

"Will you tell me everything when you get back?"

"Yeah," he said, "I'll tell you everything." He paused and looked back at her before walking out the door.

21

Asia

"So where's your ring?"

Asia met her sister's curious stare but didn't answer.

"Asia?"

Asia expelled a frustrated sigh. She needed to talk to someone, and she and Claire had always been close . . . until David. And although during the past four years they'd worked hard to repair what had been damaged, there were certain aspects of her life she could not discuss with her sister. She knew how Claire felt about David's family, including Sean.

"Sean and I are having issues," Asia said softly, praying that for once her sister would have an open mind.

Claire reached across their mother's kitchen table, took her hand, and clasped it tightly. "Talk to me, Asia. You used to be able to do that and I promise that I'll listen and only offer my opinion if you want to hear it."

"I don't know where to start," she whispered, her voice wavering and unsteady.

Claire's hold on her hand tightened. "Start wherever you like. I have all day, and Mom won't be back from choir practice for a while."

For a few brief moments Asia didn't say anything. "After David, I tried so hard to get my life together and keep it there. It wasn't easy rebuilding the confidence I'd lost, but I did. Writing helped, and it felt good to know it was not only therapeutic for me but for women in similar situations who read my books."

Her gaze drifted back out of the window when she said, "Sean asked me to marry him, and a part of me knew the problems I'd face with David, but I also knew him to be the kind of man I needed in my life, someone I could trust and grow to love. I told him I would think about his proposal."

She looked back at Claire. "While speaking in New York, I met Lance Montgomery and from the first there was this unholy attraction between us. But I refused to let another man use me the way David did. Lance's reputation preceded him, so I knew what I was up against . . . but still, I was not prepared for his relentless pursuit. The man didn't give up." She drew in a quivering breath just thinking about all the ways Lance had worn down her resistance.

"Why do you think he refused to give up?" Claire asked, releasing her hand.

"For several reasons," Asia said softly. "But the main one was that he saw me as a challenge. In one of my talks he heard me say I'd been abstinent for a year and decided that he would be the one to change that status. I was nothing but a game he was determined to win, and he focused his efforts on doing just that."

Claire wished she could smooth the lines of pain that fanned from her sister's eyes. "And did he win, Asia?"

Asia sighed, slumping her shoulders disgustedly. "No, but he could have. I was that much of a fool and—"

"Let me get this straight," Claire said, interrupting her sister. "I've seen you and Lance Montgomery together. I felt the heat the two of you generate. I saw the way the man was looking at you, and I felt a sense of intimacy, something intensely sensual surrounding the two of you." Claire leaned in closer. "Are you telling me that the two of you have never slept together?"

"Just like there are different levels of love, there are different levels of intimacy. Let's just say when I walked out of Lance's bedroom, I was still celibate. Technically." Asia knew her sister would probably draw her own conclusions, but she refused to give her every little detail.

Claire stared at her, her eyes widening some. "You want me to believe that after that *relentless pursuit,* Lance Montgomery didn't go all the way when he had the chance?"

Asia dropped her eyes, not able to handle her sister's intense stare any longer. "Yes, that's what I'm saying."

"Asia," Claire prompted. "Look at me for a second."

When she did as her sister asked, Claire reached out and took Asia's hands in hers. "Think about it. Playas don't leave any job incomplete if they have the opportunity to finish it. Montgomery wrote that in his book himself." At Asia's arched brow she said, "And yes, I read the book. It wasn't one of his top ten rules, but it was one of the implied ones. So if you left his place technically untouched, there was a reason for it. Maybe he cares for you more than you think."

"A man like Lance doesn't know how to care for anyone, and yes, there was a reason for it. I told him that I would never let a man use me for his pleasure again."

Claire lifted a brow. "And?"

Asia felt awkward. "And he said that he wouldn't use me for his pleasure but was willing to let me use him for mine . . . and he did." When Asia thought about just how he had done so, the memory made her breath catch. A shadow of pain crossed her features when she remembered how that night had ended.

"There's more, isn't it?"

Asia stood and walked over to the window and looked out. "Yes. Later when I woke up, he threw in my face what he'd done, made me aware he could have done more but had chosen not to because he knew there would be another time. Then he got a visitor, another woman, and he asked me to leave."

Claire heard the hurt in her sister's voice, the humiliation. "Are you saying that he tossed you out of his place to sleep with another woman?"

Asia turned back to face her sister.

"Yes, although he now claims otherwise. Lance wants me to believe that he didn't sleep with anyone else that night and the reason for his unforgivable actions was because he felt things for me that he'd never felt for a woman before and it scared him."

Asia's laugh was laced with anger. "He even wants me to believe that he loves me."

Claire shot her sister an incredulous look. "He told you that?"

"Yes. Can you believe it?"

Claire knew that it didn't matter whether she believed him or not. It was apparent that Asia didn't. She shook her head. Lance Montgomery had screwed up big time, but unlike Asia, Claire believed the man was in love with her sister. She had been present that night at the *New York Times* party. She had watched from the sidelines the moment he had taken Asia into his arms to dance. She had seen anger, bitterness, and hostility etched in her sister's face but the only thing she had seen in Lance's features had been love. She hadn't believed it that night, nor had she understood it. But Asia had explained everything, and now there was no doubt in her mind that what she'd assumed was true.

Lance was in love with Asia, and he wasn't playing a game.

"Now you see what I'm up against?"

Asia's question intruded her thoughts. Yes, she saw what Asia was up against, but she doubted that Asia truly did. If her sister thought Lance was relentless before, there would be no stopping him now in his determination to get her back. No wonder he had sent a dozen roses to Asia practically every other day for the past couple of weeks. That was probably just a small part of his strategy. "And what do you think you're up against?" She decided to let her sister answer her own question.

Asia crossed the room and sat back down. "A conceited-ass jerk who has convinced himself that I'm in love with him. Can you believe his gall? He actually had the nerve to show up at my conference two weeks ago in Atlanta and manipulate a limo ride with me to a dinner function." Asia snorted. "He said I didn't love

Sean and that he was the one I loved and had the nerve to ask *me* to prove to him that I didn't love him."

Claire inwardly smiled. The good doctor certainly had her sister rattled. "And how are you supposed to do that?"

"By spending a week with him, somewhere secluded, just the two of us. In his arrogant mind, he actually believes during that week that I'm going to realize and accept my true feelings for him. He actually dared me to go along with it."

Claire considered Lance's dare for a moment. She didn't want to tell Asia that she had a feeling at the end of the week, after being alone with Lance, that her sister would realize that same thing. What Lance had done—or what Asia was convinced Lance had done—had caused her deep intense pain. But in Asia's present state of mind, she couldn't see that if she didn't love him, she wouldn't be hurting this much.

Claire said, "So, are you going to take him up on his dare?"

Asia looked aghast. "Of course not! There is nothing to prove. I'm marrying Sean."

Claire gestured toward her sister's hand and asked, "Okay, then back to my original question—where is your ring?"

Asia told Claire about the article David had mailed to Sean and about Sean's visit to Lance. "So now Sean thinks that perhaps I don't know my own mind and need time to make sure I'm making the right decision in marrying him. He's given me until New Year's Eve to think things through."

"And will you?"

"There's nothing to think about. What I feel for Sean is solid. More than one marriage has begun with friendship, and I know that I can grow to love Sean the way he deserves."

Claire desperately wanted to argue but decided now wasn't the time and it would be pointless. Asia was convinced Sean was who she needed. She would settle for passiveness instead of passion, friendship rather than love. "So, what are your plans while you're waiting for New Year's Eve?"

A smiled rolled around Asia's lips. "I need to finish that book I'm working on and have decided after Thanksgiving to go in seclusion for a few weeks to complete it. That way I can enjoy the holidays without feeling guilty about not having it finished. When Sean and I get together New Year's Eve, we can sit down and spend time planning our wedding."

"You're going in seclusion?"

Asia chuckled upon seeing the look of disbelief on her sister's face. "Yes. I've done it before, and it works for me. I'll be alone with no one to bother me, no interruptions, and no reason to waste time." Her voice vibrated with excitement when she added, "And don't try making me feel guilty about leaving you alone for two weeks. You have plans to go visit Tessa in Birmingham before the holidays, anyway."

Claire nodded. Tessa was one of her dearest friends from college. "And you'll be gone for two weeks?"

"Yes."

Several ideas popped into Claire's head and she chewed the corner of her lips as her mind dared her to go with one of them. "When will you leave?"

Asia smiled. "As soon as arrangements can be made. When I return to New York after Thanksgiving, I plan to check with Melissa about a few writers' retreats. Considering all the cold weather I've endured this winter, a place somewhere in sunny Florida sounds nice, doesn't it?"

"Yes, it does." Claire cocked her head as another thought popped into her mind, one she really needed thinking about before acting on. She moistened her lips. The more she thought about the idea, the more she liked it, but . . .

She looked at Asia as she took another sip of her tea. More than anything, she wanted her sister to be happy, and it would be worth the risk. Claire paused, letting the idea sink in deeper and beginning to like it when she thought of all the possibilities. At some point, Asia had to face up to her true feelings for Lance Montgomery. If she really didn't love him, then there would be no harm done, but if she really did and she got a chance to spend time with him in some secluded place, then . . .

Claire pressed a finger against her mouth. God forbid, but she was contemplating trying her hand at something she had never done before: matchmaking.

22

Carrie and Connor

Carrie had just sat down to the table to enjoy the meal she had ordered from room service when the suite door opened and Connor walked in. She glanced up, surprised. "Connor, I hadn't expected you back until after midnight or so."

Evidently, Connor thought as he leaned against the closed door. It was nearly nine o'clock, and he had a feeling that she would have ordered her meal a lot sooner otherwise, since she had a problem eating in front of him.

"Miller had plans, so we decided to call it an early night. I see you're having a rather late dinner," he said, pushing away from the door and crossing the room to the table, where she sat. He glanced down at her food. "Looks good."

She glared at him. "Yes, it does, and I'd like to enjoy it, if you don't mind."

He shrugged and one side of his lips quirked in a half smile. "No, I don't mind. Go ahead."

Carrie took a deep breath and let it out before she spoke. "Considering the fact that you're standing over me, I don't think so."

"Oh." He moved away from the table to sit down on the love seat. "Is this far away enough?"

Carrie's glare deepened. "No."

"And why not, Carrie? Why do you have a problem eating in front of me? You assured me that you know how to eat properly, so what's your hang-up?"

"I don't have any hang-ups!"

"And I say that you do."

When her lips began quivering, he knew he had definitely hit a nerve. For reasons beyond his understanding, she *did* have a problem eating in front of him, and he wanted to know why.

At any rate, as they stared at each other, he could see the battle lines had been drawn. She could retreat and not tell him anything, but he wouldn't let her do that. For once he planned to find out what was going on with her, since for some reason this issue was one that annoyed the hell out of him.

"Fine," Carrie said, standing and throwing her cloth napkin down on the table. "I just won't eat."

"The hell you won't." He was across the room and in her face in a flash. "I want to know what's going on here, dammit."

"There's nothing going on. I can pick and choose my dinner partners, and I refuse—"

"Not this time. I want to know why you're so afraid to eat in front of me."

"I'm not!"

"You are, too!"

"Think what you want." She made a move to walk around him, and he reached out and touched her shoulder. He snatched his hand back when he felt her flinch, like his very touch revolted her.

Connor saw it in her eyes—stark fear—and it suddenly made his stomach clench. And then somehow he knew. Her refusal to eat in front of him had nothing to do with him personally, but was connected to some evil in her past that she hadn't let go of. "Tell me, Carrie," he whispered softly. "Tell me. And believe me, no matter what, I would never hurt you," he added quietly. "Please tell me."

Confused by emotions that she was suddenly feeling, Carrie closed her eyes. It had been a long time since she'd reacted this way. Seeing those photographs as well as coming face-to-face with Simon again after all these years had stirred up the heinous memories she'd tried so hard to put behind her.

"Please tell me, Carrie."

She slowly met Connor's gaze. What she saw reflected in his eyes sent a warm feeling through her. There was no sickened desire and lust revealed in his eyes, nor was there loathing and pity. What she saw was compassion and desire of another kind, one she didn't understand but knew was different from the look that had always been in Simon's eyes.

She swallowed. The lump was so thick in her throat, for a moment she didn't think she could get the words out. "I knew exactly on which nights he would come to my room," she said softly, her voice unsteady. "Those would be the evenings when he would sit across from me at the table and watch me eat."

She closed her eyes again as if to close off the memories. "I hated those times. It was like he got turned on from watching my mouth move, seeing me swallow my food. The look in his eyes while I ate always frightened me because I knew what would happen later, and there wasn't anything I could do about it."

Her words tore into Connor, and in his mind he could envision her, an innocent eight-year-old having to endure a pervert like Anderson. She had been at an age where someone should have been protecting her, but no one had. His heart hurt for her so much, he ached. In just the short time he had known her, he had witnessed her fragility as well as her strength. This was one of her fragile moments, and for some reason a part of him wanted to replace it with his strength. He wanted her to feed off of it, use it, and be consumed with it.

He was hard-pressed to understand why Carrie Montgomery had gotten under his skin, but she had. He could admit that somehow she had invaded his world in a way no other woman had, and all he wanted to do was take her into his arms, hold her and remove her pain, erase the bad memories and replace them with good ones.

The silence between them lengthened, and the only sound that could be heard was the steady beating of their hearts. Connor knew what he had to do. What he wanted to do.

He reached out and took her hand in his, expecting resistance, but to his surprise, she didn't pull away although he felt her fingers trembling beneath his. "I told you earlier that I wouldn't hurt you, Carrie. Will you trust me to keep my word?"

Carrie met his eyes, studied the strong lines of his jaw and the steadiness of his gaze. Other than her brothers and father, she had never fully placed her complete trust in another man. She had tried with Ethan and hadn't been able to let him get close to her the way he'd desired, and after months of frustration he'd eventually given up and ended the relationship. She hadn't been able to feel this closeness, this peculiar connection that she felt with Connor, which was something she didn't quite understand when most of the time they seemed to be at odds with each other.

But they weren't at odds now. They seemed to be on the same wavelength. It was as if he could feel her emotions, read her thoughts, and was the calm behind her storm. She looked down at the hand encompassing hers. Warm hands, strong hands, trusting hands.

"Carrie?"

Her name whispered softly from his lips caused her to glance up. "Trust me."

Connor wanted to do more than hold her hand. He wanted to hold her. Gather her into his arms and take her pain away, shelter her from all the ugliness she had ever endured. "Trust me," he whispered again.

Oddly, Carrie suddenly knew that she could trust him. She believed he would find the person responsible for resurrecting all these painful memories. And she also believed that he would be the one person to remove those ugly fears from her mind. But still, a part of her held back. "I'm afraid to trust you," she said, fighting back the sob that formed in her throat. Her voice broke.

He leaned down closer, bringing his face just inches from hers and whispered, "Try."

She looked directly into the darkness of his eyes, and what she saw there caused a calm to settle over her. She felt her heart pounding when his lips moved closer to hers, and for the first time she was going to let a man kiss her without resisting him. More than anything, she wanted him to kiss her.

Connor tried to slow the thunder of his own heart, knowing this would be a very special moment for the both of them. He had never been this understanding, this patient with any woman, but felt compelled, driven, destined to do so with her. His fingers on hers tightened when he inched his lips even closer, filled with an overwhelming need to taste her, and to assure her that all men weren't the same.

When their lips were mere breaths apart, he instinctively snaked out his tongue and caressed hers, moistened them, savored them. He suddenly felt her lips tense but then her mouth relaxed and moments later, he actually heard her moan.

The moment she released a deep sigh, he entered her mouth, taking it slow but thorough, gently pulling her closer, wanting her to feel the steady rhythm of her heartbeat against his. And when he felt her returning the kiss, and became aware of the passion that was slowly inching through her body to consume his, he fought back the urge to plunge into her mouth deeper and kiss her with the hunger he felt. Instead he remained on the verge, although it was killing him. He wanted to place her needs before his own. So he battled for control and put in place his restraints.

Carrie wanted to get closer to Connor. She had never allowed a man to kiss her this way, and she hadn't known such an act could be done with such tenderness. With Connor she didn't feel threatened or fearful. What she did feel was a sense of urgency to continue to kiss him, savor the warmth of his tongue as it did such delicious things inside of her mouth. She hadn't known the touch of a man could bring her more pleasure than pain, intense satisfaction instead of shame and grief.

She gasped, and their lips parted when she felt him sweep her into his arms. Her heart was thumping wildly in her chest. She looked at him as a tense silence settled over the room. "Now you will eat in front of me," he whispered softly, walking toward the table with her nestled gently in his arms.

He pulled out the chair with his foot and sat down. Cradling her in his lap, he reached for the fork and begin feeding her, forcing her to stare at him with every morsel she took into her mouth. She saw the desire in his eyes as she chewed her food, but what she was seeing was so different from what had been in Simon's leer years ago. She didn't feel any fear. But she began feeling an awakening of some sort in the pit of her stomach and a slow simmer that started inching toward her crotch.

"Mmm," she groaned. Seconds ticked off into minutes as he fed her everything on her plate, in between sips of her ice tea. When that was finished, she swallowed hard when he turned her around in his lap to face him. The position put her just where she wanted to be—close to his lips. Before she could take the initiative and capture those lips, he leaned closer and kissed her deeply, causing a shimmer of sensations to flood her.

At that instant, desire took over, and she kissed him back.

Connor knew he had to get a grip or else he would be pushing everything off the table and taking her right there on it, and that was not what he wanted. He needed to go slow with her, prove to her that he could be trusted and not rush her into doing anything she might regret later. But there was a magnetic force that was at work, generating energy, fusing their mouths, spreading desire to a degree that wasn't normal for him. He knew he had to pull away.

He reluctantly broke the kiss. "Carrie," he breathed against her lips.

"Mmm?"

"Will you have breakfast with me in the morning?"

She reared back and met his gaze. His eyes were intense and very, very dark. Suddenly, breakfast, she thought, wasn't the only thing she wanted to have with him in the morning.

She shrugged her shoulders and said softly, "It depends on what's on the menu."

With her statement spoken so seductively, Connor's imagination filled the spaces between her words, filling his head with all sorts of visions. "Let's decide on what entrées we'll try out in the morning." Connor knew he couldn't treat her like he treated other women. For some reason, she was pulling emotions out of him that he wasn't used to feeling, up close and personal.

She inched her lips close to his. "You won't let me sleep through breakfast, will you?"

Connor slid her off his lap and stood to his feet, placing her in front of him. "Not bloody likely." He kissed her again, wondering how in the hell he would last until morning. He needed to give her that time but . . . maybe not, now that she wrapped both her arms around his neck and returned his kiss, stroke for stroke.

Moments later, fighting for control, he lifted his head. He had a feeling that breakfast was definitely going to be an unforgettable treat. As much as it killed him to do so, he took a step back. "I want you to be sure, Carrie, so sleep on it."

23

At six in the morning, Connor still hadn't slept a wink since walking away from Carrie hours ago. He had taken a cold shower then lay naked in bed staring at the ceiling, counting the seconds, the minutes, the hours.

He couldn't remember the last time Mr. P had been so hard, or this overcome with anticipation and desperation for any woman. But he knew what was happening to him, as well as what was happening to his body, was totally out of his control. Carrie Montgomery was rocking his world in a way that it had never been rocked before.

Damn, since he couldn't sleep, he might as well get up and shave. He rolled out of bed, grabbed for his robe, and went into the adjoining bathroom. Later, upon returning to his bedroom, he heard the sound of soft footsteps outside of his door.

His heart skipped a beat. He tightened the belt on his robe, shoved his hands into the pockets, and waited.

Would she knock or just stand there a while undecided? He started to go to the door and then stopped. The decision had to be hers. No matter what, she had to believe that she could trust him and that he wouldn't force her into doing anything she wasn't ready for.

When seconds ticked off, he inwardly stifled a groan. In his pockets his hands trembled, and sweat began forming on his forehead. He'd never been in such a bad way when it came to a woman. Sex was easy come, easy go. But with Carrie, things had to be handled another way.

Connor shook his head. What had made him think something like that? Carrie was just another woman. Different, but just another one. He knew it was a lie the moment the thought had entered his mind. She wasn't just another woman. If she had been, he wouldn't be standing here getting tortured to death while he waited for her to make up her mind about him.

And then, when he thought he couldn't take it any more, he heard it, the soft knock on his bedroom door. Without wasting time, he crossed the room to open it.

After knocking on the door, Carrie placed her fisted hand by her side. She hadn't slept much during the night. All she had thought about was Connor. She had been lying in bed when she heard his shower going, and her mind had filled with visions of his naked body standing under the spray of water as it washed down on him.

She had never actually made love to a man. She had come close a few times, but hadn't been able to complete the task. It had always set off an alarm from her past. But after last night and the way Connor had kissed her and held her tenderly in his arms while he fed her, she had wanted him so bad that she had ached during the night. For once the thought of being with a man didn't trigger bad memories.

And although it felt strange, here she was—standing in front of the door to Connor's room, ready to take a giant leap forward, and she knew why. She had fallen in love with him. She hadn't meant for it to happen, but it had. Her feelings had been wavering on the edge, but last night when he had shown her such profound tenderness, she had gone and toppled over. She didn't expect him to love her back . . . that's not what she was after. But what she truly wanted more than anything was the chance to be intimate—share her heart, body, and soul—with the man who had captured her love, and not be afraid to do so.

When she heard movement on the other side of the door she knew the day that she thought would never come had finally arrived. She was about to walk out of the darkness and into the light.

Connor found Carrie standing in the doorway. She was barefoot and wearing a pair of satin jaguar print shorts with a matching midriff top that had lace-trimmed shoulder straps. His gaze scanned her from head to toe, coming to a stop at her belly and getting turned on by the sight of her navel.

"Would you like to come in?" he asked huskily.

She met his gaze. "Yes."

He took a step back as she came into the room. "I'm told this is where I should come for breakfast," she whispered, a smile touching her lips. "But before you think of feeding me I might as well warn you that I don't like anything over-easy."

Her simple teasing made the breath catch in the back of Connor's throat. He decided not to scare her by saying with Mr. P nothing would be easy. Everything would definitely be hard. "Would you like to talk?" he asked after detecting her nervousness.

"No, I don't want to talk."

He covered the distance separating them, came to a stop in front of her. "Then what do you want?"

She felt a quivering in the pit of her stomach. "I don't know how good I'll be at this since I haven't done it since becoming a woman but . . ."

Knowing whatever she asked for, chances were that she would get it, she leaned up on tiptoe and whispered close to his ear. "I want *you,* Connor."

Connor felt himself stagger for a moment with the combination of Carrie's words as well as the feel of the warmth of her sweet breath on the side of his face. When she took a step back his gaze dropped to her mouth, and he knew he could not refuse her anything, and as far as her not knowing just how good she'd be, he knew without a doubt that she would be as good as it could get.

"If you come to bed with me," he said, reaching out and releasing the straps of her top off her shoulders, "I'll give you as much of me as you want. And," he went on to add as a smile touched the corners of his lips, "I promise it won't be over-easy." *Or over quickly,* he thought further.

He reached out, swung her up into his arms, and kissed her.

For the second time in twenty-four hours, Carrie was swept off her feet. And this kiss, she reasoned, had to be insane, but she didn't want to dwell on anything sane at the moment. She would take all the craziness Connor threw her way.

He carried her across the room and then, without breaking the kiss, placed her on his bed and joined her there. He continued to stroke her tongue with his own, and she knew the moans she heard came from her throat and not his. His hot and demanding mouth, his oh-so-gentle and tender hands, were erasing the painful memories of the past and replacing them with new ones, welcoming and everlasting ones. He was kissing her thoroughly, deeply, definitely getting a good taste of her, and she was getting a real good taste of him back.

He released her mouth and tilted his head and looked at her, admiring her decision to move forward. He didn't want to do anything that would make her regret that decision, and knew he had to tread cautiously. "I think we have on too many clothes. Do you have a problem with me removing them?" He continued to study her face to gauge her reaction.

At that moment, Carrie didn't have a problem with anything Connor might want to do. "No, you can remove them."

More than satisfied with her response, he rolled off the bed and began removing the belt to his robe. Seconds before his fingers were about to open his robe, he looked at her after noticing her watching him intently. "Are you sure seeing me without clothes won't bother you?" he asked again to be certain.

"Yes, I'm sure." Nothing about him would bother

her, she thought. Unless he decided not to quench the fire that was burning low in her belly. God help her if that were to happen. She shivered at the thought.

"Are you cold?"

She shook her head. "No, I'm not cold."

He didn't remove his robe but let it hang open, and the first thing that caught her eye was his manhood, fully erect and springing forth from the dark curly hair covering his groin. The sight of it didn't frighten her, but it did impress her. Connor Hargrove was a man very well endowed. He tossed his robe aside and, after retrieving a packet out of the nightstand next to the bed, slipped on a condom. Watching him prepare himself for her had to be the most erotic thing she'd ever seen, and it pushed her desire for him to another level—like it wasn't high enough already. Everything about him was a total turn-on, including the rest of his physique: muscular, well toned, and perfectly proportioned.

He placed one knee on the bed and reached out to remove her top. "Although it bothered me every time I saw it, I love your belly." He leaned down and stroked the palms of his hands across her stomach, feeling it quiver. Then he slowly moved his hands upward to touch her breasts, kissing them, inclining closer and taking the tips in his mouth and sucking gently and then greedily, making her shiver in anticipation even more. Moments later he leaned back on his haunches to hook his thumbs in the waistband of her satin shorts and ease them down her legs.

"If you love my belly, then why did it bother you to see it?" She saw his gaze centered on the curly thatch between her legs. He tossed her shorts aside, and she lay before him completely naked, exposed and getting wetter by the minute.

"Because," he whispered, leaning down to her belly. "If I saw it, that meant others saw it, as well, and I can be a very possessive man."

She sucked in a quick breath when the tip of his warm tongue came into contact with the area surrounding her navel, lapping at the soft skin and licking it.

Connor didn't stop there.

He slowly began kissing his way down her leg, caressing her ankle in his hand, massaging her calves, and then switching to the other leg to give it the same attention, and working his way back up until he reached her belly again. He knew what he wanted to do. It was something he had never done to a woman before, but he was driven to do it with her.

"I want to brand you mine," he said, his voice a deep growl.

He dipped his head, flicking his tongue out to taste her there at her center, and Carrie went speechless. And when his tongue slid inside of her and began stroking her in a way that drove her mad with desire, insanely over the edge, she could only reach out, firmly grasp the sides of his head with her hands, and drown in ecstasy.

Breathless moans poured forth from her throat, and with every sound his tongue seemed to thrust deeper.

"Connor!"

He continued kissing her as shivers of pleasure ripped down her spine, sending sensations escalating through all parts of her body. When he eased upward to kiss her mouth, she tasted herself on his lips. His mouth mated with hers relentlessly as tingles swept through her, over her, around her, leaving her quivering in the aftermath.

He released her mouth and then recaptured it for another taste before finally pulling back. He began tracing the outlines of her lips with his fingers, burning with an intense need to become one with her. He watched her watch him, almost fearful to consider what she was thinking, taking into account her past history. Was she absolutely sure she was ready for the next part? "I won't do anything that you're not comfortable with doing, Carrie," he decided to say softly. "And if you prefer, you can be on top."

Aware of what he was trying to do and knowing that not too many men would take the time to do so, Carrie didn't think she could love him any more than she did at that very moment. "No, I don't want to be on top," she said softly. "I want for you to be on top to replace the face that haunts me." She leaned up close to him—so close their foreheads almost touched when she whispered. "Give me new memories to cherish, Connor."

His heart suddenly felt full. "Sweetheart, I will." And then he kissed her gently while simultaneously easing her down on her back. He slowly positioned his body over hers and seductively brushed the tip of his erection over her wet folds. When he saw that she had closed her eyes, he whispered, saying, "Open your eyes, Carrie. Look at me."

When she opened her eyes and looked up at him, he ran his hand down the length of her, inhaling deeply her scent as he fought for control. "I want you so much," he whispered in a strained voice.

After probing her entrance several times, he continued

to hold her gaze and then with one smooth movement he buried himself inside of her, deep.

She gasped when the entire length of him was sheathed tight inside of her, and almost drowned in the tenderness she saw in his eyes, and she knew that this moment would be forged in her heart and mind forever.

Keeping his gaze locked on hers, Connor held his body immobile, allowing hers to adjust to the intrusion of his. Then when he thought that if he didn't move he would go insane, his hands dipped beneath her hips to lift her closer to him. Parting her legs at the same time, he proceeded to lock their bodies together while savoring the scent of an aroused woman.

"This," he said in a voice heavy with need and desire, "is how I dreamed of us every night—with me inside of you this way and giving you pleasure. I've wanted you ever since I first laid eyes on you."

Carrie leaned forward and planted her hands on both sides of his face. She whispered, "And I've wanted you, too. Ever since I first saw you."

"Aw, hell." Her words were like a match to a batch of explosives. His body suddenly ignited and he began to move, sliding inside of her on one stroke and sliding out of her on another; over and over again as he found the rhythm that would become passionately theirs. Connor was an accomplished lover, and with the skill he had acquired over the years, with his every thrust, he sent earth-shattering pleasure jolting through her, filling her again and again.

His throaty growl rent the air when he felt Carrie's body begin to explode, and knowing that he was buried thick and hard inside of her, every cell in his body ignited at the charged state of arousal that consumed him, and forced every erogenous zone in his body to come alive. It robbed him of all logical thought, except one. A determination to slay the demons associated with Carrie's bad memories and replace them with something that could be beautiful and painless.

So he did just that.

A gigantic orgasm tore through him, electrifying every single nerve in his body. He thrust deeper, hissed between clenched teeth. He was coming in a way that he had never come before, and he couldn't stop it if he tried. He groaned in sexual pleasure the same time Carrie did, and together their bodies became a unified sensation. They were carried unheedingly toward a sea of total and complete fulfillment.

Connor and Carrie lay together in each other's arms after their throes of pleasure. She wanted to lift up and look at the man who could make her lose herself so completely, but she didn't have the strength to do so. She felt drained, weak, and spent. The man who lay beside her, who was holding her so tenderly in his arms, had thrown a net over her, and she couldn't break free.

And at the moment she didn't want her freedom.

She just wanted to lie there and savor the moment, the memories, and all the good sensations associated with what seemed to be a good sexual meltdown. Her climaxes, both of them, had been overpowering and had pulled her within their clutches so quickly, that she hadn't been able to do anything but soar as high as she could while her body splintered into a thousand sensuous pieces.

While living on the streets, she had known what men wanted and she had taken great pains not to be any one's victim again. The other runaways hadn't had any such hang-ups and had used sex either for profit or for kicks, a different kind of high. It was something strictly physical and had nothing to do with emotions. But what she had just shared with Connor had been emotional. Even now her skin was thrumming, tingling, bore his scent.

She felt Connor stir, and then she was pulled deeper into his embrace. His chest felt solid, enduring, comforting. "Tell me what you're thinking," he said softly.

There was so much she wanted to tell him. So much she wanted to show him. "I'm thinking that I wished I'd known that there didn't always have to be pain."

"Oh, baby." Connor pulled her tight into his arms and hoped he had destroyed every evil image she had remembered from years ago.

Carrie's throat felt tight with emotions, and before she could say anything, Connor leaned over and kissed her and she was filled with a sense of warmth and security. Emotions welled inside of her and tears filled her eyes as she returned his kiss. She never thought she could share this sort of passion with anyone, but Connor Hargrove was proving her wrong.

"What are your plans for Thanksgiving?"

Connor's question reminded Carrie that Thanksgiving was next week. She glanced over at him. After making love again, they had showered together then ordered breakfast from room service. They had eaten while Connor brought her up to date on his meeting with Miller.

Using the connections Miller still had within the police force, he had promised to find out as much as he could about the mystery woman who claimed to be Anderson's sister.

When breakfast was over, they decided to make part of their visit to L.A. a pleasure trip and had signed up for one of the sightseeing tours. Afterward, they returned back to the hotel and ordered dinner. As soon as their stomachs had gotten filled, they turned their concentration to another kind of nourishment. They had quickly divested each other of their clothes, and Connor had swept Carrie into his arms and they had made love again and again.

Even now, Carrie couldn't get out of her mind the feel of running her hands over Connor's ribs, back, and stomach and feeling the solid strength of the muscles beneath the palm of her hands.

She had lost track of time. All she knew was that every time Connor had rolled off her, after making love to her, she had fallen in love with him that much more. He had given her pleasurable sensations over and over again, replacing all the feelings of helplessness she'd felt beneath a male body all those many years ago.

"My brothers are flying in, starting this weekend, in fact," she said, smiling. "And we're spending the day with my father. Logan and Lyle are the ones who enjoy doing all the cooking, and as usual they plan to cook an entire meal including the turkey, dressing, and potato pies." She glanced over at him. There was a lot about Connor that she didn't know. "What about you? Do you have a family?"

He grinned. "Oh, yeah." He pulled her closer into his arms and then told her about his mother and older sister and how they enjoyed getting together on Thanksgiving. For his mother, the gathering was an expectation. Even when he was working as a cop, he was expected to at least drop by and grab a plate.

Carrie quirked an eyebrow at him. "Why did you want to know my plans for Thanksgiving?"

Connor shrugged. "Just wondering." He'd been tempted to ask her to dinner at his mom's place if she hadn't had any plans. What the hell was he doing? He was a playa, and playas didn't invite women to dinner at their mama's house, for crying out loud. He enjoyed her company; sex between them was great. Shit, he had to admit that it was better than great. It was downright off the charts. And he had to accept that she wasn't like most women he'd dated. So far she hadn't given any signs that she expected anything beyond their time in bed together, so he should be grateful for that. But something, and he wasn't sure exactly what, was keeping him from feeling the intense satisfaction that he should be feeling. Never in his life had he worried about keeping a woman at bay. Crossing the boundary from casual sex to serious relationship was entirely foreign to him. There had never been a woman that he'd thought enough of to make him lose focus. He intended to be a playa until such a thing was outlawed by the state. He would still be having no-strings sex in his old age while confined in a nursing home.

So why was a part of him aching to slide down between Carrie's thighs and kiss her in what he'd discovered to be a very wonderful hot spot. Going down on her had been a first for him, and he couldn't imagine doing anything so intimate with any other woman.

For the next hour or so, Connor and Carrie stayed in bed and talked. Connor shared with her bits and pieces about his childhood, and Carrie told him things about hers she hadn't shared with anyone but her brothers— namely her friendship with Serena, who looked after her like a younger sister.

"I'm sorry you lost your friend, Carrie," Connor said, cupping her face and leaning down to kiss her. Retelling the story had left her in tears, and he knew after listening to her story that there had been a special bond between her and the person named Serena.

"Not having her around forced me to grow up and learn how to fend for myself," Carrie said softly, re-membering those days. "I became street smarter and street wiser, always remembering what Serena had taught me about being true to myself no matter what environ-ment I was in."

He smiled. "It seems that this Serena was a smart person."

Carrie smiled back. "Yes, she was." A lump formed in Carrie's throat. "I owe her a lot." She met his gaze and added softly, "And I owe you a lot, too. You didn't have to—"

Connor quickly leaned over to kiss any words of grat-itude from her lips. He didn't want to hear them. He wanted to do this instead, make love to her again. All he could think about was getting back inside of her and sharing earth-shattering passion with her.

He broke off the kiss long enough to open the night-stand drawer and grab a condom packet he had placed there earlier. He tore it open and quickly sheathed himself with trembling fingers while struggling for breath. He was about to make love with a woman . . .

He shook his head as those two words—*make love*—seared themselves into his brain, almost frying the cells inhabiting that space. A prickling of uncomfortable awareness flooded his insides once again. He didn't make love to women; he had sex with them. He knew the difference. But for some reason, he couldn't think of sex and Carrie within the same sentence. Hell, he was repulsed at the very thought.

Convincing himself that he was undergoing a mind game, the thought that he was about to *make love* with a woman instead of just having sex . . . and added to that was the fact that for the first time he wasn't fully in control of the situation wasn't good. But it wasn't anything he wanted to put a lot of thought on now. At the moment, his thoughts were too filled with Carrie, and all the things he intended to do with her before the night was over . . . and before they returned home to Indiana.

And with that thought in his mind, he leaned down and kissed her again.

24

The Montgomerys

"I understand you were out of town last week," Lyle said.

Carrie couldn't help the sensuous memories that immediately washed over her. Those three days she had spent in Los Angeles with Connor, she had done more than spend some intimate time with him; she had been able to confront her past and face up to the sensual being inside of her without the recollections of the past robbing her of any sexual pleasure.

And all thanks to Connor. If he only knew how much he had helped her in casting aside the ugliness she'd associated with sex. She had even been able to indulge in fantasies—something she'd never allowed herself to do before.

She took a deep breath, calming herself before meeting Lyle's gaze. She replied, "Yeah, I was."

"And where did you go?"

That question was asked by Logan. She shook her

head and set her diet soda on the table in front of her. Today was Thanksgiving. They had enjoyed a wonderful dinner and had been sitting around discussing politics, recent medical breakthroughs, and the best stock investments. Now her brothers' attention had shifted to her and the out-of-town trip she'd taken. Her right to privacy had always seemed to be a foreign concept to them.

Knowing she could tell them that where she went was none of their business and be through with it, she decided that the last thing she wanted was for them to worry about her. They were already pondering the reason why she had taken a leave of absence from work.

She met Logan's intense gaze. "I flew to Los Angeles to see someone I once knew." She hadn't exactly lied, but then she hadn't told them the full truth, either.

"Anybody we know?" Lance asked, coming to sit across from her in a recliner.

Before she could respond, Jeremiah Montgomery paused in the doorway. "Stop badgering your sister with all these questions. She's old enough to take care of herself."

Carrie smiled over at her father. "Thanks, Pop."

"We aren't badgering her," Lyle said, smiling, and coming to sit down beside her on the sofa. "We were merely asking for conversational purposes."

Jeremiah came into the room, his dominant presence the center of attention. He walked over to Carrie and patted her shoulder before moving off to stand in front of the polished mahogany fireplace mantel. "Then you need to change conversations. I don't see her asking any of you what you did last week."

As her father had declared, the conversation changed. Lyle began telling everyone about his feelings on what two teams would be playing in the Super Bowl in January, and that he had made plans to be right there in Detroit with them.

Everyone was about to add their two cents, opposing views no doubt, when the phone rang. Carrie quickly walked out of the room to the small hallway to answer it. She returned moments later and said, "It's for you, Lance. Your agent."

Lance frowned. Why was Carl calling him here? And on the holiday? The man knew his rules about family time. He had even turned his mobile phone off. "Excuse me." He walked over to Carrie and took the phone out of her hand. "Thanks." He then moved into the hallway for privacy. "Carl, you know I don't like getting calls on—"

"I thought you might like getting this one," the older man quickly said.

"A woman claiming to be Asia Fowler's sister called. Said her name was Claire Fowler. I didn't give her your number, of course, but I did get hers to pass on to you."

"Claire Fowler tried contacting me?" Lance asked in surprise. He had met the woman the night of the *New York Times* party, and for some reason had immediately liked her, since she had been the one to convince Asia to dance with him.

"Yes, she called yesterday, but I only retrieved the message today. If you've got a pen or pencil, I'll give you her number."

Moments after ending the call with Carl, Lance was calling Claire. A soft voice that reminded him so much of Asia's answered the phone. "Hello."

He got straight to the point. "This is Lance Montgomery, and I understand you tried reaching me."

"Yes, Dr. Montgomery, how are you?"

"Fine, and you?"

"I'm fine. I'm going to be in Chicago this weekend and was hoping we could meet and talk."

Lance quickly wondered what they needed to talk about, but then just as quickly he decided he didn't care. He was about to move full speed ahead in his pursuit of Asia, and he didn't give a damn who knew it. And no one would talk him out of it. "Yes, a meeting is possible. In fact I look forward to it."

"Can you talk now?"

A deep stirring erupted in the pit of Carrie's stomach. She quickly glanced across the room at Logan and Lyle. They had looked over at her the moment her cell phone had started ringing. "Yes, I can talk," she said to Connor. "Hold for a second."

She then glanced over at her brothers and father and said, "Excuse me for a moment." She passed Lance in the hallway, who was talking on the phone, and went into the kitchen. "Okay, I'm back. Did you find out anything new?"

"No, I haven't found out anything new. The reason I called was because I had you on my mind."

His words made a tiny flutter erupt in her chest. He had been on her mind, as well. "Thanks for thinking about me. How was your Thanksgiving?"

"It was nice. And yours?"

"It was nice, too." Carrie hated this, the strained but polite conversation. There hadn't been anything polite about what they had done in L.A. Even now her body shimmered in heat at the memory of how after one of their showers he had smoothed lotion all over her body, escalating her to an intensely aroused state.

"I'd like to see you, Carrie."

Carrie wished he hadn't said that, because heaven help her, she wanted to see him again, too. "When?"

"Tonight. Can you get away for a little while?"

Carrie smiled, thinking of her brothers, but she knew that Pop could handle them. "Yes, I can get away for a little while."

"Good. We can either meet somewhere or you can come here to my place if you'd like."

Carrie said, "I prefer your place."

"Okay." He rattled off his address and then said, "I'll be waiting."

Connor could feel the spike in his blood pressure, an actual rush of blood through his veins, the moment he heard the doorbell. He closed his eyes briefly. Carrie had pushed him beyond any limits he had ever set with women.

His mind flashed back to the time they had spent together in L.A. It had been perfect. The times they had remained in the hotel suite had been idyllic, cozy, and intimate. In addition to making love, they had talked about a lot of things including his reason for leaving the police force. And he had discovered a lot about her and her work and admired her dedication to it.

Connor answered the door, and there Carrie was, like always, the epitome of his fantasies. She was wearing a short top that didn't expose as much of her belly as the others had, but her leather jacket didn't completely hide her exposed flesh. Then there were the oh-so-tight corduroy pants she was wearing.

His gaze raked the entire length of her body before returning to her belly and then inching a little higher to her chest. The top she wore hugged her bodice, lifting her breasts into perfect mounds. He vividly recalled tasting them, taking a swollen tip into his mouth and—

"Aren't you going to invite me in?"

Her breathless voice intruded into his thoughts, and he looked deeply into her eyes. In them shone the same desire and need that he felt.

He leaned over, brushed a kiss across her lips, took her hand in his, and then whispered, "It will be my pleasure."

Connor kissed her the moment she was inside his apartment, a kiss designed to give maximum pleasure, and with each circular motion of his tongue inside her mouth, licking, sucking, and possessing, she felt her middle ache and felt a deep heated rush through all parts of her body. The throbbing need in the lower part of her stomach could only be relieved when she squeezed her legs tighter together.

When he finally released her mouth, she shook her head to clear it and discovered that had been a waste of her time. The look in his eyes inflamed her all over again, made her body tingle . . . especially her breasts. She could recall the last time he had touched them, and they ached to be touched again. He had cupped them in his hands, then kissed the nipples, sucked them, licked them, had flooded her with sensations she hadn't known existed.

"I want you, Carrie."

His words did more than linger in the air. They charged the atmosphere. Made breathing almost difficult. She actually felt blood surge through her. Hot blood. He took a step back, not to give her space but to study her, and he reminded her of a hungry cat sizing up his prey. Getting ready to devour it.

"Take off your top for me, sweetheart."

She dropped her purse to the floor and proceeded to do what he asked, pulling her short top over her head. She hadn't worn a bra, so her breasts were revealed the moment she tossed the top aside. His hot stare was causing intense heat to settle around her nipples, and her entire body shuddered with a need only he could quench.

He picked her up, gathering her into his arms. At that moment, her breath deserted her while he carried her into his bedroom then placed her gently down on his bed. He unfastened her pants then slipped his hands beneath her hips to tug them off of her.

She heard his sharp intake of breath when he realized she hadn't worn any panties either. She watched as he quickly began tearing off his T-shirt and jeans. Then he reached into a nightstand drawer and pulled out a condom. Her heart slammed against her chest as she watched him put it on. Then his attention was drawn back to her.

He returned to the bed and slipped his hand beneath her hips, lifted her and leaned over and dipped his tongue into her moist center. The moment his tongue touched her, stroked her, the room seemed to swirl. Her mind became mush.

When his body eased over hers, she felt herself melt into the mattress as more sensations racked her body, and when he slipped inside of her, the room began spinning all over again. Just when she thought she would regain her equilibrium, he began moving inside of her, soaring her to new heights. She automatically arched her back and thrust her breasts forward as her world once again exploded.

And she felt his body exploding as well. She heard the guttural moan that was torn from his throat, felt his thrusts get harder, more powerful, every shudder as he went deeper. She continued to lose herself in every sensation he evoked, driving her over any sexual limits ever established.

A cry tore from her lips and, as she began drowning in a sea of pleasure, she felt it, a sense of oneness, an intimacy that went beyond just the sharing of their bodies. She didn't know if he felt it, but she did, and as sensations continued to rip through her, she sank deeper and deeper in love with him and deeper into the throes of ultimate satiation.

Later they simply lay there, in each other's arms. Carrie was sprawled over Connor's chest, listening to the slow pounding of his heartbeat. She was aware of the slow, gentle caress of his hand to her back. His touch always soothed her.

"Miller called after I talked to you."

A cold sense of dread suddenly clutched Carrie's middle. She didn't want to lift her head and look at him. She just wanted to lie there and listen to his heart-beat under her cheek. "And?"

"And he's checking out a new lead. It seems some-one showed up to see Anderson at the nursing home. A woman."

Carrie drew in a breath. "The same one who's claim-ing to be his sister?"

"Possibly. That's what Miller is checking out."

She lifted up and fixed her gaze on his face. "When will we know something?"

He reached out and took a strand of her hair in his fingers and began absently toying with it. "Hopefully soon." His hand left her hair and stroked the side of her face, the outline of her lips. Both he and Miller had an idea who the woman was, but he wasn't ready to share his suspicions with Carrie, at least not until they were confirmed. "I don't want you to worry about anything, Carrie. Let me handle things. I won't let anyone hurt you," he whispered huskily.

He bent his head and their lips met. At that moment, nothing mattered.

"Good afternoon, Dr. Montgomery," the restaurant manager greeted Lance, smiling. "Your guest has already arrived," he continued and proceeded to escort Lance over to the table where Claire Fowler sat waiting.

"Thanks, Baron, for handling everything and mak-ing sure she was taken care of until I got here."

"It was my absolute pleasure, sir." When they had reached the table, Baron's smile widened when he said, "I'll send someone over to take care of your needs." He then walked away.

Lance's attention immediately focused on the woman who had been sitting alone while waiting for him to arrive. For the second time he thought that, like Asia, she was an extremely beautiful woman. He extended his hand. "Dr. Fowler, it's good seeing you again."

She grinned as she accepted his hand in a firm handshake. "Same here, Dr. Montgomery." Her grin then widened. "I think it will be easier if we become just Claire and Lance."

Lance chuckled as he took his chair. "You're probably right."

A waiter quickly descended upon them, poured water into their glasses and took their drink orders after giving them menus. Lance glanced up after the man walked off. He didn't need to look at the menu to know what he wanted, since he ate here often and this was the place he had suggested to Claire when she called. Besides, he was anxious to know why Asia's sister had wanted to meet with him.

After they had dispensed with a few pleasant preliminaries about the weather, the official kick-off to the holiday shopping season, and their opinions on who would eventually make it to the Super Bowl in a couple of months, Lance cut to the chase and asked, "Why did you want to meet with me, Claire?"

The woman didn't flinch at his directness. Instead she leveled him a look and said, "Because I've decided that you're the lesser of the two evils. Not that I think Sean is a bad person, but I don't think he's capable of making Asia completely happy."

Lance leaned back in his chair, surprised yet grateful for her opinion. "And you think that I can?"

"Yes, once she realizes that you really do love her."

Before any question could form on Lance's lips, she gave him a quick reply. "And yes, I believe that you love her. Although I'm as equally certain that for a man like you, discovering that fact was a bitter pill to swallow, which I gather is the reason for your present problems."

Lance had to admit that she had summed things up perfectly. "Why are you so convinced that I love Asia?"

A smile touched the corners of her lips. "Because I read your book, Lance. You're doing a lot of things true playas just don't do. The main one is admitting to a woman that you love her. No matter what, for a man of your caliber and die-hard determination to never commit to a woman, there would not have been any degree of desperation which would have made you take such drastic steps and confess such a thing unless it was true. Besides, I saw the two of you together that night in New York. I felt more than just pure lust flowing between the two of you, as Asia wants me to believe. From you I felt love." She gave a light laugh then said, "And from Asia I felt intense anger."

The waiter interrupted them by bringing a bottle of wine to their table and took the time to pour it into their glasses. As soon as the young man departed, Claire met his gaze again. "You've hurt Asia, and because of that, a part of me was very reluctant to meet with you. I was totally convinced that you got just what you deserved in losing her to Sean. But then another part of me, the one with the only romantic bone in my body, believes even you, a reformed playa, deserves another chance and I want to help you get it."

Lance was desperate to hear any ideas she had. "How?"

Claire gave him a steady look. "Asia told me about your dare, and I don't think it's as bad as it sounds. Spending time together alone without interruptions or intrusions is what the two of you need." She paused, then tipped the glass of wine to her lips and took a slow sip. "And I know a way to make it happen . . . if you're interested."

Lance was plenty interested and didn't hesitate to say, "I'm definitely interested."

"Good. But I need to give you fair warning. If I'm wrong about you, Lance, and this is nothing more than a game you're playing, then you might as well kiss your balls good-bye. And trust me when I say that I'm a woman of my word."

Lance blinked. It took less than a minute to realize the woman was dead serious. He shifted in his seat, not wanting to imagine the extent of pain that would be inflicted on a certain body part if she ever made good on her threat. "This is not a game with me. Time alone with Asia is all I'm asking for."

Claire nodded. "Okay, then. I'll help you get it."

25

Lance and Asia

Melissa James leaned back in her chair and studied the woman who was impatiently pacing her Manhattan office. She had been Asia Fowler's agent since her first book, and over the years they had maintained more than a good, strong working relationship. They were also friends. And because of that friendship, she was more than open to the suggestion Asia's sister Claire had made in her phone call this weekend.

Like Claire, she was convinced that Asia marrying Sean would be a big mistake, although she wasn't as totally convinced as Claire that Lance Montgomery was just what Asia needed. However, she could go so far and admit that like Claire she had been a witness to those sparks that definitely seemed to fly when Lance and Asia got within ten feet of each other. The chemistry between them was unreal. That day when they had been in her office to discuss the television show they would do together, it had been pretty easy to pick up on the fact that the sexual attraction between them had been instantaneous, explosive, and outrageously volatile.

"Melissa, are you listening to me?"

Melissa blinked, jerked from her musing as she met Asia's narrowed gaze. Melissa cocked her head as though she was offended that Asia thought she hadn't been hanging on to her every word. "How could I not listen to you, since you've been ranting and raving since you've been here? I've heard everything you've said, loud and clear. You're at your wits' end. You have personal issues and you need to finish your new book, which is due on my desk the first of the year. You need total seclusion and want to know if I know of a place that will give you just that."

Asia expelled an irritated breath. "So, do you?"

Melissa smiled. "Ahh," she sighed sweetly. "I think that I do, but I'm not sure if you'll be able to get it on such short notice, since it's always in high demand."

Asia's interest was piqued. "Where is it?" she asked finally, taking a seat on the black leather sofa in Melissa's office.

Melissa's smile widened. "Come here and I'll show you," she said, turning around in the soft cushion of her leather chair to her computer. "It will only take a minute for me log on and pull it up on the Internet. It's a private island, and for you it will be perfect."

Asia lifted a brow as she stood and walked over to Melissa's desk. "A private island? You're kidding."

Melissa chuckled. "No, I'm not. Just think about it. An entire tropical private island all to yourself for two weeks. When you're not plugging away on your manuscript, you'll get the chance to bask on the sugar-sand beaches, swim and play in crystal waters, and just enjoy being by yourself for a while."

Asia grinned. "Hey, I'm eager to go there already."

When Melissa pulled up the site on the Internet and it displayed a beautiful island surrounded by the sea-green ocean, Asia could only stare at the computer screen in awe. "It's simply beautiful. Where is it?"

Melissa glanced up at Asia and chuckled. "It's located off the coast of Florida near the Bahamas, and is part of a chain of private and luxurious tropical islands called Exumas. This particular island is called Paradise and encompasses one hundred lush acres. The twelve-room villa will be your own personal kingdom, and from what I hear, it's so private and secluded that it's only accessible by private helicopter, seaplane, or yacht."

Melissa flipped to another screen that showed an aerial view. "I understand the owner purchased it a few years ago for an investment and periodically rents it out to those individuals who are in need of seclusion. Word has it that Tiger Woods and his wife were there a few months ago."

Asia nodded as she stared at the computer screen. She could believe that. "I bet it's expensive."

Melissa shrugged. "Yes, but you get what you pay for. And if you really need to get away, this might be the place for you. It beats checking into a hotel for a few weeks."

"Who do we contact to see if it's available?"

Melissa's lips curled into a smile as she stared at Asia for a moment. "How soon do you want to leave?"

* * *

Lance gripped the phone so tightly, his hand almost shook with excitement and gratitude. "Thank you, Claire, for everything."

He hung up the phone. Everything had gone as planned. Thanks to an investment that had made him millions, he had purchased Paradise a few years ago, not knowing at the time just how important the island would be to his future . . . a future with Asia.

"I take it you got some rather good news."

Lance turned. He had totally forgotten about his brothers. Since they were flying out in the morning from O'Hare, it had made perfect sense for them to spend the night at his place. He met Lyle's gaze. "Yes, that was a call from Claire Fowler, Asia's sister."

"Asia has a sister?" Logan asked. His interest in the football game on television was temporarily diverted.

Lance smiled. "Yes. Why?"

"Then I definitely want to meet her if she's anything like Asia," Logan said.

Lance shook his head. "You've never met Asia."

Logan shrugged as he leaned back on the sofa. "Don't have to. She was able to blow your mind, which could only mean one thing."

"What?"

"She must be one helluva woman."

"She is," he murmured, his heart racing at the thought of just how much of a woman she was.

"Hey, you two. I believe we were discussing Carrie before Lance got that phone call," Lyle reminded them. "And if you don't mind, I'd like to go back to our conversation. I'm worried about her."

Lance wanted to think that perhaps Lyle was worrying needlessly, but in truth, he was also concerned and knew his feelings were a reflection of Logan's. Their sister had been acting pretty tense lately, and they couldn't help wondering why.

"I think that was a man who called her last night," Lyle said when the room got silent.

"Yeah, I think so, too," Logan agreed, throwing his head back against the sofa and drawing in a deep breath. "She left right after the call and it was close to dawn when she returned home."

Lance leaned against the wet bar and rubbed his chin. "And what if it was a man? We've always wanted her to start seeing someone, to get out and date. I don't consider the time she was seeing that baseball player as anything significant, since she really didn't take him seriously. He was merely someone to pass the time with until he got too arrogant for his own good."

Logan inclined his head forward and met Lance's gaze. "And you think she's taking this guy, the one who called last night, seriously?"

Lance snorted. "Within minutes of his call, she was racing out of the door. What do you all think?"

Lyle gave his head a shake and smiled. "Yes, she's taking him seriously." He glanced over at Logan. "What do you think?"

Logan heaved a small sigh. "I don't know what to think. I know Carrie is old enough to make her own decisions about things, but I think something else is bothering her other than just a man."

Lance straightened and crossed his arms over his chest. "What else do you think is bothering her?"

"I don't know. I felt it when she was in Tampa and

when I tried talking to her about it, she clammed up. Whether that call she got last night has to do with anything, I really don't know."

Logan added, "I think for now we shouldn't push her or start bombarding her with a lot of questions. We should let her know, as we've always done, that we're here if she needs us."

Lance and Lyle totally agreed.

26

Asia

This place is utterly breathtaking, Asia thought the moment she alighted off the seaplane onto the sandy beach and glanced around. It was truly a luxurious paradise.

As she was leaving New York, the forecast said snow for the rest of the week, yet here the sun was shining brightly in the noonday sky and the huge two-story villa where she would be staying was sheltering under a bevy of palm trees. The huge structure was surrounded by a wrought-iron gate and had a brick-paved courtyard in the front. The back, from every angle of the house, gave a breathtaking view of the Atlantic Ocean. She envied the person who owned the island, thinking that he was definitely a lucky man.

"You're going to love it here," John, the pilot of the seaplane, said. "I don't know of anyone ever leaving this place disappointed."

Asia smiled as they walked across the beach to the villa. "I can truly believe that."

After taking a tour of the place, she returned with John to the living room. "There's a number by the telephone for you to call if you need anything, ma'am," John said as he headed for the door. He had been kind enough to help carry her bags into the villa. "Unless you call us, for the next two weeks the only footprints in the sand here will be your own."

Asia grinned. She knew the older fifty-something man, who stood well over six feet with sun-bleached blond hair and tanned features, was letting her know just how secluded and isolated from civilization she would be. That would be fine with her, since she needed a temporary break from the rest of the world. She had talked to Sean on Thanksgiving, and he was sticking by the suggestion he had made when he'd last seen her. He wanted to give her time to be sure that marrying him was what she really wanted to do. "Thanks, John, I'll be fine and really do welcome the isolation."

"All right. In that case, I'll see you in a couple of weeks. Enjoy yourself."

"I will. Thank you."

Asia watched the seaplane take off moments later, leaving her completely alone. She sighed deeply, feeling absurdly pleased as she glanced around. The villa was large, and her New York apartment could easily fit in the living room alone. And the terra cotta floors, and the high twenty-one-foot vaulted ceilings that arched over wheat-colored walls, only added dimension to the villa's decor. The sleeping quarters were large and spoke of luxury, and she'd selected one of the downstairs bedrooms that had separate dressing, lounging, and bathing areas as well as French doors that led out to a verandah that was furnished with wicker furniture, including a day bed. But what she liked and appreciated more than anything was the office attached to her bedroom. Even it was luxuriously decorated and had a huge ceiling-to-floor window that faced the ocean's tranquil waters. How was she going to get her book finished with such a beautiful view outside beckoning her? A smile touched her lips. Although she was alone here, this was a place that was truly meant for lovers. She momentarily closed her eyes, and the face she saw looming in her mind was Lance's and not Sean's.

She quickly snatched her eyes back open. Whenever she thought of passion she automatically thought of Lance, even when she had no intention of doing so. It seemed her mind would immediately latch on to him and the feelings he was able to elicit within her.

Passion for her meant a loss of control and devastating pain. She should have learned her lesson with David but evidently hadn't—at least not completely, because Lance had been able to walk into her life and take her breath away, although she had fought to resist his temptation. But even now she had to grudgingly admit that Dr. Lance Montgomery was by far the most fascinating man she'd ever met. And he had been too experienced, too smooth, and too intent on luring her into a hot steamy affair, for the sole purpose of proving a point.

She wasn't here to dwell on Lance, but to dwell on Sean, as well as to finish up this book. Only her agent, sister, and mother knew where she was. She had thought of calling Sean and letting him know, too, but had changed her mind. She would look forward to seeing him on New Year's Eve. She smiled at the thought.

Claire was wrong. Everyone didn't need passion. She would gladly settle for the sedate degree of pleasure Sean would give her if it meant keeping her heart from ever breaking again, and in return she intended to make him a good wife.

Satisfied she still had her head on straight, she decided to go into the bedroom and unpack, and then later she would go for a swim before setting up the office to start working.

Dr. Montgomery, John thought, looked rather pleased when he saw the lights burning ahead in the villa. John found that rather strange, since after talking to Miss Fowler he'd gathered she was looking forward to being alone for the next couple of weeks.

"What time did you bring her here?"

Dr. Montgomery's question invaded John's thoughts. "Around noon. She's a nice lady."

"Yes, she is."

John knew that Dr. Montgomery had bought the island a few years ago, yet this was only his third time coming here. It wasn't hard to tell, even dressed in casual clothing, that the man had money. John had heard he was a psychologist who wrote books that sold millions, and besides that, he was involved in numerous profit-making investment ventures. Most of the people who owned these private islands were.

"Do you need help getting your luggage to the villa, sir?" John asked casually.

"No, I think I can manage things from here. Did Ms. Fowler indicate that she would need you to come back and bring anything during the next two weeks?"

John shook his head. "No. I told her to call if she needed anything."

Lance met John's gaze. "She won't be needing anything, and neither will I. And I prefer that we not be disturbed for any reason."

"All right."

Lance then politely thanked the man for the ride to the island before quickly crossing the beach to the villa.

27

Connor and Carrie

Connor felt the soft feminine body curl into his and smothered a yawn as he slowly opened his eyes. Carrie could arouse him even in sleep with even the most casual touch. But nothing with them was casual anymore . . . not since California.

He felt her hand on his thigh, eliciting sensations within him with the erotic movement of her thumb rubbing across his naked flesh. His nerve endings, every cell in his body, came alive and was acutely tuned to her; his senses were immediately assailed by everything woman about her, including her fragrance. She had the scent of a woman who wanted to make love. He reached out and took her hand, folded her fingers into his as he shifted in bed.

"Did I wake you?" she asked quietly, her voice like all the rest of her—soft and velvety.

"What do you think?" he answered, amused, hot, aroused.

She shifted closer, deliberately taking her leg and crossing it over his, to further stroke his passion. Her thigh came into contact with his erection in the process, and she smiled knowingly. "I think that you prefer doing something else rather than talking right now."

He pulled her closer into his arms and whispered, "And I think that you're right."

He kissed her, immediately feeling that connection to her. Then there was this hunger, this need, this urgency that he always felt when they were together like this. And since their first time in L.A., he had found what had usually been his stark sense of keeping things less personal with a woman slowly fading away with her. Shit, twice he'd almost lost control and taken her without using a condom, which showed just how messed up his mind was getting.

But he didn't want to dwell on any of that now. All he wanted to think about was how sweet her mouth tasted and how good he would feel once he got inside of her. For someone like him, who was full of experience and who'd in his lifetime enjoyed countless women, he couldn't help wondering what there was about Carrie that was so different that he didn't want to group her with the rest. Mainly because deep down he knew that she was in a class by herself.

Her taste continued to fill his mouth as he kissed her, putting everything that was him into loving her, making his already responding body even more responsive. She brought out things within him, things he hadn't ever experienced with a woman before. In addition to this fierce need to protect, there was also this fierce urgency to mate—only with her. It was a primitive urge, instinctive, enormous.

He pulled his mouth from hers and slipped her beneath him. "Connor?" she whispered his name, and hearing it from her lips made his body get even harder.

"I'm not going far, baby. I just need to put on a condom."

Moments later he was back, holding her in his arms, kissing her again as he eased between her legs. The moment the tip of him probed into her center, he felt her warmth, her wet yearning for him. And as he began easing inside of her, something within him jolted to awareness, tugged at the heart he'd forgotten he had and shattered through to emotions he had long ago tucked deeply away.

He loved her.

No, that couldn't be possible. Playas didn't fall in love, he thought as he fought hard for control. But the only answer he got was one he knew to be the truth. *This one has.*

His chest suddenly expanded and an accepting sigh, as well as a small moan, rose in his throat. He gazed down at her, met her eyes, locked into them as he felt the warmth of his love for her flow all through him. Even with all the issues she faced, in his mind and heart, she was perfect, and he would not let the horrors of her past come and invade her present again. She was his future. She was his now.

She was his completely.

"Connor?"

"Yes, sweetheart?"

"You okay?"

His smile deepened, his arms held her closer, his body moved further inside of her. "Yes, I'm okay," he said truthfully.

And then he began moving again, making love to her, wrapping his arms around her, holding her tight as he thrust back and forth inside of her. He felt her arch her body upward to meet his, watched as her lips parted softly as she tilted her head back, opening her body even further for him and murmured his name over and over again. The dazed look of passion on her face only stirred his desire for her even more.

As he watched her, felt her response, heated pleasure rammed through him, and he leaned down closer and took his tongue and probed her mouth, kissing her in a way he had never kissed a woman—with fire, passion, and love—branding her, stoking the fire blazing between them even more, forcing his mind to store into memory every sensation he was feeling, every moment he was experiencing here with her.

He couldn't stop what he was feeling. He didn't want to stop. And when something suddenly exploded within him, he groaned out her name as an orgasm of a gigantic magnitude tore through him and hit her. The fireworks shot off as they were plunged into a sky of tremendous pleasure.

"Connor!"

Hearing her call his name while in the throes of passion did something to him, and he gripped her hips and thrust into her deeper as his release—seemingly unending—hit him again.

And as he continued to shudder with the pleasure of everything he was feeling, everything he had accepted, he knew that he wanted to share this degree of intimacy with her for the rest of his life.

They lay side by side, facing each other, not saying anything but sharing this quiet moment, the calm after such a fiery storm. Connor wanted to tell her how he felt but knew he couldn't. The last thing he wanted was to freak her out with emotions she may not be ready to deal with.

"Do you have to go home tonight?" he asked softly, hoping she didn't, but understanding if she needed to. Other than that time in California, they hadn't spent another night together.

"Why? Do you want me to stay?"

He met her gaze, held it. "Yes, I want you to stay."

She was silent for a moment, and the only sound that could be heard other than their breathing was the sound of a car passing by with its stereo blasting. Then she said, "Okay, but I'll need to call my pop. I owe him that much respect. Since returning home I've never stayed out all night unless I stayed at my brother Lance's place in Chicago."

Connor nodded. Whether she understood what she was trying to say or not, he did. Since being reunited with the family she hadn't known she had, over the years she had tried being a good girl. In her mind, everything that had happened to her before that time was in some way her fault. He knew it wasn't true and was determined to do everything in his power to make sure she knew it, as well.

He leaned over to kiss her softly on her lips and then said, "Okay, go call your pop because I want you here with me, all night."

He watched as the corners of her lips lifted into a smile. "Okay."

She made the phone call and then got out of bed to go into the bathroom. Connor's phone rang. He quickly reached over and picked it up. "Yeah?"

"Hey, Connor, it's Miller. I forgot about the difference in time and regret calling late, but thought you needed to know something."

Connor shifted in bed and sat up. "What?"

"I think I have a positive ID on the woman posing as Anderson's sister, and it's who we thought it was, your client's mother."

Damn. Connor rubbed his hands over his eyes. "But are you absolutely sure she's the one sending the pictures and demanding money?"

"Yes. We verified that the post office box she'd been using is hers. Can you believe it?"

Connor shook his head. Yes, given the woman's history, he could believe it. Some women just weren't meant to be mothers. They gave the title a bad rap.

"So what do you want me to do now?"

Stuart Miller's question pulled Connor out of his musings. "Nothing. I need to tell Carrie and then we'll decide how we're going to handle it. Talk to you later." Connor then placed the phone back in the cradle.

"That was your friend in California, wasn't it?"

Connor's fingers stilled for a moment; then he moved his hand away from the phone and turned. Carrie was standing in the bathroom doorway, and he wondered how long she'd been there. "Yes, that was him."

He watched as a cool air of speculation filled her

eyes. "He found out something?" she asked, coming to stand next to the bed.

Connor wasn't sure just what to tell her and how much. How would she handle finding out that her own mother was the person trying to extort money out of her? He sighed deeply and decided he would level with her and tell her the truth. She *would* be able to handle it . . . with him. He would see to it.

"Yes, he did," he said, standing and grabbing his jeans off the floor. He slipped into them and zipped them up before turning to face her.

"He's found out the identity of the woman who's claiming to be Simon Anderson's sister."

He watched as Carrie's breath seemed to stop in her lungs. "Who is she?" she asked softly.

He crossed the room to her, wanting to be touching her when he told her. He took her hand in his, felt her tremble. He pulled her closer to him, engulfed her into his arms and whispered, "It's your mother."

He felt the jolt of shock that passed through her, and he pulled her closer. And then she let out a pained cry, and he wished he could wrap his hands around the woman's neck when Carrie broke down and the tears came.

As she cried, he held her in his arms, glad he was there to give her the support she obviously needed. And when she was ready to accept more, he would be there to offer it. In time, he would tell her about his love and that no matter what, he would always be there for her.

28

Lance and Asia

Lance used his key to get inside the villa. The moment he stood in the foyer, he could hear the sound of a woman humming and a shower going in the downstairs master bedroom.

The thought of Asia naked and standing beneath a spray of water elicited a number of wanton fantasies. Fulfilling those fantasies, he reasoned, would come later. The main thing on his agenda was convincing Asia that he loved her and that he was more than worthy of her love in return. No matter what, he would not let her rob him of the opportunity to prove that.

Stepping into the living room, he glanced around, thinking that the person he'd hired last year to decorate the place had done an excellent job. It looked stunning, from the sophisticated-looking furniture to the expensive-looking ceiling fans overhead.

Not ready to make his presence known to Asia, he headed up the stairs to the guest bedroom to unpack and get settled. He needed all his bearings when all hell broke loose.

Asia, beginning to relax, slipped into an oversized T-shirt after her shower. The cotton material felt soft against her naked skin, and since the garment hit midway on her thighs, she felt decent enough. Besides, even if she wasn't decent, no one was there to complain about it.

She had talked to Claire earlier, to let her know she had arrived and was all right and not to expect another call from her again for a while. Claire had mentioned the weather was horrible in New York and really envied her. Her sister had sounded so pitiful that for a moment Asia had been tempted to invite her to join her, but then she knew once Claire got on the island Asia wouldn't get any work done.

Asia glanced around and grinned. Just about anyone would envy the time she was spending here. Things couldn't get any better than this. After taking a tour of the island earlier that day she had quickly concluded it lived up to its name—Paradise.

She lifted her head, thinking she'd heard something, and then decided she hadn't. The last thing she needed to do was to let her nerves get the best of her. It probably had been nothing more than a coconut falling on the thatched roof. She was used to living alone, had done so for years without a problem in her five-room apartment.

She glanced out the huge window and saw it had gotten dark outside. A part of her hadn't wanted the day to end. She had enjoyed the solitude of spending time on the beach doing practically nothing but relaxing and thinking about things, mostly about her and Sean. Perhaps he'd been right—that she had accepted his marriage proposal without thinking things through. But then another part of her felt that Sean was the best thing to happen to her and wished she had met him before meeting David.

And as much as she didn't want to think about Lance, she had. She couldn't forget the last time she'd seen him, at the writers' conference. He had called her several times since, but once the caller ID had identified him, she had refused to take it. The two of them had nothing further to discuss.

Her eyes narrowed to slits as she brushed her hair back from her face. The man was a playa. Hell, he wrote the book. She despised the fact that she'd let him get as close to her as he had, preying on her emotions. His persistence had worn her down. His personality was too intense. He was used to getting what he wanted, and she had played right into his hands. And what really pissed her off more than anything was his assumption that he could charm his way back into her life. Fat chance!

Not wanting to think of Lance any longer, she slipped into a pair of flat sandals and left the bedroom. She decided to prepare something light to eat before buckling down and getting some writing done, determined to get one chapter completed before going to bed.

Thinking it was past time to make his presence known, Lance left the guest room when he heard Asia moving around downstairs. He found her in the middle of the kitchen, standing next to the sink. She had the blender going, churning together what looked to be her own brand of a fruit smoothie. She had kicked off her shoes and was in bare feet as she went about her task.

Lance's insides tightened and his skin got warm at the thought that she was here with him alone in this secluded place, and he was determined that while there they would reach an understanding. He leaned back against the door. She hadn't yet detected his presence, and he took advantage of the peaceful moment to study her. God, she was beautiful—and could inspire fantasies that you wouldn't believe. There hadn't been a single night that went by since they'd met that he hadn't thought about her, dreamed about her, craved her.

But then he knew there was more to Asia Fowler than just her physical beauty. There was that rare exuberance that shone deep within, which had ensnarled him from the start. He'd watched her interact with people. He'd seen how easily and confidently she worked an audience. Then later when an army of her readers had bombarded her, he'd seen how genuinely open and friendly she was.

Deciding that it was way past time for him to say something, he was about to open his mouth and then stopped, immediately captivated by what he saw. She had leaned over the sink to pour some of the fruity concoction into a cup and doing so made the hem of her already short T-shirt rise higher, showing off a gorgeous pair of thighs.

Suddenly, blood rushed through every vein in Lance's body. He couldn't stop his gaze from traveling down the length of her scantily clad body all the way down to her bare feet before moving back up to her face. She'd closed her eyes to sample what she'd made, and the most precious of smiles shone on her face.

As he watched her, love—a degree he hadn't thought was humanly possible—invaded his gut, and he was tempted to cross the room and take her into his arms. He took a step and then stopped when she suddenly went still, sensing someone's presence.

She swirled around, and then blinked as if she were seeing things. He decided to put her mind at ease. "Hello, Asia."

The ceramic mug she'd been holding fell to the floor and shattered into pieces, spilling what was left of the contents. She closed her eyes as if doing so would make him disappear. When she reopened them and saw him still standing there, all signs of shock had vanished from her gaze and were replaced by fire-spitting anger.

"What are you doing here, Lance!" She nearly screamed out the words.

He straightened when she crossed the room, got all into his face, madder than any woman had a right to be. She got so close, the tips of her breasts brushed against his chest, but she was too mad to notice. He sure as hell did. It was hard to keep his face blank and not to respond to the contact.

"You did it again, didn't you? You manipulated everything to your benefit, determined to have your way, just like you did that day you tricked me to your place for dinner. This is a game that you have to win."

Her words cut into him, and the quivering of her voice made him aware of just how angry and upset she was. "It's not about winning, Asia," he said softly, wanting her to understand. "I'm not playing a game with you."

"Yes, you are, and I won't stand for it! I'm leaving!"

Lance slowly shook his head. "You can't leave."

She took a step back, visibly shaken by what he'd just said. "What do you mean I can't leave?"

"There is no way off the island."

"Of course there is a way off the island—the same way I got here. All I have to do is make a call, and the seaplane will come back."

Lance shook his head. "They have my orders. No one comes, and no one leaves from here."

Asia couldn't do anything but stand there and stare at him when it hit her that he was dead serious. "Who the hell are you supposed to be?"

Satisfied that she had finally asked, he met her glare and said, "A man who intends to get the one thing I want—time alone with you."

"When hell freezes over."

He chuckled, the sound more intense than amused. "Then let me issue a freeze warning, because we're in for one hard blizzard."

Asia angrily pushed her hair out of her face, lifted her chin, and glared at him. "I won't stand for this. You can't force me to stay here against my will."

"And I'm not. I'm merely making you aware that there is no way off the island until I give the word. Like you, I'm here to finish a book and for rest and relaxation, as well. This place is big enough for the both of us, so being here together shouldn't be a problem."

"It *is* a problem. I refuse to spend any of my time under the same roof as you."

Lance crossed his arms over his chest. "Why are you afraid of being alone with me? Are you worried that I will force you to face the truth—that you don't love Sean Crews?"

"I do love Sean!"

A smile curved Lance's lips. "I care to differ."

Her first instinct was to slap that confident smile off his face, but then she decided she would not let him make her lose control. And under no circumstances would she allow him to make her question her emotions. "I don't care what you think."

"Then maybe you should, because as long as I'm convinced that I'm the man who should be a part of your life, I'm not going away. I'm determined to prove you wrong."

"You can't prove anything!"

"Then I will die trying."

He knew the exact moment she saw the intensity in his eyes and realized that he wasn't about to let up, which only made her more furious. "I will find a way off this island, no matter what you say, and in the meantime you better stay away from me."

Without saying anything else, she quickly walked out of the kitchen and went into her bedroom, slamming the door behind her.

An angry Asia paced her bedroom, getting angrier by the minute. She had tried calling out to the mainland, only to find the phone—the same one she had used earlier that day—completely dead. She had gotten so mad, she had crashed the receiver down in its cradle. She also tried using her cell phone, but could not get reception—something no one had warned her about.

Lance had somehow manipulated his way onto this island with her, and there was no way he could have accomplished such a feat without help . . . which meant Melissa had been in on the deceit. But then what about Claire? Her sister had known of her desire to go somewhere to be alone. Was Claire involved in this farce as well? It wasn't a secret how Claire felt about Asia's engagement to Sean.

The thought that Melissa and Claire could betray her this way was almost unbearable. She wanted to start cursing viciously and throw things but knew doing so wouldn't help matters. She had to maintain control.

She sat down on the bed and clasped her shaking hands together when the full realization of the fix she was in hit her full force. She was on an island in the middle of nowhere, alone with the one man she had been determined to protect herself from.

The only reason Lance Montgomery would not leave her alone was because for some reason, he was totally convinced that she felt something for him. In that case, she had to prove his arrogant ass wrong. He thought he had the upper hand. Maybe it was time to show him just how wrong he was. After that ordeal with David, common sense had kicked in and the healing had taken place. She had gotten an inner strength she hadn't known she had, and in the end she had grown confident in trusting her instincts. She had learned how to handle the most distressing of situations, no matter what it took or how painful things might become. And she had taken a vow never to let any man take advantage of her again. Lance thought the two of them on the island together would be to his benefit, but she was determined to show him otherwise. No matter what it took, she would ignore his very existence. She had come here for solitude and to get some work done. He had destroyed the solitude, but she still had a book to finish—and no matter what, she intended to finish it.

Lance placed the mop back in the bucket after cleaning up the spill on kitchen floor. Things had been quiet for the past hour, and he wondered what Asia was doing behind those closed doors. She would have discovered by now that the phones didn't work. He had taken every precaution to make sure any contact with the mainland was severed the moment he had arrived.

"I would have done that. I don't need you to clean up after me."

Asia's sharp tone let him know she was still pretty pissed. "I didn't mind since I was the reason you dropped the cup in the first place."

He watched her closely, studied her features, and tried to read her expression. But he found it was a total blank. She had become unreachable, erected a solid wall between them, and distanced herself. "I'm about to prepare something to eat," he said. "Would you like—?"

"Let's get one thing straight, Lance. The only thing I want is for one of us to leave, but since that doesn't seem to be an option, then I just want to be left alone. You said you came here to finish a book like I did. Then do it. You're right. This place is big enough for the both of us, and I intend to ignore your very presence and do what I came here to do. I refuse to be a party to your games." She then turned and walked out of the kitchen to return to her bedroom.

Lance sighed deeply. She was so convinced that pursuing her was nothing more than a game for him, and the first thing he intended to do was prove her wrong. By the time it was over, he would have destroyed every defense she tried using and would never let her erect them against him again.

29

Upon waking up the next morning, Asia just lay there, staring up at the ceiling. It was almost eight. Somehow she had gotten through the night, which hadn't been easy knowing Lance was somewhere in the house. Whether she liked it or not, it seemed her entire being was attuned to his nearness.

She remembered waking up earlier at dawn, to the sound of a door closing, and had gotten out of bed in time to glance out the window to see Lance, dressed in T-shirt and shorts. During the time it had taken him to do body stretches before jogging off toward the beach, she had stared at him, watched how his muscles had flexed, pulled tight with the workout he was giving them. In no time, his body had glistened with sweat, and every inch of him, from head to toe, appeared rock solid and exceedingly well fit.

While watching him, she had been filled with an enormous amount of heated desire, wanting, and lust.

She'd actually felt her head spin as her traitorous body responded to the sight of him. She had been filled with forbidden thoughts of being outside with him, running her hands all over his body, taking a certain part of him into her hands and . . .

She had gotten back in bed determined to rid herself of the madness that possessed her. But even when she'd tumbled back to sleep, her mind had been filled with the images of what she'd seen, and they were visions she couldn't forget. Even now.

It was time to start her day. She got out of bed and went into the bathroom, peeling off her nightgown. Moments later while standing under the shower spray, she became attuned to just how responsive her body was, a reminder of her celibate state. But a few months ago, she'd had an orgasm, and not the self-induced kind. It had been the Lance Montgomery kind. She paused, remembering it so well, every shudder of pleasure that had ripped through her body when Lance's mouth had done all kinds of things to her, taking her in a way no other man had.

She stepped out of the shower and began toweling dry, trying to fight the tumult of emotions that was raging through her. Only Lance had the ability to do this to her . . . even without trying.

After putting on a pair of shorts and a top, she walked out of the bedroom. The house was quiet, and she couldn't help wondering where he was. She walked near the stairs and paused, listening, and then she heard the sound of computer keys clicking. He was evidently working on his book—like she needed to be working on hers.

She went into the kitchen to make a fruit salad for breakfast. A short while later, she walked into the downstairs office ready to get started on her writing. The moment she entered the room, she saw the vase of tropical flowers. They were beautiful.

Crossing the room she gazed at them a moment before noticing the folded note that had been placed beside them. She picked it up and read the bold script words: *These were hand-picked for the woman I love. Lance.*

Asia closed her eyes as she tried to fight the emotions that suddenly consumed her. *Stop it!* she ordered herself. *Don't believe a word he says, and don't let him get to you!* He was playing a game and would do or say anything to win. He wouldn't hesitate to trample her emotions while trying to prove some stupid point.

She balled up the note and tossed it in the garbage as she fought to get her emotions back on track. No matter what it took, she would get through her time here on the island, finish her book, and move on.

She would not let Lance Montgomery get the best of her.

Lance glanced at his watch then pushed away from the computer terminal. It was four in the afternoon already. For the first time in a long time, his words had flowed easily, mainly because for the first time ever he'd been writing from his heart.

Several times during the course of the day, he had heard Asia move around downstairs, yet he'd still managed to stay focused and get a lot of work done, and hoped she had done the same. He would allow her to continue to try to ignore him, handle him with cool indifference, but likewise he planned to take one day at a time and let her know just how much he loved her. He hadn't heard the vase go crashing against the wall, so maybe that was a pretty good sign that she had liked the flowers.

He glanced out the window. It had been another beautiful day, and he intended to go outside to enjoy what was left of it.

After changing into his swimming trunks and with a beach towel under his arm, he walked down the stairs. The villa was quiet and felt empty, and he wondered if Asia was still at work. He opened the back door and walked out, headed for the beach. He didn't go far before he saw her, stretched out near the water and lying on a huge beach towel.

When he got near, she detected his presence. A dark frown appeared on her face and without saying a word, she turned away from him to look back out at the ocean.

He strolled to where she lay and placed his own towel down within a few feet of her and sat on it. "Hello, Asia."

She didn't respond. She just kept her gaze on the beach and off of him.

But he wouldn't let that deter him. "Did you get much writing done today?" he asked.

It seemed that minutes passed before she turned cool eyes to meet his. "Don't push me, Lance."

At least he had finally gotten her attention. "Trust me, you'll know when I begin pushing." *Preferably on your back,* he thought, glancing over at her. She definitely looked good in her bathing suit, and seeing her in it wasn't helping matters. It was slowly bringing out the lustful beast in him. He loved her, but hell, he wanted her, too. He was trying to be the epitome of control right now but was finding it hard as hell to do so.

"It's nice out here, isn't it?"

She didn't answer, but he refused to let up. "Every time I come to this island, it gets more beautiful and I notice something that I hadn't before."

She turned and stared at him, and asked accusingly, "You've been here before?"

His eyebrows lifted. "Yes, I've been here, and before you ask, no, I wasn't here with a woman. I came to finish a book."

Moments later he added, "I'm grilling fish and making a salad for dinner tonight. Would you like to join me later?"

She stood, brushed sand off her legs, grabbed her towel, and then reached for her tote bag. The look she gave him was still cold as ice. "No, I would not like to join you later. In fact, the less I see of you the better off I am."

He was tempted to grab her wrist, tumble her back to the ground, and kiss those words right off her lips. But he would let it go for now. "All right," he said evenly. "Enjoy the rest of your day." When she began walking off, he said, "And Asia . . ."

She halted but didn't turn around.

"I love you," he whispered.

He saw her body tense, and then she slowly turned around, glared at him. "You don't know the meaning of the word, Lance."

He leaned back on his arms and held her gaze and said, "Until I met you I hadn't. According to my shrink, thanks to my mother's desertion, I've despised women for a long time. But I'm slowly learning how to let go and get over it, and each day I'm understanding more and more what love is about."

He stood. "And the more I analyzed things, the more I discovered what a selfish and inconsiderate bastard I've been, not only to you but to other women as well. But especially to you."

He took the few steps separating them to stand in front of her. "But the one thing I do know is my emotions and how I feel. Whether you want to believe it or not, I do love you. I hurt you, and for that I'm sorry and will regret the pain I've caused you for as long as I live. I don't expect you to believe me or trust me right off the bat, but I am asking that you give me a chance to prove to you just how much you mean to me."

Asia turned away, refusing to believe what he was saying. The wall encasing her heart was too thick. "No, Lance, I refuse to let you get next to me a second time."

"And I refuse to let you push me out of your life."

She turned back around. Their gazes connected. Lock. And then without saying anything else, she turned and quickly headed back toward the villa. The realization struck him like a ton of bricks: He had hurt her deeply, and winning her back wouldn't be easy. It might even be impossible.

Asia let herself inside the villa and went directly to her bedroom, closed the door, and leaned against it. Dammit, she couldn't let herself respond to him or react to his words. She couldn't because they were just words. From the night she had decided to accept Sean's pro-

posal of marriage, she had been holding herself together, and had convinced herself that Lance, like David,
had been a mistake. But she hadn't counted on this—
his ability to penetrate the wall she had erected around
herself, especially her heart.

How could a man tell a woman that he loved her and
make it sound so legitimate while lying through his
teeth? She set her mouth in a grim line. Only a man
who was a playa of playas would know all the sweet
words to say to break down a woman's defenses; convince her that she was special. Lance Montgomery was
the epitome of smooth and slick; what did she expect?
Fury touched her face when she thought that trustwor-
thiness and honesty wouldn't be so bad.

She heard him come into the villa. If for one minute
he thought she would share his company he had another
thought coming. She would go to bed hungry first. She
crossed the room to the bathroom to take a second
shower and go to bed early.

The delectable aroma of grilled fish woke Asia up and
immediately made her aware that she hadn't eaten anything since lunch. She glanced over at the clock and
saw it was nearly the eight o'clock hour.

Getting out of bed and sliding her feet into her slippers, she went to the window and looked out. Moon-
light splashed across the ocean, and the salty smell of
the sea did nothing to calm her stomach. It was growl-
ing from lack of food. Deciding that her battle with
Lance was no reason to starve, and since he *had* invited her to join him for dinner, she walked over to the
closet and pulled a cotton sundress off the hanger.

After removing her nightgown, she slipped the dress over her naked body, kicked off her slippers, then stepped into her sandals. She took the time to put on a thong and tried to quash the fluttering she felt in her stomach. Drawing in a deep breath, she tried convincing herself that her hunger had more to do with the food being cooked than the man cooking it.

Lance glanced up at sound of the French door opening. He had set up the grill outside on the patio, where he could enjoy the view of the moonlight-kissed ocean while putting his culinary skills to work.

He watched as Asia stepped out into the cool evening air and walked straight into a pool of light. From the angle of the lanterns hitting her body, he could easily tell she wasn't wearing anything beneath her dress . . . at least nothing that mattered or couldn't quickly be removed. His pulse suddenly raced at the thought.

Deciding not to make her appearance such a big deal, he said, "Make yourself useful. The salad in the kitchen still needs to be tossed."

His words surprised her, but nonetheless, she tipped her head up, ready to square off with him. "You didn't say I had to do any work."

He chuckled, thinking she was a regular little smartass. But he loved her anyway. "You're going to share in the work if you intend to eat. I apologize if I didn't make myself clear, but that's the way things go around here. There's no free ride."

She took a step forward. "I'm not looking for a free ride. I'll make the damn salad."

"Sure you know how?"

She laughed and rolled her eyes at something so absurd. "Hey, you're the one with the personal chef, not me. Maybe I'm the one who should be concerned that you know what you're doing."

"I know what I'm doing. With no mother around and a father who worked tirelessly to make sure we stayed clothed and fed, my brothers and I learned how to do plenty for ourselves. We took turns doing the cooking, laundry, and whatever else needed to be done."

Asia craned her neck to look past his shoulder to see what he was doing to the fish to make it smell so good. "Your mother never came back? Not even to visit?" she asked out of curiosity.

Lance shrugged. "She did come back once, after Logan, Lyle, and I had finished college and made something of ourselves. She needed money and asked us to lay a couple of grand on her. She said we owed her something for bringing us into the world."

Asia blinked. She couldn't imagine a mother saying such a thing to her child. "Was she serious?"

"As a heart attack. And when she saw we didn't agree with that assessment, she tried another approach."

Asia's interest piqued. She asked, "What?"

"She was willing to bargain for the whereabouts of our kid sister."

"Sister? You have a sister?"

He grinned. "Yes. You sound like you find that hard to believe."

"Considering the stuff you write in your books, I do."

He chuckled. "Touché."

Asia regarded Lance's amused expression, then asked, "What do you mean she was willing to bargain for the whereabouts of your sister? Didn't you know where she was?"

Lance furrowed his eyebrows, concentrating, remembering. "No. When my baby sister was barely six months old, my mother ran off with her lover, taking the baby with her."

"Oh."

"And from what I understand, my mother got into drugs and booze and my sister was placed in various foster homes, and at one time she lived as a runaway on the streets of Los Angeles. We had no idea where she was. We eventually hired a private detective to find her. He located her a few months before her sixteenth birthday. Once she was found, there was a big adjustment period since we were practically strangers to her."

Lance didn't say anything for a few moments then finally added, "My only regret is that we didn't find her sooner. There's no telling what sort of hell she went through all those years to survive."

Asia nodded. "How is she doing now?"

Lance released a long-suffering sigh. "If you would have asked me that a couple of months ago, I would have said she was doing just fine. She has a great job as a social worker down in Tampa, where my brother Logan lives, and like most twenty-four-year-old young women, she's into clothes, hair, and nails. But lately, something is different. There's something going on with her, and my father and brothers and I don't have a clue what it is, and she won't talk to us about it."

Asia nodded. Lance picked up a bottle of beer that was close by on the table. Asia couldn't help noticing how he moistened his lips before taking a sip. She re-

membered one kiss they had shared where he had practically sipped her the same way.

Silence grew around them as she forced her mind
away from that memory. Instead she thought about all
that Lance had said and how openly he had shared the
personal information regarding his mother with her.
No wonder he still had issues with his mother. Not only
had the woman deserted Lance and his brothers, but
she had literally torn their family apart as well.

"Are you going to make the salad, or are you going
to stand out here all night and daydream? The fish is
almost ready."

She narrowed her eyes when she saw the faint grin
that tugged at his lips. And what a nice pair of lips they
were, she thought, pulling in a quick, quivering breath.
"Okay, I'll make the salad. Just don't expect me to help
clean up the kitchen afterward," she said, tossing the
words over her shoulder as she walked toward the French
doors to the kitchen.

An unexpected rush of pleasure flooded Asia as she
slipped between the sheets later that night. She hated
admitting it, but she had enjoyed having dinner with
Lance, and for once they hadn't been biting each other's
heads off. She had merely listened while he told her
more about his family, finding every little tidbit fascinating. And although she had claimed she wouldn't do
so, she had ended up cleaning up the kitchen with him.
When they had finished, he had merely thanked her for
her help, told her good night, and then went upstairs to
bed.

Because she had taken a nap earlier, she had been

too wired up to sleep and had gone into the office and had completed another full chapter before calling it a night. Although at no time had Lance acted inappropriately, she had still managed to feel his warmth in the spacious kitchen. His nearness had reminded her that she should have been keeping her distance, but she had honestly enjoyed his presence too much to think about that. And, she reasoned, no harm would be done as long as she kept her guard up.

And she was determined never to lose her head when it came to Lance Montgomery again.

Over the next few days, the routine for Lance and Asia was basically the same. He would get up at the crack of dawn to go jogging, and she would wake up around eight, grab a cup of coffee, and start writing. And just like that first day, a fresh vase of hand-picked flowers with a note would be sitting near the computer. And just as she did that first day, she tried not to put much stock into what he'd written.

They would spend the day in their separate offices getting as much writing done as they could and during the late afternoon, by silent agreement, they would meet on the beach to relax and unwind. It was during those times they would talk about different things, always keeping their conversations impersonal. Then at night they would prepare a meal together, eat, clean up the kitchen, and then part ways, going to their separate bedrooms. But it was during those dinner times, when he would always share with her some things about himself, that, whether she wanted to or not, she was getting to know the real Lance Montgomery. She knew the music he liked, the foods he didn't like, the places he had gone and places where he still wanted to go. And despite not wanting to, he got her to talking about herself and how hard it was for her single widowed mother to raise two daughters after their father's death from a work-related incident when Asia was five.

Although occasionally she still thought about leaving the island, especially on those days she felt herself being drawn to Lance, she didn't. She rather liked not getting any phone calls, and not having any interruptions. During the day, since Lance had his own book to work on, it was as if she was alone anyway. He didn't try to invade her space, and she didn't invade his. They had respected each other's privacy. But then she knew they both looked forward to the time they spent together on the beach at the end of the day.

It seemed that this evening there would be a slight change in plans, Asia thought, as she logged off her computer and glanced out the window. There were heavy, dark clouds covering the sky, which meant a storm was coming. That also meant she and Lance wouldn't get to spend any time on the beach later that day.

She walked out of her office the same time he was coming down the stairs. "A thunderstorm is headed our way," he said, glancing out the window. "The last time I was here and a bad storm came up we lost power. I'm going to go around and gather candles just in case."

"All right." In a way she was glad he was there with her. She didn't want to think how she would have handled things alone on an island in total darkness. "And just in case we do lose power, I'm going to go ahead and fix us something to eat, like sandwiches and a fruit salad. How does that sound?"

"Like a winner."

Asia had just finished making the last sandwich when the storm hit, hammering the island with torrential rain and with it came the smell of fresh, rain-sweetened air combined with the scent of topical flowers. She glanced up when Lance walked into the kitchen.

"The candles are lit already."

"Good. I don't relish the idea of sitting here in total darkness." But then she didn't relish the idea of sitting anywhere in candlelight with Lance. There were times like these that his presence made her tense, not for anything he was doing intentionally, but because as much as she didn't want to, she was attracted to him. And she couldn't stop the dreams she had of him at night.

In one particular dream—the one she'd had last night, in fact—he had come into her bedroom and slipped into the bed with her. Taking her into his arms, he had kissed her while sliding his fingers underneath the flimsy nightgown she'd worn and easing it off her shoulders. Her head had fallen back when he had released her mouth to let his lips trail all over her. And when he had made it to her stomach and was inching lower, her body had actually quivered at the thought of how she would feel when he kissed her deeply in the spot between her legs. And when he had pushed her thighs apart and lowered his head she had—

"Asia? You're okay?"

She blinked. She was standing in the middle of the kitchen having a heated flashback of her dream. She glanced up at him and found him looking at her strangely. "Yes. I'm okay. Why do you ask?"

"Umm, mainly because you were breathing funny."

Had she been? Deciding not to go there, she said, "Sounds like the rain is going to be here for a while."

Lance glanced out the window. "Yes, it does. I don't see it letting up any time soon."

"Are you ready to eat your sandwich?" she asked, having nothing else to say.

"No, I'm not hungry. I thought I'd go back upstairs and take advantage of as much daylight as I can just in case the power does go out."

She nodded. "I think that I will, too."

Asia made a move to step around him and he touched her arm. She stopped and lifted her brow, trying to face him calmly, fighting hard to do so. But the touch of his fingertips had done something to her. It had scattered her thoughts, and had made hot pulsating desire run rampant through every part of her body.

"Yes?" she asked, fighting the fierce longing, the deep urgency, for him to touch her again. She gazed into his eyes and wished she hadn't. She saw it. Stark desire of the most potent kind.

"We've been on this island together for five days," he said huskily, like he'd been the only one counting. "And so far I haven't done the one thing I've been itching to do since I got here."

She swallowed deeply, knowing she shouldn't ask but knowing that she would anyway. "And what's that?"

"Taste you."

Her entire body felt convulsed with desire, and she felt as if she was suffocating. Suddenly she needed air.

She needed to run outside in the rain to cool off. She needed for him to kiss her.

She closed her eyes, trying to remember her relationship with Sean and her decision to marry him and thinking it was strange that he hadn't crossed her mind much lately. It seemed Lance was the only man who held her attention, thoughts, wants.

"Asia?"

Her name was a raspy sound from his lips—lips she wanted to devour hers. Her mind suddenly began spinning. What was wrong with her? Technically, she was engaged to marry one man, yet she wanted another. She loved another.

That realization hit her with such force that she almost tumbled backward, and she would have if Lance hadn't reached out to keep her from falling. But in a way, she fell anyway the moment he touched her. She fell straight into desire. It started as a slight tremble deep inside of her and then without very much effort, it escalated into something else when heat blazed to life within her body, igniting a fierce form of sexual need, leaving her visibly shaken.

Instinctively, Lance pulled her into his arms and held her trembling body close to his and she hung on to him. She knew what she wanted, and she knew what she needed, and deep down she had a feeling he knew, as well.

"Lance?"

He pulled back slightly and looked down at her. "Yes, sweetheart?"

At first she couldn't get the words out but was determined to do so anyway. "I want you."

The dark eyes that stared down at her didn't flicker when he responded by saying, "I want you, too. And I need you and I love you. The reason I wanted time alone with you was to prove to you just how much you mean to me. And even now I don't think I've actually done that."

"It doesn't matter."

"Yes, it does." He released her and took a step back. "It matters a great deal. The book I'm working on is called *No More Playas*. I've poured out my heart and soul in this book to get men to understand how a die-hard playa can change his thought processes after meeting the one woman he believes is his soul mate, which is something that I thought could never happen. I was wrong in believing such a phenomenon didn't exist. And whether you choose to believe me or not, I *have* fallen in love with you, Asia, and I haven't touched another woman—not even come close to doing so—since meeting you, and like I told you, although I wanted to paint a different picture, I sent Rachel Cason packing probably before you'd even left the building."

She stared up at him. "Then why did you do it? Why did you want me to think otherwise?" she whispered.

Lance sighed deeply. "Because being with you, being swamped with emotions I've never felt before, scared the living daylights out of me. What I felt for you that day was more than naked desire, Asia, and when I realized the significance of that, I panicked and was driven to do whatever I needed to do to get you out of my life."

He recalled that day and the hurtful look in her face when he'd pulled that stunt in front of her with Rachel.

"It wasn't until later when I realized and accepted that I'd deliberately made you hate me that I began hating myself. It was then that I also realized that I couldn't go on without you in my life and had to admit my true feelings for you."

He didn't say anything for a moment; then he added, "That night at the Pattersons' party when I discovered you had gotten engaged to marry Sean Crews, my world came tumbling down."

Stunned by everything he'd just said, Asia took a step back and sank down in the nearest chair at the table when she felt her legs folding beneath her. For a moment she just sat there, wondering how she had not considered the possibility of what he'd done that night as some devious ploy to get her out of his life because he had begun developing feelings for her . . . just like she had begun developing feelings for him.

"I know I've hurt you, Asia," he said, his voice dropping to a whisper. "But if you give me another chance, I promise never to cause you pain again. I love you and need you in my life. Not just for now, here on this island, but for forever. Will you grant me the chance to do that?"

Asia glanced up at him, and what she saw in his gaze touched her heart. There weren't just desire and longing deep in his eyes; she also saw love. This hadn't been a game to him like she'd assumed after all. The thought of that made intense heat swirl through all parts of her and love flow freely through her heart. She suddenly needed to be held by him, in his arms.

"Lance?"

"Yes?"

"Hold me."

Quicker than she could blink an eye, he was at the table, bending, gently sliding his hands around her, gathering her into his arms. And he stood there, holding her securely against his chest, gazing lovingly down at her before lowering his head to kiss her.

30

It seemed like he'd waited to do this forever, Lance thought, remembering the very first time he had kissed her that day in Dallas, as well as the last time—that night in New York. And now, like then, he was as focused on Asia's mouth as any man could be. And it wasn't helping matters that she had her hand fisted in the front of his shirt, clutching it, holding his mouth captive the same way he was holding hers as sensations after sensations hit him, literally squeezed air from his chest while their tongues dueled, melded, and satisfied an intense need that vibrated all the way to their bones. He ran his fingers along her bare arm, needing to touch her skin as her mouth opened even more under his.

He hadn't intended to possess her mouth this greedily, but he was helpless at the thought that she was here like she'd been in his dreams countless times, in his arms, reciprocating all the things he was feeling and crashing through any measure of self-control that he had. Loving her, he thought, was pure heaven, but he wanted more than the sighs of pleasure that escaped from their joined mouths. He wanted to give her more.

He wanted them to share paradise.

Lance pulled back slightly, breaking the kiss. His gaze was dark with desire when he looked at her and said, "I want to do something with you that I've never done with a woman before."

"What?"

"Make love and not just have sex."

His words made currents of desire, awareness, and need coil in Asia's belly, and she reveled in the sensations that were flooding through her. She remembered her decision to become celibate over a year and a half ago. She had always been of the mind that there was nothing wrong with a man and woman sharing a wonderful and healthy sexual relationship, but what she had found wrong was when that relationship lacked love and commitment.

After David, she had needed time to recover, and on more than one occasion she hadn't done that. She would allow some man and his sweet-talking ways to pull her back into another relationship that she hadn't been quite ready for, a relationship that was never intended to go anywhere. She couldn't let that happen to her again. That was one mistake she would never repeat.

From the first, Lance had insinuated that he intended to be her lover, but the woman in her—the one who had grown tremendously from those days with David—needed more than a toss between the sheets. He said he loved her and she needed to know, to fully understand just what that meant for them.

"What does forever with me mean to you, Lance?" she asked softly.

He reached out and touched her cheek, letting his finger softly stroke her face. "Forever with you means loving you completely, making a life with you, embarking on a real relationship, a committed one. With other women, I've always protected my emotions by being the ultimate playa; now I want to share those emotions with you. I want to marry you, give you my name, my babies, my love, my life. I want you to be the woman I wake up with in the morning and go to bed with at night. I want you to be my best friend, my soul mate. Right now I love you so much, I hurt at the thought of ever losing you again. Telling a woman that I loved her was something I'd never done, while truly meaning it, but the words flow easily off my lips for you because they are real and meaningful. And I will love you, Asia Fowler, until my dying day and even beyond that."

Asia sighed deeply, hearing the intensity in his voice with the words he had spoken. He had said what she needed to know. What she needed to hear. And deep down, she believed he really meant them.

He pulled her close to him again. "Now it's my time to ask. What does forever with me mean to you?"

She looped her arms around his neck. "It means knowing who I want and what I want. Accepting that I love you, Lance. It also means sharing a committed and loving relationship with you. Marriage. A family. Being your soul mate, lover, and wife, till death do us part." And remembering his words, she added, "And even beyond that."

She eased her body even closer to his. "It also means becoming one with you, heart, body, and soul, and right now it's the body aspect that I'm looking forward to the most."

A grin tugged at the corners of Lance's mouth. "I think I can safely say that I can definitely handle that."

"Prove it."

No sooner had the challenge left her mouth, the lights in the villa flickered. Seconds later, the electrical power went out. Everything would have been thrown into total darkness if Lance hadn't taken the time to put out lit candles earlier. Candlelight gave the villa a romantic effect, stirred up an already arousing mood, charged an already stimulating setting. And then Asia was lifted into strong arms when Lance didn't waste any time carrying her in the direction of the bedroom she was using. She glanced around the moment they crossed over the threshold. Two lit candles were sitting on the dresser. Their vanilla scent permeated the air, making the room smell heavenly.

Lance placed her down on the king-sized bed and took a step back and when he did so, the candlelight reflected off his features. The planes of his face appeared even more profound, sharp, and sensuous. "Do you have any idea of how much I want you, Asia?" he asked.

She almost asked him that same question regarding her own degree of want and desire for him. "No, how much?"

He came back to the bed, leaned over close until his mouth was mere inches from hers. "I want you so much, I quake inside. Do you know that since that time in my bedroom with you, I go to bed each night craving the taste of you again, wanting to be inside of you, going slow, and then fast, deep. Then deeper still."

He began kissing, nibbling, licking the corners of her mouth, sliding his tongue down the side of her neck. "And growing larger, harder, within the confines of your body and then the final act where I come apart in your arms, release my seed inside of you, hoping doing so will give you my baby. A child conceived in our love."

A child conceived in our love . . . Asia's pulse raced and her heart leaped as she stared into his eyes, and she could honestly admit that a piece of her had fallen in love with him that day after her speaking engagement in New York at the Betty Shabazz Center. He had approached her, more handsome than any man had a right to be—arrogant, confident, and sexy.

She released a breathless sigh the moment he leaned closer still and connected his mouth to hers. Her mind and body went on sensory overload, taking her to the point of no return when he joined her on the bed, gently pushing her onto her back. He continued to kiss her deeply, thoroughly, exploring the insides of her mouth with his tongue, taking possession, staking his claim. Her muscles trembled, her insides quivered and when he finally lifted his head, her breath came out hot, damp, forced.

The vanilla-scented candles in the room continued to flicker, providing a degree of light that was purely sensuous. She watched as his fingers slowly began working at the spaghetti straps on her sundress, pulling them down her shoulders and finally removing the garment completely from her body. After removing her bra and panties, he kissed the mounds of her breasts, tormenting them the same way he had tormented her mouth earlier, and causing an ache to build up between her legs.

"What about your clothes?" she asked as she tugged his T-shirt from the waistband of his shorts. She gave him a gentle push back onto the bed. "The last time we were in bed together, you treated me to my pleasure. Now it's time for me to treat you to yours."

Asia's hands pulled his shirt over his head, tossed it aside and then went to the waistband of his shorts and unbuttoned them. He lifted his hips for her to remove both them and his briefs. Her gaze immediately dropped to the area below his waist, and the only words she could think to say were, "Oh, my." He was hard, huge, hefty.

She returned her gaze to his face and as he watched her, she lowered her head to his nipple, taking it into her mouth, licking it with her tongue, while letting her hand drift lower, down his belly, and taking him into her hand. He jerked against her palm, said something that sounded a lot like, "holy shit," while she ran the pad of her thumb over the sensitive head of his staff.

When she let go of his nipple and moved her mouth lower, and worked her way down toward his belly and began circling his navel with her tongue, Lance knew what she intended to do next, but there was no time. He wanted her now. He needed to get inside of her fast. He reached out, grabbed her around the waist and switched their positions, placing her on her back beneath him. "My pleasure will always come from treating you to yours, baby," he whispered, taking her mouth again in one hell of an erotic kiss.

After freeing her mouth, he whispered, "Look at me, Asia."

She did, held his gaze.

"I've dreamed of making love to you so many times, prayed one day that I would. I love you. Every damn thing about you," he said in a hoarse voice. "You are perfect."

He begin easing inside of her, while holding her gaze, almost losing control when his staff came into contact with her hot, wet center. She began making arousing little sounds deep in her throat as he went deeper and he felt her muscles tighten, pulling him in. And he continued to sink into her heat, feeling her lift her hips for him. And when he had gone all the way, connecting with her in a way he had never connected to another woman, a feeling of urgency slammed into him, jerking his body into movement. The slow pace he had intended was suddenly forgotten and he gasped, bucked his body, feeling pushed over the limit.

He threw his head back and released a primal cry when he began thrusting into her. And when she started moaning, groaning, begging him for release, he gave her what she wanted as he continued to slide in and out of her, deep and fast.

"More, Lance."

She raised her hips to him, arched her back, locked her ankles around his waist while he thrust urgently inside of her, giving her what they both wanted. His passion. His love. More.

A scream tore from her lips at the same time his body exploded, his entire being shook, splintering into a multitude of sensations, ecstasy of the most prolific kind. But he didn't stop. He continued to push forward, needing to give her everything that was him. And she took it. Milking him with her muscles, grabbing his butt tight in her hands to make sure he didn't go anywhere before she got it all.

She screamed again . . . and again, and he lowered his mouth to kiss her. Not to quiet her but needing the feel of his tongue thrusting inside her mouth the same way his staff was thrusting inside her body. And then it happened again, this orgasm more explosive than the first. The only thing he could think about other than the sensuous feelings shaking him to the core was that the woman he loved more than life itself was finally his.

At some point during the night, Lance awakened to find the power was still out. He also noticed that he was alone in the bed. He glanced across the room and saw Asia, wearing his T-shirt and standing at the window looking out, gazing at the moon-lit ocean. The raining had stopped and the musky scents of sea and sex hung in the air. He thought the two were one hell of a combination.

He closed his eyes, remembering the exact moment he had slid into Asia's body, hopelessly and helplessly falling even more in love with her. Last night had been a huge turning point in their relationship, but he knew there were things they hadn't yet discussed. Things they needed to lay to rest.

"What are you thinking about, sweetheart?" he asked her quietly. He watched as she slowly turned away from the window to meet his gaze.

"Sean."

He hated thinking it, but knowing the woman he had just made love to—and shared at least three to four orgasms with—was thinking of another man didn't sit too well with him. Not bothering to put on any clothes, he slid out of bed and slowly crossed the room and pulled her into his arms and kissed her lips.

"Talk to me. Tell me why you're thinking of him," he said, trying to keep any sign of jealousy from his voice.

"I'm going to hurt him, Lance. When I tell him about us."

He noted her voice was raspy and hoarse. Probably from screaming so much, he thought. "If you had married him, without truly loving him, you would have eventually hurt him anyway."

"Yes, but he's been such a good friend."

He skimmed the tip of his thumb along her jawline. "And if he truly cares for you, he will accept your decision and continue to be a good friend."

A soft smile touched the corners of Asia's lips. "I hope so, Lance. I know you don't like him but—"

He pulled her to him, wrapped his arms around her waist. "He was my competition, Asia. No, I didn't like him, but I never saw him as a threat."

"You didn't?"

"No. I was determined that no matter what it took, I was getting you back. Even if it meant kidnap. But I didn't have to go that far, since you made things easy for me by coming here."

She frowned up at him. "And from what I gather, you had help."

He chuckled. "Hey, can I help it if others thought we made a fantastic pair and wanted to get us together?"

He then added, "But on a serious note, Melissa and Claire were concerned about you. About us. They love you and wanted you to be happy."

"And they thought I'd be happy with you, with the reputation you had?"

"Only because they saw something you refused to see. My love for you. And I'm glad they did. My life would be nothing without you in it, baby." He leaned down and kissed her again, needing the intimate contact of their lips. Slowly he released her mouth.

"I don't think I like the idea of you leaving my side to think about another man," he said, backing her toward the bed. When they reached it, he gave her a little push and together they tumbled onto the mattress.

"Umm, what do you prefer that I think about?" she asked, after he had tugged the T-shirt over her head, leaving her naked.

"Ways you can scream again. You're getting pretty good at it."

Asia laughed. "Sex. Is that all you think about?"

He shook his head. "No. At the moment I'm thinking about how soon I can make you my wife."

She went still and met his gaze. "Are you asking me to marry you?"

"Yes. I want to marry you, Asia. As soon as we can arrange things."

"Oh, Lance," she breathed quietly. "I want to marry you, too. But I have to talk to Sean first. I can't accept your marriage proposal until I've told him about us. It wouldn't be right, and I owe him that much. It's bad enough that you and I have slept together."

"There's nothing bad about what we did. You aren't

wearing his engagement ring. Claire said he took it back."

Asia raised her eyes to the ceiling. "Claire was wrong. Sean merely gave me time to think things through until New Year's Eve. He believes there is a possibility that we still might work things out and marry in April."

Lance cupped her jaw. "Then that's his problem, because the only man you're marrying is me. Here. On this island."

She smiled at his arrogance. "I'd love to get married to you on this island, but don't you think we'd need to clear it with the owner first? From what I hear this place is constantly in hot demand. I can definitely understand why after spending time here. It's beautiful."

"I think so, too, but I never realized how beautiful it was until I spent time here with you. For that reason, I think I'm going to keep it."

She quirked a brow, trying to follow his conversation. "Keep what?"

"This island. Especially since you like it so much. I was thinking of selling it after Tiger Woods made me such a fantastic offer."

She considered his words as she stared at him and watched his dark eyes twinkle with sexy humor. She then remembered the little information that Melissa had provided about the person who owned Paradise. "Are you telling me that you own this island?"

He grinned wryly. "Yes, I guess that's exactly what I'm telling you."

Mildly exasperated, she wondered how he could have kept something like that from her. "You, Lance Montgomery, are impossible."

He shook his head, smiling. "No, I am the man who loves you and plans to marry you and make you happy for the rest of my life."

"And I plan on doing the same for you."

He leaned over and kissed her lips. "You can start by agreeing to spend Christmas with me. It's a tradition now that Carrie's back home with us that we spend Christmas in Gary with my father. I want my family to meet you."

"And I'd like to meet them. Since I spent Thanksgiving with my mom and Claire in South Carolina, spending Christmas with you and your family won't be a problem."

He smiled. Very pleased. "Now that all of that is out of the way, I think it's time to turn my attention to other things."

"Such as?"

His hand drifted to the area between her legs. "Making you scream."

31

Connor and Carrie

Connor glanced over at Carrie. They had been sitting in the rental car for almost an hour, watching the house where Carrie's mother was supposed to be living. After arriving in Los Angeles earlier that morning, they had checked into a hotel, rented a car, and then met with Stuart Miller. He had been keeping tabs on Edwina Montgomery for the past week, and according to him, the house across the street was her place of residence.

"You okay?" he finally asked Carrie, not standing the silence any longer.

"No, Connor, I'm not."

He nodded. She didn't need to elaborate. She hadn't been very talkative since finding out the identity of the person who'd sent her those letters trying to blackmail her. Several days ago, he had noticed the dark shadows under her eyes, which meant she hadn't been getting much sleep. He had tried remedying that by talking her into staying over to his place a couple of nights. After wearing her out by making love, she hadn't had any choice but to sleep soundly. But on one of those nights she had awakened in a sweat and with tears swimming in her eyes. While she had sobbed against his chest, she had kept asking him over and over, "How could your own mother do such a thing?"

Finding out that her mother was the one behind the extortion attempt had rattled her something awful. He inwardly shuddered, thinking that for the life of him, he couldn't imagine such a thing. Good mothers protected their kids, not used them for profit.

Connor pushed back the car seat to stretch his legs. He glanced around, thinking that this wasn't the best of neighborhoods. More than once a group of teens, who gave the appearance they were looking for trouble, had walked by, eyeing the car's hubcaps and tires. But after looking Connor in the face, they must have figured the hubcaps and tires weren't worth it if it meant tangling with a mean-looking bastard like him.

A cab pulling up caught their attention, and a woman quickly got out. "I think that's her," Connor said quietly as they watched the woman let herself inside the house.

Carrie shrugged. "I wouldn't know. I really don't remember much about her, and what I do remember is foggy. For years I tried forgetting she existed and pretty much had. I guess she decided to show me."

Connor heard the sadness in Carrie's voice as well as deep disappointment. He reached out and skimmed the tip of his finger on her cheek, loving the feel of her soft skin. "Don't worry, babe. Evidently she doesn't know the seriousness of what she's trying to do. I'm sure the mention of jail time will be a deterrent, and she'll go back to whatever rock she crawled from under."

Carrie smiled, a little more relaxed than she had been a few moments ago. "I hope it will be that easy."

"And if it's not, we will deal with it, okay?"

She sighed deeply before saying, "Okay."

He checked his watch. "We might as well go get this over with."

Carrie took a deep breath and knocked on the door. She had asked Connor to let her handle things by doing all the talking. After all, it was her mother they were dealing with.

The door snatched open. "Go away! I'm not buying nothing!"

The woman blinked as she stared at Carrie. Carrie stared back at her, and she hoped she wasn't seeing an older version of how she would look in another thirty years. It was evident from the harshness of her mother's features that she'd had a rough life. But then, too many men, booze, and drugs were known to do it to you. Her earlier visions of her mother were as a beautiful woman who wouldn't hesitate to use that beauty to get what she wanted. Carrie couldn't even start to count the number of relationships she remembered her mother being involved in when she'd been too young to care or understand.

"Well, if it isn't my long-lost daughter," the woman sneered, recognizing Carrie. She moved her gaze from Carrie to Connor. "And who might you be?" The smile on her lips was plastered.

"My name doesn't matter. All you need to know is that I'm with her," Connor said in an irritated tone of voice.

The woman shrugged and leaned in the doorway. "Whatever. So why are the two of you here?"

Carrie met her mother's nonchalant gaze. "I know what you're trying to do, and it won't work. You're not getting a penny out of me, and if you keep it up, I'm taking everything to the police."

The woman's eyes narrowed. "You have nothing on me; can't prove a thing. Even if you did, what good will it do to turn me over to the cops? Being behind bars won't stop those photos from getting posted, trust me. I'm sure your brothers will get a kick out of—"

"Leave my brothers out of this!" Carrie snapped.

"Protective, aren't you? Hey, that's good. But I won't leave them out of this. You adore them, and you will pay me whatever amount I want for them not to find out about you and Simon."

"You act like I wanted him to touch me. I was only eight years old. You exposed me to a pedophile, and I will never forgive you for doing that."

Edwina Montgomery tossed her gray, stringy, streaked hair over her shoulder. "Simon had been my man, and I refuse to believe you didn't want him coming into your room all those times. I can't believe he'd been taking those pictures and had actually kept them over the years. Now I'm going to cash in. You owe me."

Connor had heard enough. Although he had promised Carrie he would let her handle things, he refused to listen to another minute of this bullshit. The woman had one hell of a sick mind if she blamed an innocent eight-year-old for sleeping with a rusty-ass thirty-something-year-old man.

"Come on, Carrie," Connor said, angered beyond belief. "Let's get out of here before I forget this woman gave birth to you, which is probably the only decent thing she's ever done in her entire life."

"Now you look here, son," the woman snarled at Connor.

"No, you look here," Connor snarled back, taking a step forward, getting into the woman's face. "And I am not your son, thank God. If you send Carrie another piece of correspondence, I will contact the authorities. It will make me extremely happy to see your ass locked up and rotting in jail."

Connor grabbed Carrie's hand and had turned to leave when the woman called after them. "Go ahead and have me locked up. I don't give a damn. The police will have to find me first—since I'm extremely good at hiding when I want to get lost—and then it will be too late, Carrie. Listen to lover boy if you want, but I'll make sure your brothers know the truth about you. Don't pay me that money, and I'll make sure they know about that Web site as well as sending those pictures to the newspapers for them to have a field day with them. Take your chances if you want. It will be your loss. Just imagine what your brothers will think of you then, their precious baby sister. Mail the money to that post office box no later than New Year's Eve midnight like I said, or you'll be sorry." She then slammed the door.

*　*　*

Back at the hotel, Connor paced the room, cursing. He stopped his pacing. "Tell me I heard you wrong and you aren't going to pay that woman a damn dime."

Carrie flinched at his harsh words but kept packing. She knew he didn't like her decision, but it was something she had to do. She had the money, although it would nearly completely wipe out her savings. "Connor, try to understand that—"

"I'm not going to try and understand, dammit. You're letting her manipulate you into doing whatever she wants. You were the one who was the victim. Why are you letting her do this to you?"

Carrie closed her luggage and glanced over at him. "Because if I don't give her what she wants, she will do as she says she will do, and I can't let that happen. My brothers are professionals. They are known worldwide for the work they do. I can't let what my mother plans to do shatter their lives."

Connor crossed the room in a flash and was in Carrie's face. "What about your life, Carrie? Do you honestly think your brothers will blame you for what happened all those years ago?"

"Of course they won't blame me, but that's beside the point. It did happen, whether I was an innocent victim or not. If a newspaper reporter gets wind of this, it won't matter to them that I was only eight years old. They will see a story, and it will be a story that could possibly destroy my family's lives."

Connor stuffed his hands into his pockets because he was tempted to shake some sense into Carrie. "Don't you see that you're playing right into her hands? If you pay her that won't be the end of it. She'll demand more money out of you. And who's to say she won't post the photos anyway, even if you were to pay her off? Don't you think it's time to face your past . . . along with your brothers and father? Don't let anyone make you a victim again."

Carrie ground her teeth. "No, Connor, I will handle this my way. It doesn't concern you."

"Like hell it doesn't."

At that moment, Carrie's emotions were frazzled, and the last thing she needed was Connor on her case. "Dammit it, Connor, it *doesn't* concern you. My mother is my problem. I paid you to do a job—to find out who was blackmailing me—and you did it. I'll handle things from here. Your services are no longer needed."

Her words cut into Connor. He stood there staring at her, not believing that the one time he had finally fallen in love, the woman was dismissing him like he was yesterday's trash. "Is that the way you want it, Carrie?"

She lifted her chin. "Yes. That's the way I want it."

He took a step back. "Fine. I'm going to give you what you want. I plan to stay here for a couple more days, hang out with Miller. Have a safe trip back to Indiana. I'll see you around." He grabbed his jacket off the back of the chair. "On second thought, maybe it's best if I don't see you around."

As soon as the door closed shut behind him, Carrie fell on the bed and cried.

32

The Montgomerys

Connor stood outside Carrie's father's house. For the past two weeks, he had tried putting her out of his mind, getting on with his life, but had discovered he couldn't do that. He loved her and had learned a painstaking lesson—you didn't give up on those you loved. He refused to walk away like she wanted him to do and let her handle things, and he refused to let her be any person's victim again. The woman he loved had spent the majority of her life trying to get over a bad episode in her life and now of all people, her own mother was keeping the past looming over her head. Connor wasn't having any of it. One thing a man did was protect his woman and he intended to do just that, whether Carrie wanted him to or not.

Connor raised a hand to knock on the door.

A jubilant Jeremiah Montgomery made his way to the front door when he heard someone knocking. This was a very happy Christmas Day with his three sons and daughter here, and what made it even more special was that the one son he thought would never settle down and fall in love had done just that. Lance had brought a girl home and introduced her to everyone as the woman he planned to marry.

Jeremiah thought that Asia was such a pretty thing and was just what Lance needed. Now if only Logan and Lyle would follow in their younger brother's footsteps and find good women.

The older man sighed when he thought about his daughter. Something was bothering her, but until she told them what it was there was nothing they could do about it. But his heart ached for her, and he could tell from the bags under her eyes that she wasn't getting much sleep. She had announced to everyone that she would be leaving right after New Year's to go back to Tampa and start back working. No one knew or understood why she had taken nearly a month and a half off work, anyway. That was still a mystery.

He opened the door to find a young man standing there. "Yes, may I help you?"

"Merry Christmas, sir, and sorry to bother you, but I was wondering if I could see Carrie?"

Jeremiah hadn't known Carrie to have any male friends in Gary, although a couple of nights she had stayed out all night. He studied the man, deciding he looked decent enough. "Merry Christmas to you, too, and it's no bother, and yes, you can see her. Come on in. She's in there with her brothers opening presents."

As soon as the man walked over the threshold, Jeremiah offered his hand in a warm handshake. "I'm Jeremiah Montgomery, Carrie's father."

"How do you do, sir? And I'm Connor Hargrove, a friend of Carrie's."

Jeremiah was just about to ask the man how he had met Carrie when Logan's voice stopped him. "Who was it at the door, Pop?"

Jeremiah glanced over his shoulder when Logan entered the room. "Someone for Carrie."

"Oh?" Logan frowned as he came to stand beside his father. He looked Connor up and down. "I wasn't aware that Carrie had any close friends here in Gary."

Connor returned Carrie's brother's curious stare. "Well, she has," he decided to speak up and say. "And I'd like to see her if I can."

The sound of voices made the three men turn around. Lyle and Lance, with Asia and Carrie trailing behind, entered the room. "We were all wondering who was at the door," Lance said, seeing the stranger standing there and sensing Logan's tense stance. "Hey, what's going on?"

"This guy came to see Carrie."

Carrie glanced up from her conversation with Asia. She looked past her brothers to see Connor standing in the middle of her father's foyer. She rushed by them to stand in front of him.

"Connor? What are you doing here?" she asked, surprised. She hadn't seen or talked to him since leaving California. That didn't mean she hadn't thought about him, though. She suddenly felt nervous about his unexpected visit and didn't have to look around to know everyone's eyes were on them.

"We need to talk, Carrie."

"No, there's nothing we need to say."

"I care to differ."

Logan made a move forward. So did Lance and Lyle. "Hey, we don't know who you are, but if our sister says the two of you don't have any business to discuss, then that settles it," Logan said.

Connor's gaze moved from the worried look on Carrie's face to that of the man he knew to be her oldest brother. "No disrespect, but Carrie and I do have something to discuss, and I'm not leaving until we do."

He shifted his attention back to Carrie. "Don't do it, Carrie. Don't let her use you this way."

It was Lyle who came to stand next to Logan. A dark frown had settled on his face. "What is he talking about, Carrie? Who's trying to use you?"

Carrie's gaze slid from Connor to Lyle. "It's nothing that concerns any of you."

"Again I care to differ," Connor said, as he leaned against the closed front door with an angry expression on his face. He met Carrie's hostile glare. "And as your brothers, they have a right to know."

Lance spoke up. "We have a right to know what?"

Biting back a curse, Carrie glared at Connor. "You've said enough, Connor. Please leave. You have no right coming here."

"No, I'm not leaving. Either you tell them or I will, Carrie."

Carrie took a step toward him. "Connor, no! Please don't. I hired you to do a job and you did it. Whatever happened to client confidentiality? You have no right discussing my business with anyone." Then in a softer pleading voice she said, "Please don't do this."

Connor took a step forward, which placed him standing in front of her. He lifted his hand and ran his thumb along her cheek. "Any such client confidentiality between us ended the day you became *my* woman, Carrie. I love you, and I refuse to let her hurt you again."

"I think someone should tell us what is going on here."

Those words, spoken in Jeremiah Montgomery's deep voice, demanded that someone comply. Connor's gaze moved from Carrie to glance over at her father and brothers. When he looked back at Carrie, he saw the tears in her eyes. "I do love you, Carrie, and you're not alone in this. Trust me to know what's the right thing to do in this situation. You have to trust me, sweetheart."

He then pulled a crying Carrie into his arms and as her family looked on questioningly, he held her while she sobbed into his chest.

"You okay, baby girl?" Jeremiah asked his daughter after they had all gathered in the living room to sit down.

"Yes, Pop, I'm fine," Carrie said, wiping her eyes on the handkerchief he had given her earlier. "And Connor is right. I should tell all of you what's going on."

She was sitting on the sofa beside Connor and he was holding her hand, giving her the support she needed. His support and his love. Even now she had a hard time believing what he'd said earlier in front of her father and brothers. He loved her. The man she loved had announced to everyone that he loved her back.

She sighed deeply and glanced around the room at

her brothers. They were sitting in various chairs, all facing her. Lance's fiancée, Asia Fowler, who Carrie had just met last week, was also there. Asia had volunteered to leave, but Carrie had stopped her, wanting her there although they would be discussing family business—as ugly as it could get. But she liked Asia. She also knew how much Lance loved her and since Carrie figured that Asia would soon be a part of their family anyway, Carrie saw no reason for her not to be included in this private family discussion.

"Now will you tell us what's going on, Carrie?" her brother Logan asked.

She met his gaze and nodded. "I don't know where to start," she said, refusing to cry anymore. She felt Connor's hand tighten on hers, and then he said, "Just start at the beginning, sweetheart."

The room got quiet while Carrie inhaled deeply. She glanced over at Connor, saw the love in his eyes. She then began talking. "It all started when I received this huge envelope at the office. . . ."

After hearing Carrie's story, the Montgomerys were furious.

Connor was still holding Carrie's hand. He knew her telling her brothers what their mother was doing had been hard, as well as admitting to them what Simon Anderson had done to her all those years ago. He had watched her father's and brothers' faces and had seen the moment their anger had reached boiling point. Connor had been a police officer on the streets for a long time; he was used to seeing anger, but what knocked him back was seeing the kind of rage that flared between the men when Carrie had told them about Anderson and what he'd done to her all those years ago. It was only after Connor had spoken up, assuring them that in Anderson's present condition he wouldn't be able to hurt Carrie or another child again did they decide not to catch the next plane to California.

"You would think Edwina had learned her lesson from the last time she tried getting money out of the Montgomerys," Jeremiah said in an angry tone. He thought what she was doing was so horribly low, he was ashamed to admit she'd ever been his wife.

"Has she tried doing something like this before?" Connor asked after hearing Jeremiah's comment.

Logan was the one who answered. "She showed up years ago—before we knew Carrie had been taken from her and placed in a foster home—and our mother offered to tell us where Carrie was if we were to pay her money. We told her we wouldn't give her a dime and instead we hired our own private investigator to find her. We knew then what sort of person she had become."

Logan switched his gaze from Connor to Carrie. "And Connor is right, Carrie. You can't let her manipulate you into paying her money. Once she starts getting it out of you, she'll never let up."

"But I can't let her go to the newspapers and—"

"Damn the newspapers!" Lyle said, coming to stand in front of his sister. "Do you think we care about her threats? You are our sister. We love you. Nothing that has happened in your past will ever embarrass us, Carrie. You were an innocent child. Let her take it to the newspapers. I will gladly see her rot in jail."

"And so will I," Lance said, sitting beside Asia on

the sofa. "And I agree with Logan and Connor. If you start paying her off, she will only come back. I say let's call in the authorities and let them handle her."

"I'd like to make a suggestion," Connor said, glad Carrie's brothers were rallying behind her and giving their support like he'd known they would do. "The only reason she is pushing Carrie is because she knows how much Carrie loves all of you, and she's banking on it. She's using Carrie's love for all of you as a weapon. But if Edwina knew all of you were behind Carrie and that you wouldn't hesitate for Edwina to serve jail time, I believe she would pull back and leave Carrie alone . . . with a little convincing."

Lyle smiled. "Sounds like you might have a plan."

Connor chuckled. "I do. Do you want to hear it?"

Logan leaned forward in his chair. "Hell, yeah, We're all ears."

"Thanks for coming home with me. With it being Christmas night I'm sure you'd made plans to spend time with your family," Connor said, closing the door and locking it.

"Thank you for inviting me over."

They stared at each other for a long time. This was the first opportunity they'd had to be alone since Connor had shared his feelings with her. Even now he fought the urge, his most fervent desire, to pull her into his arms and kiss her and let her know things were going to be all right. Together with her brothers they had come up with a pretty good plan, and hopefully it would end this nightmare she'd endured for the past months.

"Your brothers are pretty nice guys," he said to break the silence.

"Yes, they are. And just think that Lance knows your cousin, Marcus Lowery. This is a small world, isn't it?"

"Yeah, small."

And speaking of small, Connor was ready to dispense with the small talk, and without another thought he closed the distance between them, took Carrie's face in his hands, and kissed her.

There was nothing like kissing the woman you loved, Connor quickly concluded as his tongue made a thorough exploration of Carrie's mouth. His mouth was demanding and she was clinging to it, giving him what he wanted, what he needed.

When he finally drew away, he looked down into her face and whispered the words he had told her earlier that day: "I love you."

His stomach clenched at the tiny smile that curled her lips as she gazed back at him and said, "And I love you, too, Connor. I think I fell in love with you that day when I walked into your office. I was so attracted to you that it was downright scary. I'd never felt that sort of chemistry with a man before."

"Yeah, I know the feeling. I was right there with you, since I was attracted to you off the bat, as well. I'd always considered myself a playa, but now I'm seeing things differently. I want forever with a woman, something I thought I'd never want. But I do now with you."

His words made a shiver move all the way down Carrie's spine. And even now with him standing so close, the scent of his cologne was teasing her nostrils, making her aware of him even more. Today had been perfect, but she didn't look forward to what lay ahead with her mother. Connor had come up with a pretty good plan; she just hoped it worked.

"Promise that you won't worry about anything."

She met Connor's gaze again. He'd known what she was thinking. "I didn't want my brothers to know, but now I'm glad they do. It's like a huge weight has been lifted off me, and I can breathe again."

"I wanted that for you. I didn't want you to continue to go through life blaming yourself for what happened. No matter what your mother believes, you were an innocent victim."

At that very moment, Carrie suddenly felt drawn to Connor, filled with desire to a degree she hadn't before. This man, this beautiful man, had decided that she, even with her complicated past, was worthy of his love, and she knew that no matter what the future held for them, she would always love everything about him. He was assaulting her senses, propelling her into a need she had never before experienced to this degree. And at that moment, a fierce craving took over her and she wanted him—inside of her. "Connor?"

"What, sweetheart?"

Her lips trembled when she said, "Make love to me."

Not intending for her to ask twice, Connor picked her up into his arms and carried her into the bedroom, determined that they would both experience the greatest explosion ever.

33

Connor wasn't surprised when he got a call from Miller the following day to let him know Edwina was packing to move out of the house she was living in. The good news was that, unknown to her, Miller would know of any change in her residence. The plan was in place, and the Montgomerys were ready to get Edwina out of their lives once and for all.

It was decided that the best course of action was for Carrie to revisit her mother, seemingly in an attempt to talk her out of her blackmail scheme. Unbeknownst to Edwina, Carrie would be taping their entire conversation on a mini-recorder. Logan, Lyle, Lance, along with Connor and an agent for the FBI, who was a good friend of Miller's, would be in a van two doors down, and would be recording Edwina's and Carrie's entire conversation. Jeremiah had wanted to come along, but his sons had felt that they were the ones who should deal with Edwina and had convinced him to stay in Gary.

After Carrie had knocked several times, Edwina yanked the door open and when she saw Carrie standing there, an angry scowl appeared on her face. "What the hell are you doing here?"

Carrie walked past her inside the house. "We need to talk."

Edwina slammed the door shut. "The only thing we need to do is get an understanding about the money you're giving me. You evidently didn't understand the terms I laid out. I said not to get anyone else involved. You broke the rule with your boyfriend, so it's going to cost you another five grand per photo."

"Fifteen thousand dollars! I don't have that kind of money."

Edwina snorted as she walked across the room to the glass of gin and tonic she had sitting on the table. She picked it up and took a swallow before saying, "Sure you do. Use your brains. You have three brothers who are rolling in dough. Just ask them for the money. I'm sure they'll accommodate you."

"I'm not asking them for money."

Edwina fired up a cigarette and blew out smoke. "Then try earning it on your back. With Simon as a teacher, I'm sure you're pretty good at it."

Carrie placed her hand on her hips. "Does it not bother you that the man who you thought was your boyfriend was molesting your daughter right under your nose?"

Edwina tossed her drink down and set the glass aside. "Yeah, I was real torn up about it when I found out," she said, chuckling. "But he didn't have anything on me, since I was screwing his best friend behind his back." She smirked. "Old Charlie and I used to make out like a couple of dogs in heat. It's a wonder I never got pregnant again."

Carrie shook her head, not believing that was something her mother wanted to boast about. "Why? Why did you do it? Why did you leave Gary in the first place? Pop loved you. He would have given you anything."

She took another drink, swallowed deep. "Is that what you heard? Hell, Jeremiah didn't give me anything. I wanted to go out and have a good time, but he was always working and when he wasn't working, he was too tired to party. He thought working and paying the bills was all that mattered. He knew when he married me that I was a party girl, but he figured I would change. He thought if he kept me pregnant, I wouldn't have time to think about going out and having a good time. Hell, it lasted five years, but then I decided enough was enough."

"Is that why you had an affair?"

"Damn right. But even that backfired on me. Met a man named Patrick, we went at it for six months and then I got pregnant with you. I convinced Patrick to take me away with him when he split town, and he did. But once he found out you weren't his kid, he dumped me."

Carrie, who had been flipping through some outdated magazine, looked up. "If I'm not this person named Patrick's child, then are you saying I'm really Jeremiah's daughter?" she asked, hoping she'd heard right.

"Yeah, it must have happened one of those nights I felt obligated to fulfill my wifely duties so he wouldn't find out about Patrick."

Joy and elation raced through Carrie. They were

emotions she couldn't show at the moment, or Edwina would find a way to use them against her. Jeremiah had always said she was his. He had believed it, and so often she had prayed it to be so. "How did this Patrick guy find out I wasn't his child?"

Edwina blew out more smoke. "You got sick, almost deathly ill, and needed blood. Your bloods didn't match. Didn't even come close. Boy, was he pissed. Raped me the same night he found out, beat the crap out of me the next day, and then he ran off, leaving me high and dry while you were still in the hospital, without a dime in my pocket."

Carrie met her mother's gaze. "You could have left me too, deserted me. Why didn't you?"

Edwina shrugged. "I thought about it then changed my mind. I figured you were my meal ticket. One of the nurses in the hospital felt sorry for me, took me home with her, and offered me a place to stay until you got better. Even convinced me I needed to go to church. But that soon got old and I split town after she found out I'd gotten into her bank account and took money out of it, almost five thousand dollars."

Carrie shook her head. Her mother had just admitted to being a thief. Not a nice admission to have recorded. "I remember all the men there were in your life."

Edwina chuckled. "Yeah, so many I lost count. But it didn't matter. I kept a roof over your head and food on the table."

"And now you want money from me or you'll let everyone know that I was sexually abused as a child. Doesn't the thought of that bother you?"

Edwina shook her head. "Not in the least. Worse

things could have happened. Mary's man had her daughter pimping for him at one time, so consider yourself blessed. I took care of you pretty good in your early years, so you have no reason to complain. But now I need money."

"For drugs?"

"Yeah, for drugs and for whatever else I want to use it for, not that it's any of your damn business. Just make sure you pay up by the first, or I'm sending those pictures to the newspapers as well as this company on the Internet that posts those kinds of photographs."

"And you would actually do that? Send those pictures off to them unless I pay you one hundred thousand dollars? Not only ruin my life, but your sons' lives, as well?"

"In a heartbeat because none of you were my children. You belonged to Jeremiah. He worked day and night for his children and not for me. And as far as the money goes, don't forget it's been increased to fifteen thousand per photo. And I won't take anything less than one hundred and fifty thousand."

Carrie slowly crossed the room to stand before her mother. "I hate to tell you this, but I don't plan to give you one red cent."

"Yes, you will or your brothers—"

"Already know," Carrie said smiling. "I told them, and they don't love me any less."

Rage appeared on the woman's face. "Then let's see how they deal with the entire world knowing. I'm sending those photographs to the newspaper. I'm sure the reporters will have a good time with it. In the course of their investigation, I can see them hounding your brothers at their offices, asking for statements, giving you all kind of grief and such."

"I don't think so," Carrie said slowly, opening her coat and easing out a mini-recorder. "Our entire conversation was captured on tape. This is your ticket to jail if you try doing that. If those photographs end up with the media, so will this tape. I don't think you'll want to see yourself on television that way, as one of the *America's Most Wanted*."

Without saying anything else, Carrie walked to the door and opened it. To Edwina's horror, six men walked in. She recognized her sons immediately. She also recognized the man who'd come calling with Carrie the other day. The one she figured to be her boyfriend. The last man she didn't know. He was the one who stepped forward and spoke.

"Ms. Montgomery, I'm Agent Mills with the FBI. It's a good thing for your sake that I'm here on unofficial business; otherwise, I would be hauling you in for extortion attempts. But we've recorded some pretty damaging material, and I want to advise you of your fate if you proceed with your plans to expose those photographs."

Later that night, back at the hotel, Carrie stood at the window and stared out into the quiet night. She couldn't help but think about what had happened after her brothers, Connor, and Agent Mills had arrived at Edwina's place.

Edwina had gotten scared shitless after Agent Mills had advised her of what could become her fate. She had dashed into the bedroom and gotten what she claimed were all the photographs along with any negatives. She had almost sworn on her mother's grave to leave the Montgomery family alone.

Carrie had felt sorry for her brothers. If they had been secretly harboring any pleasant memories of their mother, she was sure those memories came to a silent death while listening to their taped conversation. She had not only ruined the life of a hardworking man who had loved her but had tried to destroy her children's lives, as well.

"Come back to bed, sweetheart. I miss you keeping me warm."

Carrie turned and smiled. Connor was sprawled on top the covers, naked and fully aroused. "Are you sure that's why you want me to come back, to keep you warm?"

"That's part of it."

When she walked back toward the bed, he grabbed her wrist and tumbled her down on the mattress with him. "It's been one hell of a day, hasn't it?" she asked, thinking that things had been pretty hectic since arriving in L.A. that morning.

"Yes, but we got a lot done today. I honestly believe Edwina won't be bothering any of you again. Agent Mills was pretty convincing."

Carrie remembered. "Yeah, he did lay it on rather thick. But that's what Edwina needed to hear. Any judge and jury would gladly toss her in jail and throw away the key. She always talked bad, but when it came right down to it, she was nothing but mouth."

Connor had to agree. "And now you know Jeremiah is your real father."

Carrie smiled. "Yes, but the possibility that maybe I

wasn't his never bothered him. From the time I returned home, he had opened his house and heart to me as his daughter, not knowing the truth, and for that I will always love him. He's a good man. It's too bad my mother never appreciated him."

"Yes, it is a shame, isn't it?" Connor's hand slipped beneath her gown to caress her breast, the tip of his thumb teasing her nipple. He liked the sound she was making with his touch. It was a sensual sigh. "You like that?"

She chuckled. "I like everything that you do to me, Connor."

"That's good, because over the course of the next one hundred years, I plan to do a lot." He stared deep into her eyes. "I love you."

Carrie thought there weren't any words for what she was feeling at that very moment. "And I love you, too."

He removed the gown from her body and tossed it aside. "Are you ready to discuss wedding plans?" He asked her the question at the same time he slipped his hand between her legs.

"Umm, yes, but not at this particular moment," she said, sinking back into the mattress. She sucked in a sharp breath when his mouth began teasing her at the corner of her lips before lowering farther to her chest. There his lips found her breasts and he began feasting on them, laving the nipple with his tongue. And when his mouth moved lower and trailed a hot, wet path down her chest to her belly, her entire body began trembling.

Carrie cried out in pleasure the moment he slipped his tongue inside of her, and it was at that moment that she lost touch with reality. As shudders raced through her, he shifted positions, mounted her, and entered her body, and when he began moving back and forth, a fresh wave of desire washed over her again, making her need just that much stronger.

She closed her eyes as the man she loved made love to her. He had helped to destroy her demons, and now he was fulfilling a need that only he could satisfy.

"Connor!"

When the explosion hit the both of them simultaneously, Carrie knew that they shared a bond that would never be broken. Any reservations about marrying him, not being good enough for him, melted away. She was his, and he was hers, and that was all that mattered. Tomorrow was New Year's Eve, and she wanted them to start the New Year off right. And deep down inside, she knew that they would.

34

Asia, Sean, and Lance

Asia glanced over at the door when she heard the knock. It was New Year's Eve, the day Sean was to come for her decision. She inhaled deeply before crossing the room to open the door. Telling him about her and Lance wouldn't be easy, but Lance was right. She owed him her complete honesty, and the truth was that she was in love with Lance and would marry him.

As soon as Asia opened the door and Sean saw her, he knew. *I've lost her* began echoing in his head. In a way, he had known it the moment he had stepped off the elevator. He knew he had gambled, but more than anything he had wanted her to be sure of her feelings, to be certain of them.

"Hi," she greeted him.

"Hi, yourself."

She moved aside. "Come on in. I've been waiting for you."

He walked into her apartment and glanced around.

The place looked the same, but he knew things were different, things he couldn't see.

"Would you like something to drink?"

He gave her a smile. A forced one, but a smile nonetheless. "No, I'm fine." Deciding not to prolong the inevitable, when she closed the door behind him and turned around, he came out and asked, "What's your decision, Asia?"

He studied her, how she nervously began toying with her watch and felt it, a cloak of guilt was draped over her shoulders, weighing her down, which could only mean one thing. But he had to hear it from her anyway.

"I appreciate our friendship, Sean, you've always known that," she said, holding his gaze. "You've always wanted more, but I never thought I could give you more, and then something happened and I convinced myself that I could, but it was a lie."

She sighed deeply before continuing. "The reality of it all is that I'm in love with someone else, and I can now admit that I fell in love with him months ago, although I tried fighting it. I have now accepted my feelings for him."

"It's Montgomery, isn't it?" he asked, his tone low yet direct.

She nodded. "Yes. I love Lance. I've seen him, spent time with him, and I'm certain of my feelings for him and of his for me."

"And if he were to hurt you again?"

"He won't. He's changed, but then so have I. We want to be together. We want to get married."

Sean felt his world come tumbling down. He wanted to hold her. He needed to touch her one last time. He reached out and took her hand in his, knowing this was all the touching he'd get. "I love you. All I ever wanted was for you to be happy."

She shook her head. Tears formed in her eyes. "I know, and I appreciate that. I appreciate you."

"But you don't love me."

"No, I don't love you. At least not that way. I love you as a friend and always will."

For the longest moment neither of them said anything. Then Sean broke into the silence and spoke again. "If he ever hurts you, he'll have me to deal with. Let him know that, okay?"

Asia wiped a tear from her eye. "Trust me, he already knows it."

"Good." He then leaned over and placed a kiss on her cheek. "Take care and have a happy New Year." Without giving her a chance to say anything else, knowing there really wasn't anything left to be said, he left.

Lance paced the confines of his condo, checking his watch for the umpteenth time. He had arrived back in Chicago from Los Angeles hours ago and had tried to call Asia but didn't get an answer at her apartment in New York or on her cell phone.

Today was the day she was supposed to talk to Sean. Had she done so already? Had the man accepted what she said? Was he giving her a hard time? Damn, where was she? He knew they had decided to see each other New Year's Day, but he wished they could be together when the New Year rolled in. There was a chance that Sean would have wanted to take her out to dinner, though.

Jealousy was a new emotion for him, but he knew that when it came to Asia it would be one he would undoubtedly feel every so often. She was his, and he was possessive and didn't care who knew it.

He turned when he heard a knock at his door. He cursed. The last person he wanted to see was one of his brothers. They had departed ways at the airport and they had headed to Gary to tell Pop what had happened in Los Angeles. That was hours ago. Had one of them decided to drive back to Chicago to spend the night on the town as a way to bring in the New Year?

Knowing it had to be someone he knew—otherwise, the person would not have gotten past security—he snatched open the door.

"Hi, expecting someone?"

A surprised smile curved the corners of Lance's mouth. Instead of providing his visitor with an answer, he pulled her inside, slammed the door shut, and began kissing her like a starving man. After that nasty episode in Los Angeles involving his mother, he needed this, the expulsions of certain emotions that only Asia could bring out in him. Not breaking the kiss, he bent and picked her up in his arms and headed straight for the bedroom.

"No extravagant dinner this time?" she asked when he finally let go of her mouth to place her on the bed, referring to her first visit to his home.

The corners of his lips turned up in a smile as he began removing his shirt. "No, we go straight into dessert, Chocolate Temptation."

"Oh." Asia remembered Lance's brand of the dessert, including just how he'd served it.

The feminine scent of Asia engaged Lance's already heated senses, and after removing all of his clothes and proceeding to remove all of hers, he began kissing her all over, feeling her body tremble beneath his lips. Her coming to him today was a surprise, but one he was overjoyed with.

Tonight he planned to taste every inch of her, and then he would join their bodies in the most special way possible. He needed her. He wanted her. He loved her.

She moaned his name. And he loved the sound of it from her lips. He shifted positions to settle between her legs, covering her body with his warmth. The tip of his shaft touched her hot womanly core, and its moistness confirmed she wanted him as much as he wanted her.

"Asia?"

She met his gaze the moment he entered her, screamed out his name as he went deeper inside of her. She arched her body as if she couldn't get enough of him just like he couldn't get enough of her. She felt good. She felt like heaven. She felt like his.

He thrust, holding her gaze, whispering words of love to her, establishing a special rhythm with her, setting the pace, the tone, the passion. Giving them what they both wanted.

He groaned out her name when his body became a mass of red hot desire. He needed her like he needed his next breath, and he would spend the rest of his life making up for all the pain he had caused her.

Every cell in his body felt fired, ignited, and ready to explode. His heart began pounding in his chest, and every emotion he possessed began swelling out of control. "I love you!"

He groaned out the words and then threw his head back as his body continued to stroke her, love her. And when he felt her body buck, knowing the same passion that had overtaken him was consuming her, he felt her muscles clench and tried to waylay another orgasm that was ready to pound into him. He gritted his teeth, but it was no use. More desire than he'd ever experienced before ripped through him, and there wasn't a thing he could do to stop it. He spilled into her at the same time that he brought his mouth down to hers and kissed her deeply, thoroughly, and completely.

And then he felt her, her firebrand of heat, and then she had him tumbling all over again.

"Sean took the news better than I had expected."

They were still in bed, had been there for a couple of hours after making love just as long—nearly nonstop. To say his stamina had gotten tested was an understatement.

A smile touched the corners of his lips. "He didn't have a choice. Once I had made up my mind to get you back, he didn't stand a chance."

"You were that sure of yourself?"

Her words made him shift his gaze over to her. "No, but I was that sure of my love for you. I just had to make you believe me." He thought of all the things he'd done to convince her, and another smile touched his lips. "You didn't make it easy, but it was worth every moment I tried. You were too precious for me to lose."

She shifted her body to lean over him. "Okay, so what's next?"

He chuckled. "No more lovemaking, that's for sure.

I can barely move." He reached out and pulled her face down to his for a kiss. "Now we plan our future. Like I told you, I want marriage, babies, forever."

She smiled. "So do I."

"What's so amusing?"

"All you playas who are turning in your cards, ready to settle down with one woman and produce kids. Amazing."

"Yeah, amazing." Lance couldn't help but think about his best friend Sam, who would be getting married on Valentine's Day, and then there were Phillip and Marcus, who had spring weddings planned. He then thought of Connor Hargrove, the man who had proclaimed his love for Carrie. According to a recent conversation Lance had had with Sam, if Connor had fallen in love with Carrie, then it was shocking news to everyone, since Marcus's cousin had a reputation as being a playa.

Lance grinned. People would begin shaking their heads wondering why there were no more playas. Well, they would just have to read his new book to find out.

Sean stood at the window in his home and looked out at Boston Harbor in the distance. He refused to feel sorry for himself, since he had known from the beginning that falling in love with his brother's girl had been wrong, but he hadn't had any control of his emotions. Besides, Asia was such an easy person to love.

Here it was New Year's Eve, and he fought hard to avoid wallowing alone in self-pity.

He almost smiled when the face of someone floated across his mind. Liz. If she wasn't working at the hospital, chances were she was at home curled up reading a book. He wondered if she would go out with him tonight.

He picked up the phone and dialed her number. "Hello," she answered.

"Hello, Liz. This is Sean. How would you like to go out tonight and celebrate a New Year?"

Epilogue

No More Playas

It was a beautiful June day on the island of Paradise, and it seemed that everyone was present to see the man who had been tagged as the ultimate playa turn in his playa card and say "I do" to the woman he loved.

Lance's new book, *No More Playas*, was selling like hotcakes because both men and women wanted to know what had happened, although for different reasons. The women thought the book gave them insight, hope. The men thought the book would give them a clue as to what pitfalls to avoid so they wouldn't land in Lance's shoes.

But Dr. Lance Montgomery wouldn't back down. He went on radio and television talk shows, did countless interviews, and all with the same message. Any playa could meet his match and fall in love. Hopelessly so.

With their diverse backgrounds and doctorate degrees in clinical psychology, Lance and Asia decided to create the Montgomery Marriage Institute, which would specialize in working with couples in crisis or on the brink of divorce. They thought that Paradise would be the perfect place to hold marriage seminars, where they would work with couples to build, repair, and strengthen their marriages.

Lance and Connor were standing together talking, waiting for their brides. Carrie and Connor had decided to skip all the hoopla and had eloped to Hawaii over the Easter weekend, but to make her brothers and father—as well as Connor's family—happy, they had agreed to a small reception, which had been held a couple of weeks ago.

"Well, well, the two men who are no more playas," said a voice from behind them.

They both turned and smiled when they saw the newlyweds, Sam, Phillip, and Marcus. "Look who's talking," Connor said, chuckling. "I recall a time the three of you were playas, too."

"No, we were playa wannabes, but like the two of you, we got smart and met beautiful women and fell in love."

Lance and Connor nodded in agreement. The men's wives—Falon, Terri, and Naomi—were beautiful women. Lance then glanced across the way and saw his own wife talking to Pop and thought his wife was beautiful, as well. His gaze shifted, and he caught sight of his brother Logan talking to Asia's sister, Claire. He found that most interesting. Lyle, it seemed, was bored as hell and kept glancing at his watch as if counting the hours, the minutes, the seconds, when he could haul ass. Lance shook his head. He would give both his brothers less than a year to find the women of their hearts.

"Think we ought to go claim our wives for a dance?" Sam asked when the music began playing.

"Yeah, it won't hurt. Will definitely earn us brownie points," Marcus said, chuckling.

"You guys might settle for a damn brownie, but I want the cake with all the icing," Connor said before walking off toward his wife. The four men watched as he pulled her into his arms and kissed her completely, in front of everyone.

"He's always been an arrogant ass," Marcus said, laughing.

"Yeah, but he might have something there. You're never too old to learn how some things are done," Lance said. And with that thought in mind, he walked straight to his wife, thinking he had something even better than a brownie or a cake. He had the most tantalizing dessert to ever be served. He had something called Chocolate Temptation.